first-timers

first-timers

true stories of lesbian awakening

rachel kramer bussel

alyson books
NEW YORK

AUTHOR'S NOTE: SOME OF THE EVENTS DESCRIBED HAPPENED AS RELATED, OTHERS WERE EXPANDED AND CHANGED. SOME OF THE INDIVIDUALS PORTRAYED ARE COMPOSITES OF MORE THAN ONE PERSON AND MANY NAMES AND IDENTIFYING CHARACTERISTICS HAVE BEEN CHANGED AS WELL.

"LIGHT MY FIRE," BY ALISON TYLER, WAS ORIGINALLY PUBLISHED IN *Bondage on a Budget*, EDITED BY ALISON TYLER AND DANTE DAVIDSON, MASQUERADE BOOKS, 1997 (SUBSEQUENTLY PUBLISHED BY PRETTY THINGS PRESS, 2002).
"FTF," BY RADCLYFFE, WAS ORIGINALLY PUBLISHED IN *Change of Pace: Erotic Interludes by Radclyffe*, BOLD STROKES BOOKS, 2004.
"RUNWAY BLUES," BY RADCLYFFE, WAS ORIGINALLY PUBLISHED IN *Change of Pace: Erotic Interludes by Radclyffe*, BOLD STROKES BOOKS, 2004.
"THREE'S A CROWD," BY BARBARA JOHNSON, WAS ORIGINALLY PUBLISHED IN *The First Time Ever: Love Stories by Naiad Press Authors*, EDITED BY BARBARA GRIER AND CHRISTINE CASSIDY (NAIAD PRESS, 1995).

MANUFACTURED IN THE UNITED STATES OF AMERICA.
THIS TRADE PAPERBACK ORIGINAL IS PUBLISHED BY ALYSON BOOKS,
P.O. BOX 1253, OLD CHELSEA STATION, NEW YORK, NEW YORK 10113-1251.
DISTRIBUTION IN THE UNITED KINGDOM BY TURNAROUND PUBLISHER SERVICES LTD.,
UNIT 3, OLYMPIA TRADING ESTATE, COBURG ROAD, WOOD GREEN,
LONDON N22 6TZ ENGLAND.

FIRST EDITION: JUNE 2006

06 07 08 09   a   10 9 8 7 6 5 4 3 2 1

ISBN 1-55583-947-9
ISBN-13 978-1-55583-947-5

LIBRARY OF CONGRESS CATALOGING-IN-PUBLICATION DATA HAS BEEN APPLIED FOR.

COVER PHOTOGRAPH BY PUNCH STOCK.
AUTHOR PHOTOGARPH BY CELESTE SMITH, WWW.KILLERBEAUTY.COM
COVER DESIGN BY TAYLOR JOHNSON.

contents

introduction

Do you remember your very first time ever? The first time you kissed a girl, the first time you picked up a stranger, your first one-night stand? What about your first butch, your first femme, your first strap-on, or your first threesome, your first phone sex, your first fisting? Or the first time you fell head over heels, the first time a girl really shook you up, the first time you realized you might be something other than straight? All of these and more are in *First-Timers,* a collection of stories for which I've pushed authors to go beyond the typical "first-time lesbian sex" story.

Why? Because, to be honest, the first is not always the best. First times are often filled with nerves, jitters, and inexperience. They're often so hyped up in our minds that when we actually get to them the moment may be more symbolic than anything else. So when I asked for "first times," I wanted, and received, firsts of various stripes; I wanted the best first times, the ones that made you know you were in exactly the right place, the ones that made these authors melt with pure, dripping desire. Some are downright sexy, the kind of first time you'd be happy to relive over and over again, like L. Elise Bland's wild strip scene in "Sugar Daddy," or Alison Tyler's hot wax exploration in "Light My Fire."

I open the book with Joy Parks' "Coming When You Call" for the simple reason that her story blew me away. The words practically burn off the page, sizzling with anticipation, tension, and arousal. "My legs are open wider and I can feel the wetness cooling against my thighs. Wet enough to take as much of her as she wants me to. Wet enough to take all she can give," writes Parks, setting off this collection with a sexual first that is clearly the precursor to many more hot encounters with her lover. Other first times are sweeter, more tender, but no less magical. They take place between friends, new lovers, strangers, and sometimes, like in Tara Alton's "What Makes Her Tick?" or Kate Dominic's "Yolanda's Sports Bra," they don't even really take place at all (but, oh, these women's erotic imaginations!). Kate Freed's "The Pick-Up" explores the power of seducing a woman for the first time, showing how inciting her yearning can fill us with joy, pride, and lust.

These stories take place in all kinds of settings, including two at sex conferences. In Jane Vincent's "Wear Me Home," she gets a very special kind of sex education when she joins her very first transman for an encounter neither will forget, while Elaine Miller gets some "First Hand Knowledge" at a kinky dyke sex conference.

What we learn from our first times can be profound, simply sexy, or mindblowing. Sometimes the woman who rocks our world and our pussy, vanishes soon after she's thrown our body into a frenzy, such as in Lynne Jamneck's "Thank You, Frannie, Wherever You Are."

Some firsts are ones we plan for, ones we feel incomplete without having accomplished. Other firsts sneak up on us, providing us with the chance to get it on with our best friend, only to find that we have more in common than just talking and giggling. Sometimes it's a coworker, or partygoer, or neighbor who comes into our life seemingly out of nowhere and makes us ache.

Other firsts can change the course of our lives, making us see sex, and ourselves, in entirely new ways, such as in Jen Cross's "The Organic Orgasm" or Gina de Vries's "Questioning Youth." Sex can be the path to redemption, to healing, to loving ourselves, and that first step is often profound for body, mind, and soul.

Sometimes the chances we take with firsts can lead us to the love of our life, the one who we'll continue to share many firsts with for years to come. Radclyffe, who proves her erotic writing proficiency in "Runway Blues," closes the book with "Meeting FtF," in which two online lovers take their relationship to the next level, and—proving that truth is not only stranger but often way hotter than fiction—proceed to pick up where their steamy emails have left off.

What I hope all these first times capture is both the wide array of lesbian firsts that are out there (along with many more waiting to be discovered and captured on paper), and how those firsts make us feel.

Finding a new lover, using a new seduction skill, or being shown that the body you've grown used to can reveal itself in utterly unexpected ways can leave us feeling elated, horny, orgasmic, breathless, blown away.

So here's to an erotic and memorable collection of firsts. May all your firsts be as hot as these!

Rachel Kramer Bussel
New York City

coming when you call

●

joy parks

"You must be tired."

Her voice is soft and close in my ear, almost as if she is right here. "I forget about the time difference sometimes."

It's a three-hour difference. If she calls when it's eleven there, it's two in the morning here. Nearly 2,700 miles apart and most nights it does feel like the other side of the world. That's why we've been calling so much, talking for hours, sometimes until daylight here. And that's why I feel like I'm sleepwalking through my days.

I murmur "no," that I'm fine, that our conversations are worth missing a little sleep. Then I yawn accidentally and it becomes a sigh. She sighs too and whispers my name, three times, like a charm. Always three times. We're both quiet for a moment. I feel my whole body curl towards the phone. I want to be with her that badly.

"I wish I was there with you," I say.

Then I feel embarrassed because I sound like a homesick child. And I tell her that too.

"Did I ever tell you that before I heard your voice I expected Joni Mitchell?" she says. "Who could have known I was going to end up talking to Peggy Lee?"

She's told me that before, a couple of times, and I love it more every time she does. Love to think of her on the end of the line, holding the receiver, hearing a sensual mature woman, not the young girl she remembered. Peggy Lee. I barely knew who she was, but I ran out and bought some of her CDs. Her voice was low and raspy and wonderfully teasing. It sounded like smoky bars and slow dancing in the kind of places where my love had grown up and come out. A singer who sounded like experience and like danger and just a little bit haughty, like sex and want and secrets, which is what we had to keep right now. I love the fact that that's who I remind her of. I want her to want me. Badly.

"What time is it there, anyway?"

I roll over and push a stack of books away from the alarm clock. Sigh again. I'm getting used to being late for work and being tired, and having even less patience than usual.

"Almost one here." She's called a little earlier than usual. That costs more. We both have unbelievable phone bills each month.

"Then how about we pretend I'm there to tuck you in?" That's what she says when she's worried about it being so late. Morning comes three hours earlier for me than for her.

"You're sounding parental again."

And I laugh. She does that all the time. Tells me I need to get more sleep. That I need to eat better and stop worrying about work. It's the age difference. Fifteen years. I know she can't help it and I don't dare say "maternal," she's way too butch to allow that. Still, there's something about the tenderness in her voice, something so pure when she pretends to tuck me in, pull up the sheets, kiss me goodnight, that makes me snuggle deeper under the covers and feel safe. Cherished.

I sigh again, loudly this time, frustrated because I really don't want to hang up. I've got a million things to say, anything to just keep her voice surrounding me like warm sheets. Still, we begin to say our goodnights, when she pauses and whispers my name again. I can feel her need stroking me. The want wells up in her voice. I know I make her feel desires she hasn't felt in years. And that sometimes neither of us knows what to do about it.

I say her name. My breathing starts to get louder, more jagged, and I know she can hear it. I can hear her sighing too, and it's almost magical, as if she's really beside me. I reach over and turn off the light, then slide back into bed.

"…I want you. I want you. I want to touch you. Oh God, I want to feel you under my hands. You're wearing a nightgown, aren't you?"

I whisper "yes," barely audible. I don't mention that it's flannel. And pink and faded. I'm not exactly sure what's happening; she's never been this bold before. She's skilled at couching want with charm. It's all the hiding and games she's learned in order to survive.

"Baby I want to unwrap you like a present. I want to lean you up against the pillows and slide that gown off over your head, throw it down on the floor. I don't want anything between us."

The nightgown is already pushed up to my thighs from sliding between the sheets. With one hand, I grab a handful of flannel and slide it over my head, keeping the phone receiver planted to my ear. I don't want to miss a word of this.

"Nothing between us," I whisper.

She sighs. "I want to kiss you. I want to lie there beside you and press my whole body up against yours. Can you feel me baby? I want to feel your heat, know how smooth your skin is. Would you let me do that?

I whisper "yes." Yes. I can feel the heat coursing through my body. Feel the pressure of her fingers on me.

"That's my girl." I shudder. I love when she says that. My girl. I lie on my back. My legs part slightly as if to make it easier for her.

"I want to kiss your neck, kiss down your shoulders, kiss a line down between your breasts. I want to feel your nipples harden under my tongue. I want to kiss and suck and lick your breasts until you can't stand it any longer."

I can't. My hips are moving, rolling, grinding on the bed. At some point, I must have pulled back the sheets. I can feel her hands on my breasts, my belly. My cunt is spilling over, thick and creamy, wetting the bedding beneath me.

"Do you want me? Do you want me inside you? Do you baby? Do you want me to take you? Do you want to feel my fingers?"

"Yes," I whisper, murmur, "I want you. I want you. I want you deep."

My cunt hurts from need. My legs are open wider and I can feel the wetness cooling against my thighs. Wet enough to take as much of her as she wants me to. Wet enough to take all she can give.

"Tell me. Tell me what you want."

I can't stop my hips from rolling. I can hardly speak, but I have to. I have to tell her what I want. Make it real.

"I want to take you inside me," I moan. "I want to feel your fingers deep. I want to grind against your hand, I want to open up, let you slide in deeper, further.

She sighs. Moans.

"I want you to fuck me."

I can't believe I said that to her. Not her. She's not the type you'd say that to. She's quiet for a minute. Then I hear her exhale. Breathe hard. It's almost as if she's panting.

"No woman's said that to me in a long time," she whispers. She's silent again. Finding the words. Her voice tightens. Drops lower. Like a growl.

"I do want to fuck you."

All I can hear now is her breathing and my own, and my hips don't stop. I'm grinding against the sheets as if I can feel her hands on me, inside me, her voice, her sighs steady in my ear, as if she's here, so close, her hand deep inside me. I feel a wave of heat flow over me, building.

And, as if she can feel it too, how ready I am, she croons, "Come for me, come for me baby, come on, let me take you baby, let me make you mine."

Mine. Mine. Hers. I want to be hers.

"Fuck me…harder."

I sing out, arch my back, I can feel her, I can feel the waves coming faster and faster, feel the heat break in my cunt, up my back, my brain, I come screaming into the phone for her to take me, fuck me, make me hers. I can feel her, the closeness of her, her voice taking me up and up then shuddering and straining and crying my release.

And it's quiet again.

I can hear her breathing, so she must be able to hear mine. I can't believe she's made me feel like this from so far away, without even touching me, with just the sound of her voice in my ear, just the words of her need for me. But it's real, it happened, and I ride wave after wave of aftershock, my mouth parched, my body drenched in sweat, my knees shaking. I'm so wet; the sheets are soaked around me. And I tell her that.

She whispers, "I know what I could do about that."

Again, I think. Yes. I want more of her. I want as much of her as is possible this way. Whatever is possible. I cradle the phone between my head and the pillow; my arms are too weak and shaky to hold it any longer.

She is talking low and soft as if she is holding me. She tells me to take a sip of water, and I do. I would do anything she told me to do right now.

Once I settle back into the bed, she begins.

"I want to taste you."

I moan. She pushes on. I feel her words cover me, press me down hard on the bed.

"Do you want me to taste you? Do you want me to make love to you with my mouth?"

I whisper unintelligibly. Yes. Oh yes.

"I want to. More than anything. I want to start with your mouth, kiss you, kiss you, kiss you."

Her words feel like kisses. I open my mouth to take hers.

Her voice is low and sure of herself. So much more confident than usual. "I want to kiss a line down your body. Here. Kiss your breasts all over." My nipples are firm and tight against the night air. "Kiss your little belly." I want to giggle.

"Then baby," she whispers. I breathe. "Then I want to part your legs wide. Wider. Open up for me baby. That's my girl. Let me have you. All of you. I want to rest my cheek on your thighs. They'd be all sticky and wet now and smell so good. Smell of you. You smell so good. I love that smell, love the way a woman smells right after she's been fucked hard."

I shudder again. Feel a ribbon of heat tighten inside my cunt. I can't believe she's saying this. I'm getting wetter, I feel her breath and her tongue and her mouth, feel my body start to move again, my hips churn as if she's there, my legs open even wider as if she's spreading me open. One foot falls on the floor, knees raised, waiting. For her to speak.

"Then, I touch you with my tongue. Lick you all over, lick your thighs. Lick your cunt up and down and up and down until you can't take it anymore, then slide my tongue deep into you. Can you feel it baby? Can you feel my mouth? Do you want me to fuck you with my tongue?"

Desire bubbles up my belly. I feel my body open, roll with her words. I'm writhing and moving and rolling on the bed and I forget where I am and that she's just on the phone, and I open my legs even more, thrust my hips up to meet her, and my breathing is hard and loud and I know she can hear me. I know she knows what her words are doing to me. And I know what that's doing to her. I want her to make me come again so she can hear me scream out her name into the phone. I can hear the tremble in her voice as she sighs. I know she's coming from making me come, just as if she were here.

"That's it baby," she says. "Open for me, let me have you all. I want to take your clit in my mouth, open you with my hands, fuck you with my fingers while I suck your clit until you come. Come baby, that's it darling, oh baby come." Her voice goes high, she sounds sexier, younger, wilder than I've ever heard her before.

And I do. I come. When she tells me to. I come, feel a rush of wet and heat, feel myself screaming her name, screaming out all my lust and wonder of how she can do this to me, how just her voice and her words can make me scream and cry and grind and come and wet the sheets. I don't understand how my body can simply release when she tells it to, don't understand this power she has over me, to make me come, screaming into the phone, without touching me, fucking me so good and complete and doing it with just her voice on the phone from across a whole country. I can tell she's in a state of wonder too. I hear her whisper how beautiful I am and how she can feel me, hear me, almost taste me through the phone. We talk some more, just words and sounds. I murmur how good she is, how wonderful she has made me feel. And she whispers how much she wants me before I finally drop the phone in the cradle.

It's after four and I fall into a dead sleep, spread across the bed.

I wake up when the sun rushes through the curtain and shines into my face. No point in trying to hurry, I'm already late for work. And I'm exhausted. I lie there in the bed and feel the wetness under me. And it all comes back. Her words, how my body opened and moved for her, how good it was. And how real. My legs feel as if I've had a workout and my lips feel bruised. I run a finger along my clit. It's swollen and sensitive and I'm drenched with cool wetness between my thighs. I lay back in the bed with my arms by my side, totally spent and sweaty, lying in a pool of my own juices. I don't know how we did it, but we did, and it was wonderful and I can't stop grinning.

I think about calling her tonight to tell her how she made me soak the sheets. I know how that will make her feel. That it will make her want to do it again. And I yawn and snuggle back into bed, touch myself one more time just to be sure. And I sigh.

8 mile

●

therese szymanski

Okay, so now here's the thing: Folks who know me—really know me that is—know I sometimes do things purely for the adventure of them. And that was about how and why I first picked up a woman on a busy street— 8 Mile (as in the*) to be precise.*

Do you remember a few years back when the power grid went out in huge chunks of the Midwest and East Coast? New York was down. And so was Detroit. And I almost went to Detroit that weekend, when it was wicked hot and there was no air conditioning to be had, but, fortunately, I decided not to.

See, I'd just lost my job. Well, actually, I knew exactly where it was— with someone younger who made less than I had. And who also didn't have a back problem due to stress from her boss continually firing folks and handing her their workloads in addition to her own. My boss pretty much broke me so I was unemployed with a really sore back.

I'd decided if my back didn't get better immediately, I'd go to Detroit to see my old masseuse, who was absolutely fabulous. Maybe she'd be able to fix me. Always gotta go for the dream, y'know?

Anyway, my nonmonogamous girl and I went to Gettysburg that first weekend, so I couldn't go to Detroit, and that turned out to be good, since there was a heat wave in Detroit and no power. So I went the next weekend.

I like driving at night. And although my speedometer died before I even left Maryland, I kept on driving—sometimes using others to pace myself. There were more than a few amusing times when I was following someone—so I wouldn't get pulled over for doing a hundred and fifty—and they ended up thinking I was auto-stalking them, so they'd start driving really erratically. (It reminded me a lot of this time in college, when I hit a deer in the middle of the night in winter and lost both my headlights.)

I arrived in Detroit at about four in the morning. Since I no longer had keys to my mother's residence, I parked in her drive and had a beer, as it was an unseemly time to waken her. When I finished that beer, I had another, and another. And a few smokes as well. (God, I still miss smoking. Quite a bit, actually.)

When I tried to sleep in my car, I was quite unsuccessful at it. Finally, my mother came outside. She talked at me while I drank more beer and sorted through all the state quarters I had brought her.

I tried to sleep in the brightly lit, too-warm spare bedroom. Of her condo. See, she had finally sold her house—after I came out on CBS evening news—and had gotten a condo. When I awoke, I detailed my car, even though I had to buy a buffer because my mom refused to admit she had the one my brother gave her somewhere in her house.

When I finished, I took a shower, started sweating, took my mom out to dinner, and she finally turned on the air in her condo, but it was too little, too late. I had to bail for cooler climes.

I went out to the bar. But it was Thursday. So it was dead. And so I went to the next bar. Which was closed as well for some odd reason.

En route back to Mom's House of Outrageous Heat, Sweat, and Torture, traffic was backed up for a train.

I noticed the car in front of me had its gas cap open and hanging.

I thought about getting out and letting the driver know about it, but I was in a really bad neighborhood, and if I got out of my car there, it'd get stolen.

It was A Really Long and Slow-Moving Freight Train.

So I sat and listened to CDs.

And the train went on. Slowly. And the traffic grew more congested.

And I sat. And listened to tunes. Flipping around. Dance-mix to Simon and Garfunkel.

If someone wanted to steal my car, they couldn't. Not now that I was boxed in—plus, the car in front of me seemed to be inhabited by two females (profiles and how folks sit can tell so much about them). So I really didn't have anything to fear from them. Unless they were armed to the teeth.

I left my car running and went to the car ahead of me. When I was still several feet away, I realized the driver's window was open, so I called out, "Excuse me, your gas cap is open and hanging. I'm just gonna close it all up, all right?" And then I did so. And walked back to my car and got back in and went back to listening to Simon and Garfunkel.

A back door of their car opened and someone I hadn't seen before got out. She swung her hips slightly as she sashayed back to my car.

She looked cute. Young and slender, brunette and cute.

I quickly lowered my window.

She leaned in, smiling, and said, "Hey, thanks for that. That was really nice of you."

I grinned back, and allowed my gaze to look her up and down. "No problem. Always try to help out."

"It was sweet. And anyways, we were wondering…are you going to the Rainbow Room?"

"Yeah, I am. You goin' there?"

"Yeah, we are. We'll buy you a drink. I'll buy you a drink, too." She smiled and went back up to her car.

Everything had just suddenly gotten A Whole Lot Better. I was just hoping these gals were at least twenty-one. I was thirty-four, so even twenty-one was way too young for me, but I was in a juvenile delinquency mood, so…I could live with twenty-one. But not a day younger. That'd be Bad and Obscene, and there really was a chance of that, considering the appearance of the young flirt who'd come back to my car.

They all got through the bouncer, which was a good.

So I joined them.

"So, Reese," Stacy, the blonde driver, who appeared to be the eldest of their group at a wizened twenty-six, said to me, "Are you from around here?"

I set up another pool game. "Originally. Now I live in D.C."

"So you're back here visiting family or something?" Sarah said, breaking in.

"Mostly visiting my masseuse, but I'm staying with my mom," I said.

"So you all are from around here?"

"I'm from California," Roxie said, taking her shot. She was my partner and was much better than me. "I met Stacy and Sarah and a bunch of other folks at this rally sort of nature thing in Oregon a few years back."

"Roxie came to visit and say goodbye to me and a few other friends before we move," Stacy said. "I'm moving to Long Island."

"There's a party tomorrow night at Emily and Lessa's," Roxie said, handing me a shot and letting our fingers twine slightly. "You should come."

I stared at Roxie. "Not theater/POW Lessa, right?"

"Hell yes, Lessa does theater—she's moving to Chicago to work for some troupe there," Sarah said. "Hold on, how do you know about POW? Pissed Off Wimmin?"

"Fuck," I said, "I wasn't a founding member or nothing, but I got in early on, and I was the earliest member who was still involved when the last POW production went up."

"You did theater?" Roxie asked, looking me over like a farmer judging a bull.

"Backstage stuff, mostly," I said. "Playwright. Stage manager. Director. Only acted when absolutely necessary. Like when Lessa forced me to." When I revealed my real name, not the nickname they now knew me by, Sarah and Stacy knew who I was.

These were all teeny twenty-something femme-type hotties, and I was feeling wicked oversized and old and butch... But they were the ones buying me drinks, so I just tried to live up to my cool black leather pseudo-cowboy hat.

But fuck, you don't really care about all that. What you want to know is…well, a bit past midnight, they decided it was time to leave. I walked them to their car and they decided en masse they needed to drive me those last ten long, lonely feet to my car. During that lengthy drive, Roxie produced a bong.

At the tender age of thirty-four I succumbed to peer pressure and took a hit off the electric bong (did you know they make them in electric now?), even though I never much cared for the stuff even when I was in college. And then I turned to Roxie, who was sitting next to me, raised a hand to cup her soft cheek, leaned in, giving her ample time to pull away, and kissed her.

She parted her lips, allowing me access to her mouth even as she raised a hand to twine into my short, dark hair, pulling me closer. I wrapped an arm around her, beginning to map the contours of her body with my fingers.

"Come home with me," I whispered. We'd pulled up next to my black sedan. Her friends were looking at us in the rearview mirror.

"Can you drive me to Hamtramck in the morning?" she asked. "That's where my bus is. With friends there. I'll need a ride back to it in the morning."

"Yeah, I can take you there," I said. "I can take you to a lot of theres." I ran my hand up her thigh, pressing my thumb into her inner thigh. When she moaned, I leaned forward and gently tugged her lower lip between my teeth, darting my tongue out to slide against hers.

"I'll catch you two tomorrow night at the party," Roxie said to Sarah and Stacy.

"Yeah, we kinda figured as much," Stacy said.

Once we were in my car, I was wicked glad I hadn't drunk much. Roxie leaned over to lick my neck as her hand crept up my leg.

"Tell me what you want to do to me," she said, even as she grabbed my crotch and nibbled my earlobe.

"Oh, baby," I gasped, taking her hand in mine and guiding it down my leg. "Let me get us home first. Then I'll have my fun with you." Sometimes it sucked being a sober adult.

She grinned at me, licking her lips, as her hand worked its way up my arm to squeeze my bicep. "I like the hat." She pulled her cell phone out of her purse and dialed. "I have this routine with a friend that I have to call. She's from back—" She spoke into the phone, "Hey Jenny, it's me, Stephie. I'm giving you the call. I was with Sarah and Stacy at the bar, and we're doing Lessa and Emily's party tomorrow night but tonight I'm…with Reese." And then she hung up.

"Stephie?" I asked, glancing at her, still carefully doing just five miles over the speed limit.

"Doesn't matter. I like *Chicago*. I like Roxie. Call me Roxie."

We shared a smoke in my mom's garage, since my car was non-smoking, then I lit another for her and went to get us beers while she smoked.

When I returned I put our beers on my mom's car, took the smoke, and hit it, then pushed her against the car.

I held her hands up behind her while I shoved my thigh between her legs.

She spread her thighs, opening herself up to me. "Oh, god, Reese."

I kissed and sucked down her neck, gently biting at her succulent pulse point, nibbling at her flesh.

I reached down, wrapping my arm just under her ass, picked her up and carried her inside.

I threw Roxie on the bed. Her legs were still entwined about me, so I fell on top of her, pushing down into her. She ground up into me, groaning, while our tongues and mouths fucked.

"Damn, you feel good," I said, lifting myself up on my arms to look down at her.

She raised her pelvis up against me, arching her back. "Mmmm, goddamn, I want you to touch me all over."

I kept my thigh between hers, and knelt, pulling her with me. "You're overdressed." The lights were still on and I stripped off her shirt and bra. I laid her on her back and kissed down her collarbone and caressed her breasts, running my thumbs over her nipples.

"Oh, god," she said, writhing under me, twining her fingers in my hair and pushing me toward her breasts. I kissed and licked one, then the other. But she wanted more contact. Direct contact.

So I grabbed one breast in my hand even as I licked the other nipple into total erection. I teased with my teeth as I tugged with my fingers. I bit even as I squeezed.

"Yes!" she cried, bucking against me.

She was moaning and squirming underneath me, her hands running up and down my back, twining in my hair, trying to guide me to where she wanted me...

I was squeezing and biting and she was writhing and riding my thigh like a big, bad Harley. "God, Reese, please," she said, starting a chant with the yes's and the please's.

I knelt at her feet, this time quickly undoing her jeans. I pulled off her boots and socks, then her jeans and panties, leaving her naked and exposed in the light of the room.

I lay back on top of her, rubbing all over her, then ran my hand down over her breast, her nipple, down her tummy, up her inner thigh…and then between her legs, sliding up and down her wet clit.

She squirmed and moaned and writhed, begging and pleading and moaning.

I spread her lips and fingered her clit, then slid a finger into her.

"Uh, yes…"

I nibbled on her neck. I kissed down to her tit and slipped a second finger into her. I licked her tit like a lolly and slid yet another finger inside of her.

I fucked her. I bit her nipple and pulled it. I teased her and was inside of her, slipping and sliding in her warmth and wetness and enjoying making her squirm and writhe and twist and turn.

I knew she was young, and she was tight. She hadn't been around the block quite yet. But this was likely the only time we were ever gonna be together, so I wanted as much of her as could be mine right now.

I'd put my toy bag right under the bed, since I believe in Being Prepared, and now I reached for my Astroglide, still fingering her pussy and lavishing attention on her breasts even as I opened the bottle one-handed. I quickly slathered my other hand with it.

She was wicked wet and turned on, but I knew she'd never had this done to her before, so I wanted to make this as easy as possible for her.

So I lubed my hand and slid yet another finger into her, working her cunt, fucking her with four fingers. I brought my other leg between hers, spreading her open farther. And she was tight. Wicked tight. I was surprised I'd gotten so much in her as it was. But I knew I could do it. And I wanted to do her right, and I wanted to be there first, and so I knelt between her legs, looking down at her in the light so she'd feel open and exposed and …

… I shoved my fist into her.

"Fuck!" she screamed, practically sitting up as her eyes went wide, then she threw herself back onto the bed and her pelvis totally left the bed.

I left my hand in her. Letting her get used to the feel of it. Then I started moving it around, inside of her.

"God, yes, fuck me, please," she said. Squirming. More. A tear ran down her cheek.

I pulled her up into a sitting position. "Look at this," I said, making her see how my entire hand disappeared inside of her.

It was a pretty fucking hot sight, if I do say so myself.

"You have your entire goddamned fist inside of me," she said. Panting. Her muscles clenched around my fist, making me fear the breakage of bones, even as I felt her add to the lubrication.

"Yeah. I do."

"Goddamned it feels good," she said, lying back down, her face as wet as her sweaty body. "And it looked hot as hell."

It did. So I fucked her. With my fist. My entire fist. In and out of her slender and lithe body. I felt her inside and out and then I lowered my mouth to her cunt so I could taste her. I kept her legs open wide, nice and inviting, even as I licked her up and down, and sucked on her clit, pulling it into my mouth.

I ate her and I fucked her and I used my spare hand to twist and tease her nipples. But I made sure I kept my right arm tucked in tight so she couldn't dislocate my shoulder.

"Oh god, yes…yes…please…harder…more…"

She bucked against me. I thought my hand would break, the pain almost made tears come to my eyes. She writhed and I fucked her and I ate her, enjoying every bit of it.

"Fuck yeah!"

Afterwards, we had a couple beers and a few smokes. We sat in the garage, smoking, with her wearing my dad's old robe. Over dinner that night, my mom had mentioned that the robe was in the guest room closet, so when Roxie asked if I had a robe, I had a ready answer.

I'm sure Dad would've approved. If he lost his homophobia and all, that is.

the pick-up

●

kate freed

It's the end of spring and just warm enough so that I don't need a jacket, not quite nearing the melting-sidewalk heat that will engulf the city in only a month's time. I am on my way to meet my coworker Alan at a gay bar near our office. Alan works with me part time, is maybe nineteen, and has a thing for men older than his father. We have taken to drinking together some evenings at establishments where, despite being a few years my junior, he likes to school me on romance. When I arrive, I find Alan sitting among a loud group of admirers. We exchange air kisses, and he tells the crowd to make room. As they do, I slide into the booth next to the only girl at the table. She stubs out a lipstick-covered cigarette and offers her hand. "I'm Carrie. From Alan's Spanish class." I shake, introduce myself, and light my own cigarette.

Sipping a margarita, Carrie looks like a pretty, fresh-scrubbed sorority sister. She has shoulder-length blond hair and the tube top and miniskirt that all the underage college girls trying to get into the local bars seem to favor this year. Despite my own lipstick, Carrie is so girly that I feel positively butch next to her. Realizing that Alan is deep in conversation with an admirer, we begin to chat. I find out that Carrie is twenty, from the Midwest, studies English, and has just broken up with her high school boyfriend. I offer my sympathies, commiserate over shitty relationships, and then ask her the question that has most piqued my interest: How does she get her top to stay up? She giggles and pulls it out an inch to show me the elastic band that is holding it in place over her breasts. I get a quick flash of flesh before she lets the material snap back.

We order another drink, and Carrie comments that Alan has disappeared into the bathroom with a new acquaintance. "Boys are so good at that," she sighs. "They just go for it. I'm always too nervous to do stuff like that." I'm not sure if she is trying to tell me something, but I decide to hedge my bets and suggest that, since Alan is obviously occupied, we might as well take off. Carrie looks at me for a second, adjusts her tube top, and says okay. We leave the bar, and she wonders where we should go. "My place," I suggest, half expecting to hear her now familiar laugh and a decisive no. But, to my surprise she says, "All right." I decide that this is an indication that I can kiss her. So, I lean her against the bar's fence, the night air surrounding us, and slide my tongue into her mouth. She kisses back, then stops. "How'd you know I'd be into that?" she asks coyly. "Just a good guess," I answer as I slide my hands down her butt where they easily find the end of her skirt and trail the edges of her underwear.

It actually is just a guess, as I do not make a habit of picking up girls in bars—especially not girls in tube tops who smell like vanilla and have recently broken up with their boyfriends. In fact, I have only ever been with girls who made the first move and seemed far more worldly and experienced than me. But Carrie appears available and open and I am feeling bolstered, so I say, "Come on. Let's get out of here." We walk through the streets, fingers linked, until we reach my apartment. I lead her inside, and as I am closing the door behind us she asks, "Do you pick up a lot of girls at bars?" "No," I tell her. "You're the first." "Uh, huh," she smirks. "I somehow doubt that." Her doubts are unfounded, but I decide not to press the issue. I am liking the novelty of being the seducer and want to play with it some more.

I decide not to worry about the formalities that usually accompany bringing a guest to your home for the first time and lead Carrie straight to my bedroom. "Lie down," I say, and motion towards my bed. She complies and looks at me expectantly. I sit next to her and put my mouth on hers, tasting cigarettes and fresh lip gloss that she has managed to apply on the walk over. "Take off your top," I tell her and lean back, propped on one elbow to watch her pull the tiny strip of material over her head. She isn't wearing anything underneath, and I see she has two heavy rings dangling from her nipples that for some reason I hadn't noticed earlier. "Not what you expected?" Carrie asks as I find my hand drawn towards her naked chest.

"Nope," I answer, suddenly wondering if this young ingénue is actually such an innocent after all. "But, I'm not complaining." I push her back again gently. My mouth finds her nipple and pulls on the ring. A few minutes later I have hiked up her skirt and slid her panties down to her ankles. They are white and cotton and I wonder how many people have caught a flash of them throughout the day under a skirt that I decide I would never have the courage to leave home in. With her underwear crumpled at the bottom of the bed, I see a small, perfectly groomed thatch of dark blond hair and the tops of her smooth thighs. I trail my fingers down between her legs, slowly opening her lips and edging up to her stiffening clit.

She reaches for my shirt and starts to pull it over my head, but I stop her, saying, "Maybe later." I let her settle back onto the bed and run my tongue down between her breasts, over her navel and to the top of her mons. I remove my mouth and lick my fingers until they are slick. Then I slowly slip my hand back between her legs and work my fingers into her pussy. I am not used to being such a top and preventing my partners from reciprocating, but I am getting off on my new role.

She begins to moan softly, and I take this as my cue to continue my tongue's descent between her legs. I find her clit and begin to gently suck on her while rhythmically rocking my hand into her body. A few minutes later her breathing becomes more rapid, she begins to moan with greater intensity, and, sooner than I expect, I feel her stiffen and shake. I am a little stunned. My sorority girl pick-up has just come on my mouth and hand.

I remove myself and slide up next to her. She is still on her back, eyes closed, her breathing slowly returning to normal. I grin at her, kiss her face and eyes, and then flop back on the bed. Deciding I am happy to remain clothed for this encounter, I light us each a cigarette. It's still early, so I suggest we go grab another drink down the street. She gets dressed and we walk outside to the bar. We sip a few beers and make out in the corner of the half-empty room. After a few drinks we agree to go our separate ways; some things are best simply taken for what they are. So, I hail her a cab and return home, where I crawl into my rumpled bed and fall asleep wondering why I'd never tried to pick up a cute girl in a bar before and how long I'd have to wait before doing so again.

law school and lesbians

●

rachel kramer bussel

Before you take the law school preparatory exams, the LSATs, they tell you not to change anything in your life too much. Don't suddenly alter your schedule, get a new job, or start a new relationship. They probably also meant "don't have sex with a woman for the first time," but I didn't let that stop me. It was my senior year of college, and I was a very young, naive, and whimsical nineteen. I'd been slogging away at practice test after practice test, trying to learn the ins and outs of logic problems, trying to outsmart my examiners. In the meantime, I was hanging out with Jenny, a tougher, older chick in several of my classes. We were totally different; I was sheltered, nerdy, my head permanently stuck in a book. I'd never been to a pride parade, and my only dyke acquaintances were older family friends who seemed far removed from campus life. But Jenny was exciting; she'd lived on her own, she'd bedded who knows how many girls, she plowed through class and campus totally unashamed of taking up space, while I was trying to shrink myself, holding back at every turn lest I become too visible. I was alone in more ways than one, and having someone so larger-than-life interested in me made me feel pretty, wild, exotic. I was fascinated and, yes, a little frightened of Jenny. She'd grab my breast as we walked to the supermarket, pull me into unexpected public displays of affection, challenge me to go outside my little insular comfort zone.

That first night, our kisses turned into something more, and one of my first thoughts as we embraced in my upstairs room on College Avenue was, *I can't believe I'm doing this.* And I couldn't. It just wasn't me—not the kissing a girl part, but the breaking the rules, deliberately disobeying the standards set for me. I was totally nervous, yet excited;

all the weeks of our flirting and stumbling and silly fun had led up to this. We moved over to my bed, a typical simple college twin, and she showed me how to touch her. I started off tentatively, playing with her clit, examining her pussy, admiring her body's combination of hard and soft. I'd never really touched myself too much before, so stroking her clit and feeling her react was something new. She kept her tampon in, so I was on the surface, but that didn't seem to stop her from getting totally aroused. I was amazed, but didn't have too much time to dwell on the novelty. She knew it was my first time, but like everything I did back then, I wanted to play it cool, to dive right in and act like I knew it all. And maybe that's the best approach to sex one can have, because confidence breeds skill, or at least is a necessary precursor.

I went slowly at first, my fingers prowling through her pubic hair to get to her clit, then dipping lower, exploring her lips, tracing, tugging, brushing over the white string and wondering what she felt like inside. I went back to her clit, two fingers circling, pressing, rubbing, trying to get it right. My heart was pounding, and it was dark so I couldn't really see, but I loved the way I made her moan and move and push back against me, loved how lost I was clearly making her feel as I stepped over into my own personal pussy wonderland, one so different from everything I'd known before. In a few short minutes, I'd made her come. "Damn girl, you're good," she said, and pulled me on top of her for a kiss. I slid my leg in between hers while she cradled me in her strong, powerful arms and I felt more than a little like I'd stepped into some strange, brave, new, uncertain world.

Of course, the next day, as page after page of standardized test questions rolled across the desk, all I could think of was the previous night. Of our embrace under my dingy light bulb, of that sublime satisfaction of her short, simple, breathless words, "You're good," after I made her come. Somehow, I pulled it off, a 660 if I recall, though looking back , I certainly deserved to have bombed the LSATs. I cracked the test, but wound up retreating from her, scared by either Jenny's boldness or my own misgivings. Her girlness was so big, so overwhelming, and it didn't feel like I could keep us in our safe, special private box anymore. Before I gave up entirely, though, I tried my best to make it work, wanting to see just where we could go—together.

Jenny had a tattoo above her pussy, and this was the first of either one I'd really seen up close. We took a shower together one day at her place. I took the soapy sponge and rubbed it all over her body, the white foamy suds clinging to her skin. She put her hand over mine, leading my way down, down, down, until the sponge hovered over her tattoo. I knelt down, looking up close at her colored skin, her pink lips, as water sluiced over both of us. I ignored the stream beating down on me and positioned myself between her legs, my own tucked underneath me as my tongue parted her clean, slippery entrance. I felt her pubic hair nestling against my skin and wondered if I was doing a good job. But soon her taste shifted, and I could tell when she heated up from the inside. I tasted her salty, special flavor, felt the way her pussy's entrance greeted my tongue, sleek, slippery, not giving me any single place to cling to. I pulled back, looking up at the tattoo, an image that's faded in my mind after a decade's worth of licks; was it green? Tribal? Big? Small? The details escape me, but that ink's what I saw before I returned my mouth to her clit, holding one hand steady on her hip while she moaned and tried not to fall as I suckled her hard nub for all I was worth. Here was something I could latch onto; I could be rewarded by feeling it harden beneath me. The water still trickled around us, growing colder, but I didn't care. I liked being down on my knees, liked feeling the tub's hardness against my shins, her womanly body, all muscles and curves, strength and power, a sturdy beauty, above me, reassuring. Already, then, I liked getting other people off, liked the sense of power and submission, approval and desire, test and reward all rolled into one. In that shower, I let go, in a way I hadn't done before; I lost the nerdy girl who wanted to please everyone in the world in favor of someone who simply wanted to please one special woman. I let the water fall around me, my eyes closed as I tasted her while she pressed down against me, giving me the only feedback I truly needed.

The rest of our courtship is a bit of a blur. I remember watching Dr. Katz on TV, playing with her cat as I teased him with catnip, sitting in a restaurant on Shattuck while we analyzed whether looks had anything to do with one's queerness. I remember laughing with her at huge, snorting private jokes that turned into kisses once we were alone. I remember her sneaking me into the gym where she worked, and sharing jelly beans on campus. I remember being nervous when she came in and kissed me before class, sure that everyone around me knew what I was doing in my off hours. I remember her telling me, casual as could be, that an old friend was coming to town. They might have sex, but it would be no big deal, no strings. No big deal? No strings? I was far from conversant in the language of polyamory at the time, and had been starting to feel trapped, confused. We worked on one level, but on another things were starting to feel strange in a way I wasn't sure I could handle.

Eventually we parted ways, and only saw each other a few more times around campus. I remember she had a girl on her arm as her graduation cape flowed around her, while I felt timid, hovering in a corner in mine, changed by our relationship, but thus far only on the inside. Is it a coincidence that I got to know my dykey side while in law school, sneaking out from the rigors of torts and contracts to explore other kinds of mysteries, to wade through crowds of hot girls until I found another one who wanted to come home with me and teach me a thing or two about getting and giving it from another woman? Maybe, or maybe the two became inextricably linked that first night as visions of pussy and passing scores mingled in my mind while Jenny made me dizzy with her tongue. Either way, she made my world orbit in ways that I could only imagine at the time. Wherever she is, and whether she realizes it or not, I owe her one.

what makes her tick?

●

tara alton

I had been trying to figure out what makes this girl tick for weeks. Everyone at work says she is stuck-up because she is so beautiful, but I'm starting to think it's not true. It's not her fault she's in the small percentage of truly attractive people in the world. You know how beauty weaves itself through the population, leaving some women gorgeous or cute as button or like the girl next door, and the rest of us get one or two good parts, like me.

Then there was Maxine, the jaw-dropping girl at work who seems to have everything from looks to grace to self-confidence. I always thought people would flock to someone like her, that she would have loads of fans, friends, and admirers, but I am starting to think quite a few people secretly resent her. People will say hardly a word to her. That was why I volunteered to sit at the desk opposite her, because I knew what it was like to be singled out, mostly because everyone thinks I'm shy.

For the first few days, I tried not to study her face when I thought she wasn't looking, but it was hard. Mostly it was the space between her eyes that drew me in. She reminded me of Marilyn Monroe, and she had full lips like her, too. Her creamy skin always seemed perfect. Her eyelashes were long and curled. She knew how to dress as well, choosing tailored silk blouses that she tucked neatly into skirts or slacks, emphasizing her full breasts and tiny waist.

To be honest, she fascinated me. I hung on her every word, watched her every move, and wondered what she looked like naked when she took a shower. This wasn't the first time 1 had been attracted to a woman, but it was the first time it was a real, live person. Before it had been crushes on women like Bettie Page and Jayne Mansfield, in which

23

I would spend hours looking at their pictures online, not sure what to do with my feelings. Now with Maxine, I wanted to know everything about her, from what went on in her head to what her pinkie toes looked like when they were bare.

Gradually, we started talking more as we worked. Our conversations were a little guarded at first, mine from my shyness, hers no doubt from being snubbed all the time, but soon we were sharing jokes and gossip from around the office.

As the workdays passed, I began to sense she was beginning to let her guard down around me, because I noticed that she wasn't exactly working all the time. She was doing things like calling psychic hotlines and asking about her future. And two or three times a day she was calling someone and asking them if they were dead yet before she hung up the phone.

One day, she asked me to dial her pager's number. I asked her why. She said to just do it. Unbuttoning the top button on her slacks, she slid the pager down inside them and motioned for me to start dialing.

"What are you doing?" I asked.

"Having some fun," she said.

I looked around the office to see if anyone was watching. I wasn't the best-behaved employee, but I still didn't want to get in trouble.

"Can't you do this yourself?" I asked.

"It's sexier when someone else does it."

My mouth opened in surprise. She thought it would be sexy for me to vibrate her. Trying not to blush, I took a deep breath and let it out before I dialed the number. She closed her eyes as the pager vibrated.

"You're insane," I said, watching her remove her impromptu sex toy.

After that, she must have asked me to vibrate her a couple times a day. No one ever caught on, and I had to admit it was getting me aroused. My panties were feeling as if they were caught in a permanent knot between my legs, and things were always a little moist down there after a pager session.

I wanted to ask her to vibrate me, but I didn't have the balls to ask nor could I afford my own pager. Borrowing hers seemed a little too personal for work friends.

A week later, she asked me out to lunch. Imagine my elation. I felt so cool leaving the office with her as everyone else looked on. I thought we would hit a fast-food place and eat in the car, but she announced we were going to the Mushroom, the fanciest restaurant in town. Of course, I panicked. I hadn't worn the most stylish of clothes, only a sweater over khakis with loafers, and I confessed to her that I only had five dollars in my wallet. She told me not to worry. We were meeting a friend of hers.

All the cars in the parking lot were extremely classy, and my knees were actually shaking as we stepped inside. I had never seen a place this elegant, with its expensive linens and gleaming china. I was relieved when we were swept down one flight to the cellar where there was a less formal tavern atmosphere.

I was expecting to meet another beautiful girl like her, so I was more than a little freaked out when I saw it was a classy but ancient old man. It turns out he was Greek and owned a few restaurants in Greek Town. There was a wedding ring on his finger, but he was looking at Maxine as if she were the angel of his life.

My heart sank a little as I considered the possibility that she was having an affair with him. As I ordered the roasted polenta with vegetables, I noticed how he kept trying to put his arm around her and she kept shrugging him off. The lunch conversation consisted of him telling me all the rotten things she had done to him, like stealing his credit cards and charging up a storm, and how he kept forgiving her.

As he spoke, I felt my food sticking in my throat. She had to be sleeping with him, I thought, and it chilled my soul. With a pang, I realized I wanted to be the only one sleeping with her.

There was no time for dessert. She gave him a peck on the cheek, and I noticed that he slipped her some money.

Holy cow, she was a prostitute! The moment we got back into her car, I gave her a quizzical look.

She held up the money.

"He paid me fifty dollars just for having lunch with him," she said. "You can't beat that."

"Are you sleeping with him?"

She shook her head. "No. Just torturing him. He's the one I call all the time and ask if he's dead yet."

There was a pause. I wasn't sure what to say.

"I really enjoyed watching your face during lunch though," she said. "You're so easy to surprise."

It became a sort of game between us after that lunch. She would tell me something shocking, like how she would buy Coach handbags on sale at one department store and then return them for full price at another store, making herself a nice little cash bonus in the transaction. Or how she once got into a threesome at a house party in the upstairs bedroom that was being used as a coatroom, and how she enjoyed the sex with the woman more than the man because she was better. Even though he was the one who picked her up in the first place, she let him know the truth.

These stories were becoming the high points of my work days. I was getting an education I never knew I would have, and she was having me call her pager even more frequently, but now she didn't close her eyes. She looked into mine.

Winter came early this year and with it a terrible snowstorm. Our company was so worried that they might not have employees there to operate the phones the next day that they were willing to put us up at a nearby hotel, two to a room, with a dinner and a breakfast voucher.

"Do you want to stay? I'm afraid to drive home, but I don't want to room with anyone else," Maxine said.

I knew I could easily get home in this storm because I used to live up north, but I feigned being afraid of the snow as much as she was just so I could stay in a hotel room with her.

At the hotel, I was nervous, but it turned out to be just like a pajama party. We ordered room service, watched cable movies, and ate junk food we bought from the vending machine at work. Soon it was midnight. I stifled a yawn.

"Time for bed," said Maxine.

I prayed for a moment that she might suggest sharing one of the double beds, but she chose the one by the wall. I started to get undressed, opting to go the underwear-as-pajamas route, feeling a little self-conscious about my lack of curves, when to my amazement, Maxine stripped down to nothing right in front of me and strode into the bathroom.

I was stunned. Her body was as gorgeous as her face. She had full breasts, a heart-shaped ass, long, lean legs, and iridescent skin. The familiar aroused feeling I got at my desk was back in full force. My legs feeling weak, I sat on my bed.

Maxine came out of the bathroom, her face full of worry, and she stopped right in front of me. I could smell her skin.

"Do you think my right nipple points off in a weird direction?" she asked.

Was this a ploy to get me to look at her breasts? She didn't need to do that. I was already trying not to look.

"I used to work as a stripper and the men were always saying this one looked off in the wrong direction," she said.

"You were a stripper?" I asked.

She nodded and pointed at her nipple.

I stared at it. It *was* slightly pointing away. I nodded.

Sighing, she flicked off the lights. I heard her slide under her sheets.

The room was deathly quiet. I knew this was the time to tell her how I felt about her because there was a fluttery feeling in my stomach that wouldn't go away. I looked over at her bed. My eyes had adjusted to the darkness of the room and I could make out the shape of her. The sheets were draped over the curve of her hips.

"Maxine?" I asked. "Do you really like girls?"

Sitting up in bed, she looked over at me.

"There was this one girl who I thought I was in love with. I confided in her. I told her the real stuff, the stuff that really mattered, and she betrayed me. I haven't touched another girl since."

I wanted to say there was no way in hell I would ever betray her, but she let out this sigh that sounded as if she was tired of the entire world.

"How about I let you in on a little secret," she said.

I held my breath. She was going to confess she liked me too, even after that horrible experience, because I meant so much to her. She wanted to climb into my bed, slide her naked body on top of mine, and kiss me deeply where I was throbbing so painfully now.

"Everyone in the world is a shit," she said "Everyone is simply out for what he or she can get. You have to take what you can get before someone else takes it first. There is no such thing as true love or true anything. To be honest, I can't even be friends with anyone. I can barely tolerate people I hardly even know because it's all just bunch of shit."

Letting out another sigh, she lay back down and turned her back to me.

In shock, I turned away from her as well, playing her words back over in my head. What did she consider me? Certainly not a friend. Was I an acquaintance she could barely tolerate? I thought back to all the times when I thought she was confiding in me, but it wasn't true. She wasn't trusting me, I realized. She wanted the entertainment value of shocking me.

I felt so hurt and used, and yet when I slid my hand between my legs, I found I was still throbbing because she was naked in the bed next to me.

Listening to the sounds of her breath becoming even as she fell asleep, I said her name once just to be sure. She didn't stir.

I closed my eyes, imagining a different scenario with her, a simpler time and place, in which I hardly knew anything about her other than that she was pretty. I was at a strip club and we were in a private booth in the back room. All I knew was her fake stage name, and she would rub her naked body on mine because I had some money, and because she thought I was cute she might let me kiss her nipple that pointed away.

Sliding my fingers in and out of my hot wetness that had been building for months, I masturbated to a fantasy about a real woman for the first time. I could feel my clit swelling up, and I let my thumb rub it back and forth while I kept my middle finger inside me. With my other hand, I squeezed my nipple.

In my mind, she was straddling me now, her breasts in my face, and my hands were on her hips as she ground herself down on me. She let me lick and bite her delicate nipple, and I held it between my teeth as if it was a precious morsel. It was like having gourmet chocolate for the first time, and realizing what you had been missing all along.

Holding my breath, I concentrated on rubbing harder, the tingles starting around my clit, causing it to spasm, little jolts of electricity jumping through my skin. Even more frantically I rubbed, thinking about her dry-humping me with abandon. It sent the tingles into a massive eruption up my legs, up my thighs, up my torso, and throughout my upper body, even to my fingertips. This surreal feeling came over me, and for a moment I felt like I was outside myself, looking down on the hotel room from the ceiling, my body in wild sexual torment and her beautiful body asleep, lost in her dreams where everything seemed dark and bitter.

I didn't want to know what made her tick anymore, nor did I want her to know anything else about me either. I buried my face in my pillow as I came so she couldn't hear me.

first sight

●

laren lebran

Three pairs of eyes probed my naked flesh. Hers were remote blank discs of impenetrable blue, so impersonal as to leave a chill in their wake. His were clinically appraising—studying me with curious neutrality, making me wonder if my heart still beat.

Only your eyes were alive—slow-dancing over the hills and valleys of my body, dipping into my secret places with unfettered abandon. The satin-covered marble beneath my thighs was slick and unforgiving. If I moved at all, every fragile dream would be exposed.

"Uh…we need a model…for the special class I take at night…to pose," you said, looking past me out the window to the quadrangle far below. "Nude."

I laughed. We'd been roommates for eight months, and you were still shy with me. I suppose it was because when we all showed up for the fall semester and got our room assignments, there'd been whispers about you. Lesbian, they'd said. Carefully polite, but with just that little hint of prurient excitement. Sure, everyone seemed cool about it, but you must have known that everyone was just waiting to see who would be in the bed across from yours, ten feet away, for the next nine months.

I sensed the others stare at me when first your name, then mine, was called. But I was watching you. Your eyes darted to my face and then away, and then cautiously back again. I was still looking at you when you finally searched my eyes for the answer. The uncertainty in your expression made me want to hold you, and I'd never felt that way about anyone before. I wanted to say, "I don't care what they say. I don't care who you love. Just don't look so scared." But I didn't know if the words would hurt more than help, so I said nothing. But I smiled, and that must've been all right, because you smiled back.

"Nude, huh?"

You nodded silently.

"Sure, I'll do it."

"Bend your knee up, please," the faintly accented voice of the instructor requested from just beyond my field of vision. "Very nice. Open just a little…yes, just like that. Perfect."

It was my fourth session, but only the first time I could see you clearly as you worked. I'd been aware of you before, sitting expectantly with charcoal in hand as I removed the white robe and let it drop behind me before settling onto the dais. The room was always very quiet as I bared myself, but the very first time, I imagined I heard a small hitch in your breath. You were careful not to look at me then, at least not until I could not see you.

You were always so careful around me. Careful not to walk in while I was changing. Careful to keep your eyes on the ceiling while we lay naked in our respective beds, talking late into the night or delaying the moment in the morning when we would have to separate. Careful not to ask me about the dates I went on, when I returned to find you still awake, sitting cross-legged on your bed with a book in front of you that I was certain you had not been reading.

I was careful, too. Careful not to tell you that I'd rather stay at home with you, laughing about our day, or bitching about our classes, or confessing what we thought about and dreamed about and hoped for in our futures. I was careful around you the way I never was around the other girls, because I understood that you weren't like the other girls. And to treat you as if you were would have been cruel, as if I didn't know you at all. I didn't tell you I was a virgin, and I don't know why. I guess because you weren't like the other girls, and I liked that.

I liked that a lot, and sometimes, sometimes I wished that you would look at me as if I weren't like the other girls, either.

Once I became "the model," a breathing still-life, I couldn't watch you any longer. I was a prisoner, unbound but restrained nonetheless. I could not turn my head to see if the heat I felt building inside was the result of your charcoal tracing the line of my skin on your paper. And always, when I was finally released from my invisible bondage, you had already risen, and were hurriedly packing your things with a downcast gaze, rushing to leave. I was forced to walk home beside you as if I had not just spent an hour with the promise of your hands upon my body. We never talked about it, and you were so careful not to look at me.

Not so tonight. Tonight your eyes were everywhere.

Tonight, you'd shifted your easel to a new spot. I could look at your face, and you, it seemed, could look directly into my soul. You sat upon a stool, and a rectangle of canvas propped upon wide-spread wooden legs was the only barrier between us. Your face was unmasked, your emotions as exposed to me as my body was to you. Your hands moved out of sight, sliding over my breasts, down my belly, between my legs, with swift sure strokes. Your eyes, wide and dark and unknowingly hungry, swept over my body in the wake of your touch with far less restraint, grazing my nipples to hardness and teasing my inner thighs to a soft sheen of welcome. To everyone else I was a profile, an abstraction, a study in light and shadow. To you alone I bled and breathed and quickened.

You did not know what your expression revealed, and I did not disclose what I saw, lest you hide your passion and your desire. Thus we sat, souls on display, pretending we were blind.

"Thank you, that will be all for tonight."

I read the disappointment in your face, felt the loss of our connection immediately. You did not, as you usually do, immediately begin to gather your charcoals and pencils. I rose slowly while the others prepared to leave. Within minutes, we were alone. I held the robe before me but did not yet put it on.

"You're not finished, are you?" I said at last.

You gave a start, as if surprised that I had spoken. Then you blushed.

"No." You indicated the canvas with a sweep of your hand, your voice laden with frustration. "Tonight was the first time I felt like I might capture some part of…you."

"Why tonight?" Although I knew.

You looked up from the image of me and into my eyes. "Because tonight was the first time I let you see me. Before tonight, you've been the only one brave enough to do that."

"All the other nights," I whispered as I moved closer, "you looked at me, but tonight, you touched me."

You nodded and I saw you shiver. Your voice when you spoke was urgent and low. "I could feel you lead my hands over your body, guiding me, teaching me." You held my gaze so desperately, your longing so open and pure, I ached. "I was almost there."

In the distance, I heard a door close as the others left. I let the robe fall, a ribbon of white gathering between us on the dark floor. "I want you to finish."

You stared for an instant, a soft groan escaping from somewhere deep inside, then you turned with outstretched hand toward your charcoal.

"No." I grasped your wrist and brought your hand to the center of my chest. The edges of your palm nestled against the inner curve of my breasts. "This way. I want you to look at me. I want to watch you looking at me."

Your fingers were hot and trembled on my skin. "Oh god," you whispered as I shuddered.

I focused on your face as you softly traced my breasts, my heart pounding wildly as the wonder rose in your eyes. You stepped closer until your jeans brushed my thighs and you brought your thumbs to my nipples, fingers splayed to cradle the weight of my breasts. I tilted my head back as pleasure bowed my spine, and when you put your mouth on my neck, warm and wet, I made a sound I'd never heard before. A whimper, a plea, a paean of delight. My legs quaked, and I sagged into you, trusting that you would not let me fall.

You pressed your face to my throat, your breathing ragged, while your hands, those sensitive wonderful hands, explored my body with slow reverence. I was your canvas and you painted me with desire.

"Don't be careful anymore," I begged. "Tease my nipples. Touch me. Touch me before I shatter."

You whimpered then, long fingers clamping around the hard points of my breasts. Sharp, pure, delicate pain. My clitoris hardened and ached. I braced my arms on your shoulders and sought your mouth with mine, needing you somewhere far deeper than my skin. Your cheeks were damp, and I kissed away your tears. You drove a thigh between my legs, and I soaked the denim. Seconds, minutes, hours passed as we thrust and moaned and gasped, until I couldn't stand the slightest barrier between us. I curled my fingers in the thick damp hair at the back of your neck and put my mouth against your ear.

"I need you. I need you inside me."

With your mouth fused to mine, you wrapped an arm around my waist and turned me until my hips hit the stool. I sank gratefully upon it and you pushed between my legs, one hand knifing high between my thighs. I arched to take you in, and you hesitated, fingertips dipping into me, but going no further. I framed your face with my palms, my fingers trembling over your cheekbones and your mouth.

"I've been waiting for you," I whispered. "Please."

You kissed my fingers as you parted my swollen flesh, caressing my clitoris with swift, hard strokes, making me come. So close now, I succumbed to the hunger in your eyes as you slid deep inside me. Filled with you, surrounding you, coming for you, I saw what you hadn't wanted me to see all these months.

Desire. Passion. Love.

You touched me, and, finally, I saw.

what's a little fisting between friends?

●

audacia ray

I'm a bit of a nerd, and sex is one of many things I obsessively gather information about. Reading about sex is my most often employed form of procrastination, because, you know, it's totally valid and useful research for my work as a sex educator, writer, and what-have-you. I often read all about sexual practices that I'm not especially interested in for myself, but find really interesting from the anthropological perspective (and this is how you spell n-e-r-d). Fisting fell into the anthropological category for me—I read all about it, asked friends who'd done it a million questions about it, and then stored the information in the sex library of my brain. I didn't think I'd ever be on the business end of a fisting, but it was a good thing to understand, you know, just in case I got asked about it at a dinner party.

One of my longtime partners in the obsessive collecting and sharing of sexual information is Jane. Just like me, she has an insatiable curiosity about all things sexual—and she's also more than happy to make the research personal. Though Jane and I agreed early in our acquaintance that the whole dating thing was not a good idea for us, we didn't exclude the possibility of becoming friends-with-benefits. However, our sexual relationship was like many sexual relationships I've had with women—lots of talking, including talking about fucking, but no actual fucking.

We told each other and ourselves that we just hadn't gotten around to sex yet, not that we were falling into the territory of premature lesbian bed-death. I'd been in a monogamous relationship for the first two years of our friendship, so that had a legitimate barrier to the consummation of our experiments. When I was unbound from monogamy in the new year of 2003, we vowed to fuck each other's brains out, and then carried on with our talking.

It was spring, and my roommate and I had fallen into the lovely and delicious habit of making big dinners every Sunday and then lounging in front of a movie, bellies full, ready to take on the new week. One Sunday we decided spontaneously to add some other folks to our low-key tradition. We made a round of phone calls and then set to cooking a big pasta dinner. The smell of garlic wafted through the house as our guests arrived. Jane was among the first to appear, bearing a loaf of fresh bread and a bottle of wine. We cracked open the wine and sat in the kitchen, keeping the bubbling pasta sauce company. Maybe it was the warm smells of the kitchen or the inner warmth the wine was producing, but there was a palpable, sexy tension in the room with the two of us.

As I served the pasta to my guests, my eyes met Jane's and we exchanged a knowing glance—this would be the night. Later, when the party started to dwindle, Jane boldly declared to our group of friends, "Dacia and I are going to finally have some hot sex. Anyone want to join us?" Our friends, undaunted by this offering and accustomed to our debauched lifestyle, all declined, citing the fact that it was, after all, growing late on a Sunday evening and there was work to be done in the morning that required rest. You know you're friends with seasoned perverts when the decision for sleep instead of an orgy is made so easily; there will be other orgies.

The house rid of non–sex-wanting friends, I smirked at Jane, "Don't you think it was a bit presumptuous of you to tell everyone that we're going to fuck? What if I just want to talk and cuddle?"

She looked at me, and, using sarcasm that rated up there with her best bedroom eyes, said, "Talking and cuddling are fine. Sex is too much work anyway."

I grabbed her by the hair and slammed her against the wall next to my bedroom door. Grinning wickedly and with lust in my eyes, I said, "Can we do the kind of cuddling where we pull each other's hair and fuck really hard?" She answered with her soft, wet mouth, gently sucking my lower lip and biting it slightly—she held onto it for just a few more seconds to let me know she meant business. Squinting through one eye so that I could clear any obstacles in our way, we waddled towards the bed, unwilling to break our horny liplock.

I turned Jane so I could grind myself against her luscious ass as I pushed her onto the bed, a beautiful wood four-poster my dad had made for me—the perfect kind of bed for tying someone to, the perfect height to bend someone over and expose their ass for a solid spanking or fucking. Conveniently, she was wearing a skirt, so I asked her to pull it up around her waist. The ass I'd see so many times at our platonic—or at least well-restrained—sleepovers was there before me, awaiting my ministrations. I bent to my knees, lightly running my hands up her legs, and felt her shiver from my touch. She could surely hear the smile in my voice when I asked, "Now, what do you like, little girl?'

The thing about having sex with someone with whom I'd discussed my own and her sexuality for two years is that we pretty much knew all there is to know about each other's sexual responses, but we just had to try it on for size. It also means that the experience was bound to be full of laughter and slightly awkward moments. Considering that, in general, Jane and I both live for awkward moments, the whole experience was halted several times for us to catch our breath from all the laughing.

After the perfunctory undressing, which we'd done together in a nonsexual context a thousand times, we fell into each other, rolling on my bed, groping, flesh straining as we became accustomed to how our bodies felt together. She pinned me on my back, letting the curtains of her hair drop down around us, tickling me slowly, teasingly. I tried to squirm away from her and giggled a bit as she put both of my arms over my head and held them in her left hand. I didn't have to tell her twice that I'm an appreciator of a fine handjob and that I prefer fingers to tongues; the fingers of her right hand brushed lightly over my belly on their way to my very wet cunt. Though I'm sure Jane could feel the wet heat emanating from my vulva, she resisted the urge to dip into the wetness. Her fingers traced around my outer labia a few times and then moved to my inner labia. She pulled lightly on my right inner labia, which is the longer of the two; I let out a sigh and tried to wiggle my pussy onto her fingers. She laughed in recognition and said slyly, "I know that pussy-hungry move, and I'm not buying it." As she said it, her left hand released my arms, which stayed over my head—I was her pussy putty, completely.

Jane moved her left hand to my pubic bone and commented, "Forget your arms, this is what needs restraining." She pressed down enough to make it tough for me to thrust my hips up at her, and resumed the teasing of my pussy, this time spreading my inner labia open. If I'd been anywhere near cognizant of our many conversations about this sexy maneuver, I would have remembered that we'd agreed that to be spread open and stared at is a truly hot thing—the exposure, the taut feeling of increasingly engorged pussy lips being parted and held open. Spreading me open like this revealed exactly how much she'd already gotten me worked up; I could feel my girl juices trickling down the inside of my thighs.

She tested the waters with just one finger and then eagerly dipped more of her fingers inside me. She expertly curled two fingers up to rub my G-spot ("Damn, you weren't kidding about how prominent your g-spot is!" she said) and thumbed my clit. Taking her left hand off of my pubic bone, Jane allowed me to rock my pelvis and grind my G-spot and clit against her ever-ready fingers. I easily rocked myself into a brief, thigh-quivering orgasm, prompting Jane to exclaim, "Oh, I know that one—that's a warm-up orgasm!" I took a big, ragged gulp of air and blinked three times for yes.

As the waves of my orgasm subsided, Jane observed that my pussy was hungry—she could feel the dull throb of my pulse as ever more blood rushed to my vulva. In those blissful post-orgasm moments, I didn't want her fingers to slip out of my pussy, but I wasn't ready to resume fucking, so she used my pussy as a convenient storage container for her fingers while we gossiped a bit about our friends who'd come to dinner earlier in the night and given the hot sex a pass. As our conversation moved along, I found that I was unconsciously starting to hump Jane's hand, ready for more. We kept making idle talk as she slipped three and then four fingers into me. We were both a little surprised to note that she was well on her way to putting her hand inside of me by the time we noticed this progression of events.

"So," she began, four fingers deep in me. "I could, you know, keep going with this. I mean, I have this thumb thing kinda hanging out here."

Without thinking about it too much, I laughed, "Give it a whirl. I'll say uncle if it gets to be too much."

Her thumb teased the lips of my vulva and then disappeared between its folds, easy peasy. Five fingers in me. But then there was the not so small matter of that wide part of her hand, knuckles and whatnot. We paused and recalled our research on the matter: tuck the thumb into the palm of the hand, scrunch the fingers together, face the palm of the hand up, have patience, don't force it, breath, relax. We resumed our conversational banter while also keeping the receptiveness of my vagina in mind. When we giggled about the absurdity of the whole situation, Jane felt my vaginal muscles relax a bit, and exclaimed, "Oh, that's it—laugh some more and I'll be able to get my fist inside you!"

We stared at each other, not laughing. "Uh, maybe you should tell some jokes or something?" I suggested hopefully.

"Okay! So a duck walks into a bar..."

Pop! My cunt opened and sucked her hand in.

I don't know what the hell was so funny about this half joke (Jane later confessed that she didn't have a way to finish it off), but my pussy granted her hand entry up past the wrist because of it. We could barely stop laughing long enough for her to inform me that I'd quite thoroughly swallowed her hand up inside of me. The success of our endeavor started to settle in as Jane tried to describe what having her hand in me was like from her side of things.

"There's a mirror on the desk at the foot of the bed," I said. She squealed, "I wanna see! I wanna see!" We carefully wiggled closer to the foot of the bed so Jane could grab the mirror with her free hand. I snatched the mirror away from her and aimed it at my cunt, which took me back to the time my mom left a copy of *Our Bodies, Ourselves* and this very same mirror on my bed soon after I'd gotten my first period. Looking at my cunt full of Jane's hand was like that discovery of seeing the folds of my labia for the first time—I felt just as gingerly about looking as I had when I was eleven. "Wow, that's really...in there. My cunt looks...different."

"Of course it does, silly, you've got my hand in there up to the wrist!"

My laughter made the muscles in my vagina contract, sending Jane into gleeful descriptions of the soft, squishy, living wetness of the inside of my cunt. She cupped her fingers around my cervix and described the different textures of my girl-innards as I lay there in bliss, feeling full of her hand and very, very bonded with her. We kind of hung out with her in me to the hilt for a while, until we decided that it was best to leave our first fisting adventure at that. We slowly and gently disengaged. After a few minutes of recovering, reminiscing ("Hey! Remember when you had your hand in my cunt? That was awesome!"), and fading into a sleepy delight, I decided it was high time that I give Jane a fuckworthy what-for. After all, it had taken us a few years to get sexed up together, and who knew when we'd get around to fucking again.

I reached over and squeezed Jane's boob to get her attention and make sure she wasn't drifting off to sleep. "So, why don't you examine the contents of that box underneath my bed," I suggested coyly. I've never seen a half-asleep girl rocket out of bed so quickly. She knew exactly what box I was talking about, and by her purposeful digging I could tell that she already knew what she wanted. She tossed my soft leather strap-on harness at me, hauled out the Hitachi magic wand, and then stood up and beamed at me while displaying her chosen prize: my nexus junior, the double dildo built for mutually penetrating strap-on fuckery. Though neither of us was a stranger to the joys of strapping on a colorful silicone cock (or being fucked by one), neither of us had had the opportunity to play with this particular toy.

I switched places with her: standing by the bed, I eased myself into the familiar leather of the harness and adjusted the nexus so that one end was inside of me and the other pointed its silicone hard-on ever so slightly towards the ceiling. Jane eagerly flopped down on the bed, rubbed a generous bit of lube onto her girl parts and pulled her knees up towards her chest. I crawled to her and began to lower my mouth to her pussy, but she stopped me and simply said, "Fuck me please." Her tone of voice was both straightforward and seductive; I smiled at her, appreciating a girl who knows what she wants. I reached for the lube and stroked my girlcock slowly with it, to Jane's moans of approval.

I gripped her thighs just above her knees and pressed her knees into her chest with the weight of my body as I slipped my girlcock into her with one smooth, hard stroke. We both grunted as our pelvises met.

I fucked her with slow, languorous strokes, slipping my cock almost completely out of her and then thrusting back in deeply. My deliberately slow pumps made her feel every inch of my cock as I penetrated her; when our pelvises touched, I could feel the cock inside of me twitch against my G-spot.

Jane twisted and moaned and bit her arm in delight, but I could tell that she was starting to get desperate to come, and that she wasn't going to come with me fucking her this way. Truth be told, that was kind of the point—I loved watching her writhe around, not quite able to come but loving every moment. Finally the frustration gleamed in her eyes, and she announced, "I'm going to ride you." In one deft maneuver, I bent to her, she wrapped her arms around my neck, and we rolled over so that she was sitting upright with my cock buried deep inside her. She reached for the Hitachi and nestled it firmly against her clit as she rocked my cock.

Jane was on a mission for orgasm, and I had suddenly become a prop—albeit a useful one that could twist her nipples and utter words of encouragement. As far as I was concerned, I had the best seat in the house; witnessing her orgasm was a lovely thing indeed. I watched as her body began to quake. Her head lolled back as she began to convulse. With a powerful burst, she gushed female ejaculate all over my torso— once and then twice. I'd personally squirted too many times to count, but it was so hot to see a girl shoot all over me. I lay there, grinning, covered in sweat, feeling her come pooling in my belly button.

When I rose to clean up, we laughed at the Dacia-shaped come puddle cut-out on the sheets. Her come had pooled around me to create a perfectly traced image of my hips.

As we collapsed in bed for the night, Jane rolled against me and said, "I love you." She quickly added the disclaimer, "But I'm not just saying that because you made me come. I do love you. But, you know, not in that icky emotional way. Just in that fuck-each-other-silly-and-then-eat-ice-cream way."

"Of course," I laughed, understanding completely. I reached over and patted her ass. We drifted off into a happy post-coital slumber, which would last a few brief hours before we had to get up and start our respective working weeks.

As I wearily climbed the stairs to my apartment after a sleep-deprived day at work, my landlord, who lives directly below me, poked his head out of his door. "Hey Dacia," he started his sentence softly and continued with a little hesitation. "I want you to know that I have no problem with you having fun—but we need to talk about your bed." The era of my beautiful four-poster bed—proudly made without any nails—was drawing to a close.

strap-on sex is so passé

●

aimee nichols

Sabina was the girl who looked at me and decided I was the kind of challenge she wanted to take on.

We saw each other fairly frequently; she was a friend of my friend Lou, and so group drinking sessions tended to throw the two of us together. She was the kind of woman who generally had the entire room wanting, without even being conscious of it, to take her home and do very bad things both to and with her. Sure, she was beautiful— taller than average, deep olive skin, sparkling black-coffee eyes, and a head of thick, glossy corkscrew ringlets. Plus, she leaned towards the voluptuous side of curvy, with a glimpse of soft brown cleavage nearly always visible, and the kind of ass that made a girl want to grab it and take a bite. But it was more than physical beauty. She was one of those people who emanate sensuality and sexiness; never in a way that came across as deliberate, but enough that women would stare longingly from afar and men would trip over their feet walking past her en route to the bar.

I always assumed she was out of my league. In fact, I generally assume people are out of my league and figure if they want me they'll do something about it, which isn't exactly proactive but saves me the embarrassment of rejection. In Sabina's case, though, I assumed she knew everyone wanted her and that there wasn't any point in making myself stand out from the crowd. It wasn't so much a self-flagellating dose of the I'm-not-good-enoughs as it was an attempt to avoid pointless effort. Why waste time hitting on girls who were bound to be unresponsive when I could be focusing my energies on getting drunk, right?

It was an unseasonably balmy night in April—Melbourne's weather

43

hadn't realized it was supposed to be autumn —when Lou organized another "drinks night." We met up in an intimate little bar in the depths of an alley in the CBD. It was a Friday night and I'd worked late, so I was the last to arrive. The others were obviously well past their first drinks already, and Sabina was the only one who didn't seem to be well down the road to tipsy. I gave everyone the usual greeting hug. I came to Sabina and paused. I'd never hugged her before—I didn't consider us that close—but since everyone else in the group was a good friend, everyone else had received a hug from me. I didn't want to seem rude by not hugging Sabina too.

Okay, so I wasn't entirely concerned with altruism and etiquette. I desperately wanted to touch Sabina, feel that soft warm body pressed up against mine. I have this thing, though, in that I'm terrified of getting found out when I fancy somebody. Completely irrationally, I worry that they'll be able to tell I'm interested if I touch them or stand too close to them, like I think my pheromones will give me away or something. And since I'm not the most socially or emotionally adept of people, you can see why that would cause me anxiety.

Sabina solved the problem for me by standing up and wrapping her arms around me. I returned the gesture and found myself involved in what I can only describe as a full-body hug; she pressed her body firmly against mine, our curves complementing each other, our breasts flattening to rest against each other. I had the interesting mental experience of simultaneously trying to enjoy the moment for what it was and take in everything so I could remember it later on, and desperately hoping that she couldn't tell I was enjoying the hug a little less platonically than I should have been. For the thousandth time in my life I was thankful I was not a man—only this time, rather than being grateful for not having to, you know, be a man, I was grateful that I didn't have a penis, because if I did it would have been making its presence felt against Sabina's lower belly, and that would have blown my cover. As it was, I felt myself discreetly moistening the crotch of my knickers.

She held on longer than she needed to, which was fine by me. I was trying to breathe deeply and quietly, partly because she'd brought on a major case of the butterflies and partly because she smelled so good and I wanted to savor her—the faintly chemical but pleasant odors of hair product and makeup mixed with the natural, vaguely musky smell of her skin. If she was wearing perfume, it was subtle and underscored her natural smell perfectly.

She pulled away, and I had to fight the urge to wrap my arms around her more tightly and not let go. She smiled at me as she sat down, her eyes twinkling. I retreated to the other side of the booth, taking a seat between Lou and Kelly, who rested her head on my shoulder.

The conversation was flowing as freely as the alcohol, and I took small but quick sips of my beer, unsure of where I wanted to be on the sobriety scale, not wanting to be the sole sober person at the table but not wanting to join in the drinking spree just yet. Sabina sipped a glass of white wine and sat back, taking in the conversation with the amused eyes of one who loves her friends but is well aware they can make complete idiots of themselves in public at times. The topic turned to the girl Lou had just started seeing a couple of weeks ago, whom none of us had met yet but who intrigued us, if only because she quite obviously made normally sedate and emotionally cautious Lou go weak at the knees. We started pumping her for information about this new woman.

"Does she have any really annoying personal habits?" asked Kelly.

"No!"

"That just means there're none you've found out about yet."

"Does she have good taste in music?" asked Sarah, the resident music snob.

"Yeah, if by that you mean, does she share my taste? We're aaaall about the acousticky lesbians, baby."

"I said good music, you walking cliché."

"And what might that be, Madame?" Kelly could obviously see where this was going as well as I could—any argument about music was never a good idea around Sarah, lovely as she was. Kelly leaned forward and said, "Look, Lou, I think what we all really want to know but are pretending we're too polite to ask is—what's she like in bed?"

Lou blushed, just slightly. "She's good." She paused. "Very good."

"DETAILS!"

"That would be tacky."

"Because we're none of us here tacky. Nooo, not at all."

I put my arm around Lou. I knew her well enough to sense that, despite her embarrassment, she did actually want to share with us, and was going to. You get used to reading someone after being friends with them for a while. In the case of my friends, I learn to tell when they really don't want to talk about their partners, and when they're being coy. Lou was being coy.

"Oh, I'm just not sure I should. What happens if one of you lets slip when you meet her?"

"So we're definitely going to meet her?" I butted in.

"I didn't say that…I just don't want her being uncomfortable that you guys know so much."

"I'm sure we all know how to keep our mouths shut, Louise," I said, doing my best fake stern voice. "Now spill."

"Okay. What do you want to know?"

"Everything!"

"Well…" Lou paused and took a swig of beer, considering what to tell us. "She's very skilled in bed. A great kisser. Wonderful with her hands. And she works a strap-on like nobody's business."

I'd been taking a sip of my drink, and nearly spat it out.

"She what?" I said. "You mean you actually do that? I thought one of the advantages of fucking girls was that you didn't have to put up with dicks in at least part of your life?"

Kelly turned to me. "That's a little bit retro, isn't it, Aim? You're always on about how important it is for people to express their sexuality however they need to."

"Yeah, but do we have to do that by aping heterosexual people?"

"Ooh, how very seventies of you. Perhaps we shouldn't be having sex at all, what with it being an expression of power over another person and all."

"That's not what I meant and you know it, Kelly."

The conversation was good-natured enough, but I was losing ground, and worse, starting to look like a bit of an idiot. In front of Sabina. I wished I'd kept my mouth shut.

"It just seems so…unoriginal. Boring. You know, half the time the first thing straight people ask when they find out I'm into girls is whether we all use dildos on each other. Because they can't possibly imagine sex being satisfying, or even 'real sex,' without a penis being involved somehow. And that's the whole porn thing happening as well, you know, 'ooh, we're fucking each other with a strap-on while we wait for you to come to us with your big manly penis. Strap-on sex is passé. There's so much we can do to and with each other but there's so much focus on that now that even dykes are obsessed with it."

"So now you're the arbiter of what's passé? Ms Vans-sneakers-are-never-out-of-fashion?"

"Fuck off, Renee."

"Oh, come on. I'm just amused. You! Thinking stuff is passé! Who'd have thought?"

"Have you ever been fucked with a strap-on cock, Aim?"

The speaker was Kelly again, but I looked across the table and met Sabina's eye. She was watching me intently.

"No. But it hasn't really captured my imagination. It's a little too straight-guy fantasy, isn't it?"

Sabina spoke up. "Not at all. I don't think straight guys ever fantasize about real lesbians anyway. I think it gets less erotic for them when they realize they're not invited."

A laugh went up around the table, and I smiled gratefully at Sabina for diffusing the situation and making me feel a little less under fire. She smiled back, eyes twinkling.

"Maybe your problem with strap-on sex, Aimee, is that you haven't met the right girl to show you the ropes."

"Or the straps, as it were," Renee interjected.

"Yeah, maybe that's it!" said Lou, eager to see both that the situation was diffused and that we were off the topic of her suddenly controversial sex life, even if it wasn't her causing the controversy.

"What? Oh, come on." We weren't here to discuss my nonexistent sex life, especially not in front of Sabina. I was supposed to look mysterious and alluring in front of her, damn it.

The twinkle in Sabina's eyes set of a slight smirk on her lips, and she leaned forward over the table.

"I bet if you found the right person, someone who knew what she was doing, you might change your mind. Perhaps you just need someone to show you the way." Her eyes held mine in her magnetic gaze, which wasn't even broken by Kelly's snort of "Hang on, are we talking about fucking or religion here?"

"Yeah, maybe," I said, and looked away. I didn't want to look away, but I was getting rather uncomfortable with everyone else around, and didn't dare even hope that Sabina was saying what I thought she was saying.

The rest of the evening passed without controversy, and I managed to get slightly buzzed without tipping over the brink into outright drunkenness. The only other person who managed that, I noticed, was Sabina; Lou, Kelly, and Renee were all well and truly off their faces by the time it began to look as though the bar staff might want to kick us out.

We wandered out onto the footpath together. Kelly jumped into a cab to head off back to the Eastern Suburbs. Lou and Renee were sharing a ride to inner-city Prahran. Sabina had offered, since we lived two suburbs away from each other, to share a cab with me. We let Lou and Renee grab the next cab that came along, and waited a few minutes in companionable, if slightly nervous on my part, silence. Sabina noted a cab a few blocks away and stepped on the road to hail it. When she was satisfied she'd caught the driver's attention, she stepped back onto the footpath next to me. She looked me full in the face, her dark eyes questioning, and said, "I meant what I said before. About showing you the ropes. What do you say?"

I looked at her, shocked and thrilled and hardly able to believe what I was hearing. There was my chance right there.

I took it.

She was grasping my hand so tightly I wondered if she'd been waiting for this for as long as I had. At the front door, she fumbled with her keys, muttering "Shit!" as she accidentally dropped them back in her bag, without letting go of my hand. I was enjoying her grip and the faint coating of sweat developing between our palms too much to let go of her hand myself, and I certainly wasn't going anywhere.

She found the keys and managed to get the door unlocked, shooting me a look of pure triumph that made me giggle. I followed her down the hall as she switched on the lights and discarded her bag and jacket. Her house was one of those cute little single-story terraces so common to the inner suburbs, but she'd decorated it with an eclectic mix of classic furniture and art prints. I caught sight of the titles on her bookshelf and conjectured that she either lived alone or wasn't too worried about housemates "borrowing" her lesbian erotica.

Together in the lounge room, we paused and looked at each other. She ran a hand through her hair, her curls bobbing everywhere. Then she strode across the room and grabbed me, pulling me into her, crushing her breasts against mine in a more forcefully sexual echo of our earlier embrace.

And then she kissed me.

I've been a fan of the kiss for a long time. A good kiss has always had the power to send sparks of electricity straight to every erogenous zone in my body. Sabina's lips were soft but her mouth was insistent, hungry, and as her hands came up to grasp my face, her tongue invaded my mouth, twisting and exploring and making me unconsciously melt against her, lean my weight against her body, surrender to her will and the power of that tongue.

She broke away long enough to push me down on the couch and climbed on top of me. Her weight pinned me down into the plush comfort of the couch, her softness pressing into me. She tilted my face up, lying slightly sideways so that her breasts rested under my chin. She continued to kiss me and I kissed back, exploring her mouth as she was exploring mine, taking smug pleasure in the staccato moans of which she was obviously completely unconscious. I reached up and ran my hand over her breast, thrilling as I found her erect nipple. I slid the flat of my palm across the curving expanse of her breast, and then ran my fingernails over her nipple in a gentle scratching motion. She kissed me harder, and ran her hand up my shirt in response. My already aroused nipples got harder, anticipating her touch, and I wasn't disappointed. She grasped my left nipple between her thumb and forefinger and pinched. Hard. I gasped, and she broke our kiss to smile down at me, that knowing twinkle back in her eye.

I tugged at her shirt. "I have to see your breasts," I said, which surely has to be the smoothest line since "Come here often?" but I wasn't exactly at my most cerebral at that point. She obliged, tugging her shirt off and reaching around behind to undo her bra. I drank in the sight of her full, heavy breasts, then pulled her to me and took a nipple in my mouth, kneading the other breast with my hand and tweaking her nipple.

"Fair's fair," she said, yanking my shirt up. I sat up and pulled it over my head, then removed my own bra. She took a breast in each hand, kneading my plentiful flesh as I continued to suck her nipple. Shortly, her hands moved lower, exploring the plane of my stomach, gently running her fingertips over my skin, provoking it into gooseflesh. I couldn't help a quick intake of breath as she slid her hand under the waistband of my jeans. Her breasts pressed against my face as she leaned to follow her hand. I reveled in their size, their weight, and her softness, the smell of her now a thousand times more potent than it had been earlier in the night. I reached up and traced patterns across her skin, following the lead she had taken with my body. Her hand found the waistband of my knickers and kept going.

I tried to bite back the gasp that threatened to erupt from my throat as her questing fingers gently stroked my outer labia, then pushed between them, discovering my wetness. I gave an involuntary moan as she found my clit and stroked it in circles. She smiled down at me, smug. I slid my hand down her pants, and delighted in the forest of curls that greeted me. Further along I came to her own wetness, slick and welcoming, and my mouth watered at the thought of how she would taste. We lay, rubbing and exploring and teasing, and she bent down to kiss me, our mouths locked in a desperately passionate embrace. I paused only so that I could undo her pants and shuck them down around her thighs. The sight of her thick, lush pubic hair with her lips shyly poking out underneath, protected by her broad strong thighs, made me moan again. I put my hand back on her pussy and inserted two fingers inside her, slowly exploring her warmth. She tightened around me, and her exploration of me became more vigorous. I changed position slightly, so I could continue finger-fucking her and rub her clit with my thumb without causing wrist damage.

"That feels good," she said, staring into my eyes, pupils wide. Our faces were level and I could see myself reflected in the shiny darkness of her eyes. "That feels really good." I smiled at her and upped my efforts. Three fingers. Faster thumb action. We were silent, verbally, but our bodies spoke for us, unable to get enough of one another's skin. Still stimulating her with my hand, I kissed my way down her body and she undulated against me. I moved lower and lower down until eventually I tasted her.

She moaned something that sounded like "yeaaaaah," and suddenly her hand was on the back of my head, gently but firmly guiding me, my tongue on her clit, pubic hair against my face, and still plunging and gyrating my fingers inside her tight, wet cunt. She grabbed a handful of my hair and yanked, and it took all my self-control not to yelp and pull away. She started to pant and grind against me and I realized she was about to come. I allowed myself a brief moment of smugness—hey, I like to achieve worthwhile goals as much as the next girl—then took her hard little clit in my mouth, sucking it in like a delectable morsel. She continued to grind against me, and after a moment I went back to licking circles around her clit.

She let out a howl and came, drenching my hand and my chin. I got even more excited then, because to me, making a girl ejaculate is quite a compliment, in addition to being a cool feat in itself, and I kept licking her until she pushed me away, smiling.

"I get sensitive after amazing head, darling."

"I bet you say that to all the girls." What can I say, I'm a line machine. Thank god it didn't occur to me to ask if she came here often.

She laughed, and leaned over to lick her juices off my face. I licked back, which did nothing but spread them around more.

She moved off the couch, smiling at me as she absentmindedly licked the juice from around her mouth. "Stay here."

"Where are you going?"

She grinned, and this time the devilish twinkle had brought reinforcements.

"I'm going to get what I wanted to show you all along."

I waited, resisting the urge to see to my throbbing pussy myself, preferring instead to alternate between fantasizing about what had just been and what was yet to come.

A couple of minutes later I heard her padding back down the hall.

She entered the room complete with strap-on attached, the silicone cock standing proudly out from her groin. I gaped. I think up until then I'd not really believed that she was determined to set me straight, as it were, about the joys of being fucked by a hot girl with an ever-hard cock. Strangely enough, I suddenly found myself very eager to learn whatever lesson Sabina thought fit to teach me. I sat up, the better to take her in. She stood still in the doorway, naked flesh luminous, curve running into curve running into curve. The sturdy leather harness hugged low on her hips and clung tightly to the tops of her thighs. The royal blue dildo was short and thick and more realistically designed than I'd been expecting to see; it had a slight upward curve and a believable head. I was surprised by her choice of dildo, actually; she didn't look like the sort of girl who'd have a short, fat little cock. I'd imagined her (yes, I'd imagined her and her kit, I admit it, when the conversation at the bar had started to lull) as having a longer, thinner cock, possibly in a lovely shade of lesbian lavender. I know. I'm all cliché, all the time.

"You like?"

"Yes," I breathed. Then I found my voice and, with more bravado than I actually felt, given that I was about to take part in a sex act that up until a couple of hours ago I hadn't believed anyone actually did, and one that I certainly thought I'd never do, said, "Why don't you come over here and show me what you do with it?"

She strode over and stepped up onto the couch, standing over me so that I could see her pussy lips pouting out from between the leather straps that went around each leg. Her cock loomed over me, ready and insistent. She got down on her knees, a leg on either side of me. I shuffled up onto my elbows and returned her gaze as she stared at me.

"Stay there, sweetie." Her mouth twisted in a wry smile. "I'm going to come to you."

"It's like Sabina's Mobile Cock Service."

"Exactly."

She grasped my legs and pulled them up, moving them so one was on either side of her. She shuffled closer to me on her knees. Staring at me intently, she rolled a condom over the shaft of the dildo, and then opened the little bottle of lube she'd brought with her and squeezed a dollop into her hand, rubbing it over the dildo as though she were masturbating. She leaned over me.

"Are you ready?"

I wasn't exactly sure if I was, but I said "yes." She seemed to sense my hesitance, and leaned forward more until she was leaning over me, and when her lips met mine she kissed me deeply and passionately. I felt my head begin to swim—the dildo was prodding my lower stomach, and the smell of her filled my nostrils, musky and warm and exciting.

She broke the kiss and moved back, trailing her fingers down my chest, pausing to tweak my nipples, which immediately stood even further to attention.

She brought her body down so that she was almost on top of me, and supported her weight with one arm as the other reached down to grasp her cock. I braced myself for the penetration. I wasn't sure why I was so nervous—it's not like I haven't slept with men before, so a cock was not an entirely alien thing—but I started to relax when I felt the dildo nudging against my pussy lips. She found my clit and rubbed the head against it, with the right pressure and movement to make me gasp. I unconsciously tilted my pelvis up to meet her ministrations, and was rewarded with a cocked eyebrow that was offset by the warmth in her smile.

"How are you liking it so far?"

"It's…great," I managed. My pussy was responding to the ministrations of her cock and my powers of thought were starting to retreat, sensing defeat. I could feel myself begin to clench as my clitoris responded more and more to the pressure of her cock. Her breasts hung in front of me, round and full, and she was beginning to sweat slightly. I reached up and took a breast in each hand, squeezing her nipples gently between my thumbs and forefingers. She moaned.

"I want to be inside you."

My pussy responded before my brain had even processed what she said.

"Yes," I finally managed.

She eased herself into me. I felt the pressure and strange sense of being filled. The cock felt thicker than I'd thought, and I could feel it push against the walls of my cunt, questing deeper inside me. She pushed further in, until I felt the pressure of her leather-clad pelvis against me and knew she was in all the way. We held the position for a moment, then slowly she began to withdraw. I caught myself whimpering, again completely unconsciously. She laughed, sweetly but with the slight edge of one who's definitely won the sex war and is preparing to take all spoils.

She began to thrust, slowly, insistently, testing my responses. I began to move against her, thrusting in my own rhythm, which melded with hers until we were in synchronicity, both of us covered in a light sheen of sweat. The dildo felt thick and warm and firm inside me, contrasting with the softness of Sabina's body. I wrapped my legs around her and we fucked like that for a while, kissing each other at random moments, my hands exploring the smooth expanse of her back, occasionally moving around to stroke her breasts again.

Eventually she pulled back slightly and looked me in the eye.

"Do you want to touch yourself?"

I could feel every nerve ending in my cunt and clit screaming for release. I managed a raspy "yes," and she smiled. Then she moved back a bit, enough so that I could reach my hand down between us and find my clit. It responded immediately to the slight pressure of my finger. I began to rub myself, and she resumed thrusting. I felt my orgasm begin to build, a gradual pressure in my nerves that made my cunt clamp down on the dildo and hold it tight as Sabina continued to thrust.

I felt the low moan of orgasm begin deep down in the back of my throat as the delirious pressure in my clit continued to grow. I rubbed faster, wanting the release, needing it, hungering for it as though starved.

I came with a moan that transformed into a howl, squeezing my legs and bringing Sabina in closer to me, the orgasm exploding into a thousand fragments in my clit and in my cunt, moving down my legs and up my body, forcing me to shake uncontrollably.

Afterwards I lay still. Sabina lay on top of me, our skin warm against each other, breasts and bellies meeting agreeably, our combined softness intermingling. We were still and silent for several minutes. I wrapped my arms around her, not wanting to let her go, thinking I didn't want this to end here. I didn't want this to be the only lesson she taught me. She burrowed against me, voluptuously warm, her cock still inside me.

I didn't want her to pull out; I wanted us, in this moment, to be joined for as long as we could be.

Eventually, though, she moved, leaning up and pulling out, unbuckling herself out of the harness and discarding it before lying down next to me again and taking me in her arms.

"Did you like that?"

"What sort of a question is that?"

She laughed. "Yeah, I know. Sometimes I like to state the obvious. Or ask the obvious, as the case may be."

"It was great. You're wonderful."

She grinned at me, and mimed tipping a hat. "Why, thank you, ma'am. You're not so bad yourself."

We held each other for a while without speaking, our skin cooling slightly, our sweat drying. She held me close.

I'm not the type of girl to start demanding exclusivity and all that jazz after one sexual encounter, but I couldn't help thinking about how long I'd been lusting after Sabina, how much I'd wanted her, and how much it felt like an amazing stroke of luck that we'd finally gotten together. I wasn't entirely sure what I wanted at that moment, except that I knew I didn't want to get off that couch and out of Sabina's arms any time soon.

"Sabina?"

"Yes, Aimee dear?"

"What else do you have to show me?"

She laughed, and kissed me.

light my fire

●

alison tyler

For our first anniversary, I planned a romantic evening for two. As romantic as ten bucks will get ya. Ella Fitzgerald crooned low on the radio. A bottle of cheap white chilled in the fridge. The lights in our apartment were dimmed (I put in low-wattage bulbs). And in the center of the dining room table stood two candles and a pack of matches.

When Eleanor got home, I took her coat for her and then led her into the kitchen. We'd watched *Body of Evidence* the night before, and no matter how silly the film is, I'll admit now that the candle wax scene with Madonna and Willem Dafoe had really turned me on. And anyway, I'd thought of this situation previously, in my own twisted fantasies, and I was ready, finally, to make my own mental movie a reality. Of course, in order to do it right, I needed my lover's consent.

I'm lucky. Eleanor and I usually operate on the same frequency. When she saw the unlit candles on the table, she knew instantly what I was telling her, what I was requesting of her. She smiled as she came toward me, taking me into her arms and kissing my forehead lightly. Then she whispered, "Get undressed. Lie down on the table."

We have a six-foot dining room table. It's like a picnic table, except that the wood has a weathered, almost silky finish to it. I followed her orders, stripping and climbing up, moving the candles to the far edge. Eleanor bent to kiss my lips before she picked up the pack of matches.

I was trembling all over, my body desperate to know what this new type of pain would feel like. My head swam with pictures of the wax dripping onto my naked skin. My cunt pooled with the thick liquid of my sex. I couldn't still myself. My hips beat a rhythm of their own against the hard wood beneath my ass.

Eleanor stood back from me, nearly laughing at the trauma I was putting myself through. I wished she'd tie me down, or at least capture my wrists. She was wearing a floral-print silk scarf. She could do it in no time.

It's easier for me to take pain when I'm tied. But she didn't. She knew that I wanted this experience. And that I wanted it badly enough that I would stay still for her. Eleanor loves it when I force myself to behave.

I watched as she opened the matchbook. The match lit on the first strike, a burst of fire that she touched to the wick of the white candle and then shook out. When I closed my eyes, the red and orange spark of flame reflected on my lids. By the time I opened my eyes again, Eleanor was magically closer, inches from me, and she kissed me as she held the candle over my chest.

"You're pretty by candlelight," she said softly, into my mouth. "You look ethereal. Angelic." With her free hand, she stroked my blonde hair, wrapping one curl around her fingers.

"Do it," I wanted to say. "Just tilt the damn thing so that I can feel it." Sometimes wondering about how much something will hurt is actually worse than the actual pain. (This is definitely true for tattoos.) Sometimes anticipation alone can make me cry. But I knew that if I begged her, she'd deny me. She loves our games, has all the rules memorized. In fact, she wrote the rules herself.

Her lips met mine again, then traveled a line down my neck to my collarbones. The candle was still upright in her hand, and I stared at the flame as she nibbled further down, licking me, biting my skin, leaving marks with her mouth. I remembered reading a story in which the main character was hypnotized by staring into a candle flame. I tried to hypnotize myself, but it didn't work. Instead, I was still, on the table. I held my body perfectly in line, trying to be good for her. Trying to please her so that she would please me.

She moved further, down my flat belly, dipping her tongue into my navel, French-kissing my cunt when she reached it, her tongue making crazy circles around my clit.

I watched the candle. My eyes seemed to blur as I looked at the flame. It was purple, then suddenly yellow, then red, then gold. Eleanor was doing naughty, devious things to my cunt. Her whole mouth was sealed against it. My pussy swam with juices, and Eleanor seemed intent upon licking me clean, as impossible as it might be. Each drop she flicked away with her tongue was replaced by ten more. My pussy was a liquid sex factory.

And still, that candle stayed upright in Eleanor's hand. The wax now was beginning to slide down the sides, though. If she wasn't careful, her fingers would get burned. As the image flickered in my mind, Eleanor tilted the candlestick and dripped the first few dots of wax onto my skin. I didn't see it coming, didn't know to prepare myself, had grown too relaxed from her tongue probing me down there. And when it happened, I lost my breath and caught my breath, and bucked up against her.

She grinned at me, her lovely face all smeared with my shiny come, and she said, "You like that, don't you?" as she tilted the candle and drew a line of melting wax down my stomach, getting ever closer to my cunt. "Oh, the girl likes that?" Eleanor continued, blowing on the wax as it hardened, creating such a wash of confusing sensations within me that I didn't know what I wanted. More. Less. For her to stop. For her to keep on going.

She continued, lapping at the generous flood of juices with her tongue, keeping me on edge with a few occasional flicks of her wrist. The candle wax drips made a line down my belly. And as I focused on the jewel-toned gold and purple flame, as I watched my lover's head bob up and down on my cunt, I shuddered and felt those spasming contractions wash over me.

Eleanor grinned when she moved away from me, watching as I began, slowly to pull myself together. Finally, she whispered, "Candlelight always does make things more romantic, doesn't it?"

wear me home

●

jane vincent

It was my third year at the national conference on sexuality research. At this point I knew to expect stimulation of the mind as opposed to the twiddly bits. However, this weekend would smash my expectations.

On the first day of the conference I spotted a young man sitting alone outside the opening plenary. I was feeling bold in my bright orange paisley vintage dress picked up at a local thrift store that afternoon.

"Hi there, lonely person. I've never seen you at one of these before."

"This is my first one. I'm Jack."

I immediately read him as gay, like 90 percent of the males under forty at the conference. Sweet, but gay.

"Hi, Jack," I said, sitting down. "So, what's your area of research?"

"I'm completing my doctorate in psychology focusing on transgender issues."

My nipples perked up. As my left leg crossed over my right, my whole body turned to him. "Really?"

"As a transman…" He went on to make very intelligent commentary on the current state of mental health services available to the transgender community. I carried on my side of the conversation, multiprocessing my fantasies.

At the student and young professional mixer I introduced him to my friends. As he walked away I leaned in and stated, "I want him."

"Sweetie, he bats for the other team."

"Actually, no. First, he mentioned his ex-girlfriend. Second, he's trans."

"Really? No…Really? No…*Really?* Wow. He's good."

"He's hot," I replied, deviously plotting my subtle seduction.

The way a sex research conference works is pretty similar to other academic conferences. There are two types of sessions: plenaries and paper sessions. At plenaries, a featured speaker lectures the entire conference body. At paper sessions, presentations go on in rooms throughout the hotel. Generally, four or five researchers (or research teams) present their findings in each room during the two-hour sessions. These rooms tend to be grouped by topic; for example, adolescent sexuality, sexual abuse, LGBT issues, masculinity, sexual dysfunction, and the occasional grab bag where street sex workers, commercial clitoral stimulants, and diaper fetishists are presented head-to-head.

Jack and I compared programs. We had several paper sessions mutually starred. As we sat together in a lecture on BDSM communities in contemporary Manhattan (great visual aides), we passed notes. I think I wrote, "You are hot." It was like junior high, only better, because this time I might actually score.

The flirting continued through the second day of the conference. Hands lingering on shoulders or waists as we passed in the hallways, searching each other out in plenaries and luncheons, the heat of anticipation overwhelming.

That evening, the featured event was a film festival of what is technically termed "educational porn." These are videos of the "how-to" variety (stronger erections and anal pleasure being two of the goals) as well as documentaries and films appropriate for college sexuality courses (examples include a duo on how men feel about their penises and how women feel about their breasts). A few films stood out, including a documentary on the Texas sex-toy laws, an educational drag show on the impact of drug use upon HIV-positive folk, and a well-edited collection of a dozen or so people of diverse age, race, gender, and shape masturbating to orgasm shown only from the neck up.

Drinks were carried into the viewing room from the bar and chairs were adjusted to form couches and foot supports as needed. There was the air of a slumber party.

Jack and I stretched out next to each other. As the screening went on to the wee hours, I decided to graduate our relationship to high school. I leaned in to his ear, "I want to fuck you." I delivered a swift nip to his lobe for emphasis.

He grinned at me and blushed, then quickly reformed his face to meet my challenge. He rose and took my hand. We waved goodbye to knowing winks as we exited at the back.

Jack was staying at a nearby motel for budgetary reasons, but had his own room. I was sharing a room with another student, also for budgetary reasons. The single room, despite the distance, won out as our rendezvous of choice.

"I need to make a quick stop in my room to freshen up." I led him up the elevators and down the hall. Once in my room he sat down on my bed. I straddled his lap and pulled his face up to mine. Tongues plunged hungrily, his hands firmly kneading my ass. He bent his face down into my cleavage, straining the buttons of another prize vintage dress.

I leaned back, afraid to get too carried away and "sex-ile" the roommate. I left him on the bed as I grabbed my toothbrush, a pair of panties, and my toy bag (just because I didn't expect partner action doesn't mean I didn't come prepared to get myself off six ways 'til Sunday). I dragged him off the bed into a kiss and led him out of the room.

We laughed down the street, speed-walk-racing our way to his motel.

Once inside, Jack pushed me against the door. With his hand on my breast as another raced up my thigh, our kisses became quick and sloppy. He traced the line beneath my breast, across my armpit and shoulder blade to the nape of my neck. He grabbed my hair and pulled my head back. I gasped.

"Now what did you say you wanted to do, little girl?" he breathed in my ear.

I looked at him with big doe eyes. "I said I want to fuck you." The hard *k* clacked in the back of my throat.

He unbuttoned my dress with one hand, the other holding my wrists behind my back. He gripped my collar in his teeth and then pulled it off my left shoulder. He mirrored the action on the right. I stepped out of my dress. I stood in my black bra and panties (simple, yet sexy) and twelve-dollar Payless pumps. He stepped back and sat on the bed, his eyes devouring me.

"You are such a...woman," he said, the word circling my birthing hips and soft stomach, caressing my breasts, tangling in my long hair, and kissing my full lips.

I slowly walked over to him. Astride his lap, back arched, I unbuttoned his shirt. I traced his red welted top-surgery scars with my nails and then my mouth. I pushed him onto his back, holding my body above his thighs, pulling off his belt and opening his pants, while staring in his eyes, daring him to look down.

I reached against his white cotton briefs, not sure what I would find. I felt a small bulge. I smiled at him, "May I?"

"Please," he moaned.

His tranny cock, a clitoris engorged by two years of testosterone and the pretty lady upon his thighs, stood erect like one of those carrots I eat by the bagful. I licked it from base to tip and pulled it into my lips, rolling it against the roof of my mouth. I flicked at the head and circled the shaft rapidly.

Then I pulled a glove and some lube out of my toy bag, which was conveniently stashed at the base of the bed by my feet. It was his turn to gasp as the first drop of lube landed on his puckered asshole. I dribbled a generous glob and snapped on a black latex glove. Still sucking his tranny cock, looking at his face tossed back against the pillow, I started tickling his ass with one finger. I teased the pucker, feeling it press and release against the pad of my finger. I gently pushed in a single knuckle deep and paused. His ass pulsed around me.

"More," he pleaded. I plunged in deeper. I curved my fingers up towards his belly button, inviting his G/P-spot to come hither. I attacked his tranny cock with a vigor previously wasted on nipples and dick. He gasped and groaned and writhed.

He came.

After kissing him, I rose and went into the bathroom. While peeing, I could not believe how turned on I was. My clit and labia were swollen like ripe fruit.

As I washed my hands, Jack stepped into the bathroom with a small bundle. "Don't you dare put any clothes back on," he instructed as he gently pushed me out the door and closed it behind me.

Like an impatient child, I rummaged through my toy bag until I found my silver bullet, possibly my most versatile toy. I popped it in a condom, not sure of the body fluids about to be swung about, and sat back against the headboard.

I was in my bra and heels, knees bent, legs sprawled, panties cast off to the corner, and bullet humming on my clit when he emerged from the bathroom, stroking a significantly larger bulge beneath his tighty-whities, which were making an encore appearance.

"You dirty girl," he scolded. "Are you going to jerk off for daddy?" I nodded a little girl "uh-huh" and continued buzzing myself. "I can see you're soaking wet from across the room. Tell me how wet you are."

I pushed two fingers in my pussy and pulled them up, glistening. "Very wet," I mumbled as I sucked off my juices.

"We're going to have to do something about that. And I have just the thing." He rubbed his bulge as he approached me. "Want to see your surprise?" I nodded and gasped as he pulled out a five-inch silicone cock, slightly curved, strapped in a leather harness. He stepped out of his underwear and kneeled above me. "Do you like it?" I smiled and reached for a condom.

I peeled the condom from the wrapper and tucked it in my mouth. The tip pressed behind my teeth by my tongue, the rim outside my lips changing my expression into that of a blow-up doll. I pushed the condom down around his dick, smoothing out the air bubbles with my lips, pulling the head in to the back of my throat.

"Good girl," he praised, pulling back. "Now I want you to tell me one more time, what do you want?"

"I want you to fuck me."

The switch of pronouns pleased him. "That's what I thought."

He pushed my ankles to his shoulders, careful not to scratch his face with the heels of my pumps. He held the head of his dick at my opening, teasing me for an endless moment. I wiggled my hips, trying to swallow the tip. "Nuh uh uh," he taunted, pulling back.

As I sighed with frustration he drove his cock into me. Deep. I thrust back. We began a grinding rhythm, like a train picking up steam. I met each plunge.

He hit my G-spot with precision. My orgasm grew with a heavy sensation, like I was going to pee or explode. I imagined my goo flung about the room, coating Jack's face and luggage. I saw him trying to explain the mess, first to the hotel staff and then the luggage inspector at the airport. I would stain him. He would wear me home.

Four positions and half a dozen toys later, the sun was up and we were late for the morning plenary. In lieu of a shower I chose a pits-tits-and-twat sink bath. He didn't take the time to shave.

We arrived five minutes tardy and suitably disheveled. As the PowerPoint flashed MRI-scans and vaginal plethysmograph readings, I leaned in to Jack's neck.

"Thank you," I whispered and kissed his cheek. I was met with the salty brine of our evening's adventure. He would indeed wear me home.

sanctuary girls

●

scarlett french

Coming out, I decided, is like moving countries: you enter a different culture, learn a new language and new customs, and try your best to integrate. Nothing can be taken for granted. I was all of three months out and I had accepted the offer to attend an event from people I barely knew. I was a bit nervous but I knew I couldn't turn it down—I had to get out there if I wanted to establish a niche for myself in the queer community. Like anything, getting out and making new friends gets easier the more you do it.

Only once a year was Sanctuary, a gay men's sex-on-site club, opened to women. Those who attended the annual 'Sanctuary Girls' event were modern dykes, many of whom had asymmetrical haircuts and wore tight tee shirts without bras—just my type. I had passed the invite on to one of my few lesbian friends, Nell, a woman I'd first met in a sociology lecture a couple of years before, who believed I was a victim of male oppression because I got my eyebrows waxed. I had hoped she might come with me but she told me that she didn't want to socialize in the environs of men's sweat and spendings. Well, I had decided that I liked the idea of a sex club and a bunch of likeminded women and I was not deterred, even by the prospect of arriving alone. Figuring I'd see a few familiar faces, I decided I could walk in on my own.

I slipped off Dixon Street and down the badly lit alleyway near the most expensive deli in town. There had been people all around me, the sound of coffee grinding and quality meats being sliced, but now I could only hear the sound of my own heels clicking on the pot-holed pavement. A life was going on back on the main street, but I was entering another one: a path less traveled. My heart thumping in my chest, I headed towards number 12. The heavy steel door had a piece of A4 paper cellotaped to it with the announcement:

Tonight
Sanctuary Girls
This is a women only event.

Under the last line was a big women's symbol, retraced in felt tip pen several times to make it more prominent. That piece of A4 was reassuring somehow in its last minute, neighborly "Jean, just popped out—Help yourself to the cake mixer" kind-of-way. Though the side street was very dark and I was heading somewhere unusual, I knew I'd see some new friends up there, good women I had met in a small city's lesbian community. I paused to take a breath and tousled my cropped hair one more time. Pushing the door open with some effort, I stepped inside. I ascended the stairs to the first floor, where the door was opened for me by a short spiky bouncer in a shiny black puffer jacket.

I stepped through the door, a little cautiously at first, but after my eyes adjusted to the sultry light, I spotted Vicki, one of the women who had told me about this night. I waved at her and gestured that I would be over in a minute. I headed towards the bar, weaving in between groups of women. The air was warm and circulating, with soul tunes undulating through it from old speakers affixed to the wall and hidden behind dragon trees and palm fronds. The main bar area had black walls, broken up with slivers of mirror glued in random clusters. The chairs and booths were upholstered in plush burgundy velvet. I had expected a club like this to be more functional somehow, but perhaps the wipe-clean surfaces were reserved for the infamous maze. Though I felt a little self-conscious, I was also charged with anticipation. I had a feeling that anything could happen. As I waited for my vodka and lime, I casually surveyed the room.

There were so many attractive women everywhere: Strong-looking women, with high cheekbones and studied aloofness; big, tough, butch women, with coiffed hair and an air of arrogance; beautiful women, surrounded by their friends, drinking out of straws; quiet women, lurking in the shadows, watching, just like me. A couple stood against the wall, in matching leather chaps over faded blue jeans, eyeing each other up then kissing hungrily, their tongues spilling out of their mouths; bulges in their trousers. As I drank in the view of many ages, aesthetics and colors, it occurred to me: I love the company of women.

A woman beside me shuffled away from the bar, trying to keep hold of five bottles of beer clasped between her splayed fingers. As she moved away, I caught a glimpse of a cute girl waiting next to me, with sandy hair, wearing a simple zip-up jacket. It was Penny.

"Penny, hey!"

"Hi!" she replied with a smile. "I wondered if you'd come tonight."

I knew Penny from the bi women's group. She'd realised she was a lesbian early on and had dropped out of the group, but we saw each other out and about quite a lot and always stopped for a chat. We were in similar shoes—recently out and both having slept with only one woman. Though we never discussed it, I think we both felt like neophytes; a lot of very new friendships and limited sexual experience made for unsure footing in this new terrain.

"Wish I'd known you were coming," I said. "It was a bit nerve-wracking walking in here alone. Have you ever been to anything like this?"

"No," she replied. "This is the first one they've done since I came out. Mind you, I know it by reputation. Apparently all sorts of wildness went on last year—I heard something about a group grope thing in the maze and apparently that strict butch/femme couple from Aro Valley actually had sex in the little side room over there—it looked like the femme woman was just straddling her partner but she had a big skirt on that covered everything and actually they were fucking."

Penny was usually a quiet sort. I was surprised by her candor. Maybe she wasn't the only one affected by her surroundings, feeling horny and reckless.

"Really? So, do you think people will actually have sex here tonight?" I asked, trying to sound nonchalant.

The corner of her mouth curled into a smile. "I don't know, I hope so. I'm sure those women from the dyke sex toy business probably will. I mean, it's the only time every year that women, just women, get to be in an environment like this."

"It will be interesting to see what happens. It's a bit of a social experiment in some ways, isn't it? I hope people have the guts to go for it tonight—it would be so typical if everyone just sat around talking. I mean, the guys do this all the time without even knowing each other's names," I said, trying to sound knowledgeable, already building stereotypes in my impressionable mind from the smattering of cynical comments I had heard in my few short months in the queer community.

"Yeah, sometimes I wonder how lesbians ever have sex," said Penny. "It seems so complicated. But then, most of my friends are having loads of sex. I guess it comes down to being brave and making the first move." She paused, thinking about what she'd just said, then noticed a woman waving at her from across the room.

"Oh, there's Cath—she's a lawyer too. She's invited me to some lesbian lawyer drinks next week. I'll catch up with you later?"

"Yeah, catch you later. I need to go find Vicki anyway." I felt like I should wander over, thank her for inviting me and say I was having a good time. Which I was, as a matter of fact.

Later, I was standing against the wall, having drifted away from the small talk of a nearby group to simply drink in the burgeoning sensuality of the atmosphere. Earlier, there had been a sex toy show, much like a fashion show, with women walking along a platform, kitted out in various sex accoutrements. Gorgeous women of all tastes had paraded wearing nothing but strap-ons and furry handcuffs, the drinks were flowing and the lights were low. The organisers were certainly going all out to create the right kind of atmosphere. Though the majority of people were chatting, there were also more and more women pairing off: whispering in each other's ears, kissing, hands on thighs. In the far corner, three women faced each other, kissing in a synchronized fashion that, coupled with the dim blue light coming from a lamp behind them, was reminiscent of a piece of art house cinema. It was beautiful to watch, erotic, but I kept looking away for fear of being caught and thought voyeuristic, when Penny suddenly appeared beside me.

"Hi there," I said.

Penny grabbed my hand. "Let's check out the maze," she said, leading me off in the direction of the infamous fucking area, complete with glory holes. Still waters run deep.

"Ok, cool." I followed her, feeling like new friends on a caravan holiday running off to hide behind a rock and giggle at skinny-dippers. Ok, and maybe feeling a bit intrigued too, and unsure of her intentions. Truth be told, I think I felt like something was going to happen to me. Or at least might happen.

We walked through the dimly lit maze, looking at the glory holes and peeking in the rooms. One room had a vinyl bench. One had a big leather sling, which we speculated on intently, suspended from the ceiling. All of them were empty. We came out of the last room and Penny just stopped and stood still. I looked at her, she looked back at me. I didn't know what to do—I didn't want to misread the situation, but she wasn't moving. So, I did it. I pushed her up against the wall and I kissed her. I kissed her full on her soft rose lips. To my relief, she kissed me right back, her tongue sliding into my mouth. That was it; we were equal now. Both of us had taken a risk and it was now safe to surmise that we were going to get our clothes off somewhere. I pulled us backwards, towards the room with the vinyl bench, and kicked the door open. We knocked each other against the walls as we clambered into the room and slammed the door shut behind us.

The room was barely lit, a warm red glow emanating from a single, colored light bulb. The bench was covered in black vinyl and set at thigh-height. The emerging 'top' in me pressed her against the bench, where we kissed passionately, endlessly. Her lips were soft and dry. They brushed mine lightly before pressing hard, deep. She grazed her teeth over my bottom lip, sucking it into her mouth. I slowly flicked my tongue just under the curve of her top lip. For me, kissing a woman is like eating peaches: sensual, delicious, soft, enveloping. To this day, kissing a woman is what undoes me. I could have kissed Penny for hours, but there was an urgency between us, along with the excitement of the newness and the sexually raw environment. Once we stepped inside that room there was no going back. The atmosphere of the whole night was magnified, then condensed, into one tiny red room with a condom dispenser and a workbench.

We hadn't spoken since we first kissed in the maze corridor. The sounds from the bar, of music and talking, seemed far away and muffled, like a dream. Penny put her hands on the bench behind her, and lifted herself up onto it. I followed silently. In between kissing, she removed her shirt and bra. Her breasts were absolutely beautiful—round, high and full. I buried my face in them, taking each nipple into my mouth in turn, curling my tongue around them as they strained to become harder still. She moaned softly, but with containment, as though making noise in the room would somehow break the spell. I began to kiss my way down her stomach as she flattened out, sliding down onto her back. I hadn't rehearsed this moment in my head, what to do with another woman. But I had no need to worry; the simpler things in life often come naturally.

My real first time had been a playful, if limited, affair a month or so earlier, with a straight woman who had brazenly seduced me. She had a wonderful curvy body and big breasts that she graciously let me explore, smiling at my innocent remarks of, "You're breasts feel wonderful!" and "My god, I'm such a lesbian!" I don't think I could have contained my joy that night, though I was a little sad when she stopped me from making her come, explaining that she wasn't over her ex-boyfriend and just couldn't let herself have an orgasm with someone else yet. But, I was delighted that I had been getting her there, obviously doing the right things.

And here I was again, going on instinct, trusting my inner dyke. I kissed my way down Penny's smooth stomach, savoring the feel of her soft skin against my lips, against my cheeks. Her fly buttons came undone easily and she wriggled out of her trousers. They made a sliding sound as they fell off the bench and hit the floor. Going deliciously slowly, I traced my finger along the elastic of her underwear and heard her breath quicken. My fingers made their way slowly under the band. I hesitated momentarily, unsure of what she would like and conscious of my fledgling fingers, but in equal measure, fearful of being arrogant or presumptuous. She raised her hips a little, as though to reassure, and a shiver of joy shot through me. Watching her face, her eyes snaking shut, I slid my hand down to find her hot and wet. I delighted in the feel of her on my fingertips, and adored watching her orgasm build as I touched her, with a skill and ease I didn't know I possessed. Her breath continued to quicken, even as she tried to stifle it, and in one glorious moment I felt her jolt beneath me, her body rippling like a rhythmic gymnast's ribbon. The beauty of that experience pervades me even now: there is something powerful and inexplicable about bringing a woman's orgasm, and it is inherent in the first time, before becoming jaded, or perfunctory, before learning how to fuck and feel nothing, or how to make an orgasm a contract. There is something arcane about making a woman come that always brings me back to what matters. It can only be a gift, it must never be currency.

Penny and I stared at each other, broad grins across our faces. I locked gazes with her as I put my wet fingers into my mouth and languorously sucked, tasting her on them, sweet and rich. She immediately sat up onto her knees and reached for me, pushing her tongue between my lips, running her hands over my rock-hard nipples. I wrenched my dress off, then my underwear, leaving my black knee-length boots on. Her hand went straight to my pussy with more confidence than I would have dared, and slid skillfully, swirling, causing my whole body to tingle with intense pleasure. We were face-to-face on the bench, sitting up on our knees, our bodies almost touching as she held my arm to brace herself and used my weight to add strength to the sliding of her hand. My orgasm came with the joy of something long-awaited and wonderful. I collapsed against her, my body shaking, with a smile so wide my face should have hurt. The warm room drew its cocoon of red light around us.

We dressed in silence, left the room and walked down the corridor of the maze. Stepping back into the bar, we stood, bemused and blinking, as much from what had just happened as the return to the lounge and light and people. We headed to the bar for a large drink each, then slowly drifted into separate groups of people, looking over at each other occasionally to exchange a knowing glance, a smile.

It wasn't until the next day that Vicki told me everyone in the bar knew what had gone on, and weeks later when it occurred to me that there were a number of glory holes in the wall that anyone could have looked through. I didn't care; what might have been experienced visually was only a snippet of what had happened. And besides, it did afford a pleasingly risqué reputation for a new girl trying to find her niche.   .

Penny and I continued as friends, became better friends in fact, never speaking of that night at Sanctuary. It had happened without words and that's where it remained, somehow by mutual understanding rather than agreement. Two ingénues in a cruise club. My first experience of making a woman come. My own first orgasm with another woman. The only sexual experience of mine to not complicate a friendship. As I write of it now for the first time, I remember the simplicity, beauty and innocence of that moment. Our little secret, shared by a room full of women.

first hand knowledge

●

elaine miller

I've never written this story out before—even though it happened over a decade ago and I am a writer and a habitual pornographer. I've always been leery of being accused of needless erotic hyperbole, like those writers for the readers' stories sections in sex magazines. You know the ones. Dear Penthouse: I never thought this could happen in real life but my wildest dream came true. So, sure, my true story is a little fantastical, and you're welcome to believe it or not, as you wish.

Her name was…well, heck, unless she was your girlfriend back then and you're just finding out right now about what I did with her, her name just ain't that important to you. I'll call her Andy. Here's what's important for you to know: I met her at a conference of kinky sexy women-loving women.

Now I'm gonna interrupt my narrative flow, which ain't even started, to pass on something I was lucky enough to stumble upon on this, my very first time out. The thing you gotta understand about sex conferences, and kinky sex conferences in particular, and kinky dyke sex conferences in ultra-amazing particular, is that when we pay the ticket price and walk through the gates and into the crowd, we're making a choice to participate in something magical.

This space, full of these women, is where you'll be spending most of your waking hours—plus a goodly portion of time stolen from your sleeping hours—until the end of the weekend. But it'll only go right if you're disposed to let the outside world stay outside, and bring the magic in with you.

In direct and nefarious contrast, in the wrong kind of mood and with the wrong expectations you can walk into a pit of madness, where every woman, womyn, or grrl either has the PMS grumpies or is actively bleeding into a bewildering array of panties, boxers, and jockstraps. You could walk into a cave of narcissists, into a haven of moody attention queens, or into a bunch of dramatists who are eager to process the meaning behind the implied classist racist ageist sizeist insult of every personal interaction until you purely forget why it was you wanted to interact in the first place.

Think of it as Schrödinger's Pussy. It's all potentially there, the horror and the joy. So you do your best to make up your mind before you walk in, hear? Leave off your poo-colored glasses, empty your mind of everything but the sexy, friendly women, take a deep breath of the leather-scented, estrogen-enriched air, and just walk right into heaven. Yes, heaven.

Like I did.

I was attending my very first conference of any kind. But keep in mind this ain't a tale of my shy coming-out or my tentative explorations. I was an aggressive, prowling femme even in those days. I was bright of eyes, warm of thighs, and pure of thought—in that I purely thought about sex.

So I walked through the gates of this conference in a high state of erotic expectation. I looked around at the mansion in which the conference was being held, with its professionally tented-in yard that made it look like the leatherdyke circus of privacy had come to town, and decided I was the luckiest daughterofabitch on the planet, and that these hundred or so yummy women must be for me.

On the first day of the conference I laid eyes on this hot butchy girl, and fell heels-over-my-head in lust with her in less time than it would take me to fix my lipstick and cock my hat in her direction. Just so my tale of too-good-to-be-true isn't too embarrassing, I'll skip lightly over the fact that she was tall and muscular and green-eyed and wore scruffy boy-jeans and great clomping black boots, okay? I lost no time in self-introduction.

On the second day of the conference, my cheerful lack of subtlety in flirting, or maybe my push-up bra—though if you think about it, they amount to the same thing—acquired me a massage from Andy. She was naked except for her boots and a soft leather dildo harness, empty of dick. The round, waiting hole in the harness offered tempting glances into a sweet spot far pinker than any of her other visible skin, and as I surreptitiously played peek-a-puss I kept thinking about whether I'd rather slip a finger or a tongue through that little hole in the leather. Also, I was angling for a chance to dither between those choices in a more realistic way.

During the massage we talked on two levels, one far more efficient than the other. Our smiling mouths talked at length and a trifle impersonally about sexual things we'd done, and things we always wanted to do. And her blunt, strong fingers on my back asked would you perhaps, and my unforced groans of luxurious delight answered yes, I will.

I held up my long-fingered hand, and told her that I'd never had a chance to fist anyone, because I'd never managed to fit. And she held my hand up against her equally large hand, shrugged, looked me directly in the eyes, and said "No problem." Her fingernails lightly drawn along the back of my neck stated alright, let's, and my light gasps and wiggles said any time.

And just like in the cliché porn stories, my head spun with desire and wanting and I managed to spit out enough blunt words to confirm all the things we were saying on all our levels of communication.

"I want to fist you. Can I fist you?" I asked, turning over so I could see her face, and holding my breath, terrified that her spoken words would belie the message in her hands.

And she answered simply, openly. "Yeah, I'd like that." And we thought of a place, and made a time, and it was a date.

I'll still skip over most of the gritty details, because you, gentle reader, don't care about me marking time until late that night, which was the official conference playtime. I attended afternoon workshops I would never recall afterwards, and stumbled around in an erotic daze, collecting gloves and handfuls of those shockingly small sample lube packets (Is this enough? What if it's not enough?). I talked to my friends in a kind of awed and whispery voice, feeling like a teenage boy about to lose his virginity. Like a dyke about to lose another kind of virginity.

At the appointed time, I walked outside into the backyard, which was transformed into a high, white cave by the festival-type tenting and electric lights. I ignored the other late-playing lezzies, and spotted Andy, dressed in black leather pants, sitting at ease in the netted sling chair that hung on an eight-foot chain from the center of the peaked tent roof. I think she was enjoying being watched admiringly by passers-by.

Andy caught my eye and smiled brightly as I, thinking helplessly of moths and flames, drew close. Despite my earlier boldness, I was scared and excited and felt a little sick. I opened my mouth to say something, anything.

Without uttering a word, she scooted her butt forward in the sling, leaned back, and pushed her long, strong legs up against either end of the overhead cross-bar support of the chair. The leather pants were actually chaps, which covered only her legs and the outside of her hips, with a belt around her waist. Chaps and boots were all she was wearing. You know I'm never gonna find a way to write about it that will convey the impact of being offered a beautiful woman's open cunt like that, okay? You're just gonna have to read the line a couple of times while smacking yourself over the head with a hefty vibrator wrapped in your lover's well-worn underwear.

The trust implicit in such a frankly sexual welcome staggered me. I melted, starting somewhere south of the belly button and spreading outwards. My fright and slight nausea had metamorphosed into tenderness and desire.

I don't remember crossing the last few feet between us. I don't remember whether either of us said anything in the next few minutes; if we did it was unnecessary, redundant.

My memory hasn't failed me on the important details, because I remember the warmth of her body in that perfect summer-night air. I remember that she smiled at me while I fumbled for the gloves in my pocket, and grinned like the sun rising when I started tearing open those silly little (blessed little) lube packets with my teeth. I remember clearly how at first I fucked her carefully, reverently, with two and then three fingers only, and how she had to encourage me to press in further, to add more lube and more fingers.

The sling chair, hung from the single overhead chain, made every movement exaggerated—simple movements becoming large, the sway of the sling becoming part of our rhythm. When she showed me that she wanted to be fucked harder, I pressed myself against her, my left arm encircling her and keeping her close, so every thrust we made wouldn't send her spinning away.

The other dykes in the yard, many close by and watching, just made it better, somehow. Their presence was not intrusive, but helpful, encouraging. Completely focused on Andy, I could still somehow feel the watchers' empathetic desire and hear their hushed murmurs, and as usual, being watched both aroused and comforted me.

From three fingers I went to four, pinkie tucked in tightly alongside my other fingers. Andy encouraged me to keep going. A final desperate attack on the plethora of lube packets stuffed in my shirt provoked giggling from Andy but allowed a generous coat of lube over my entire gloved hand. And when I tucked my thumb in the hollow of my palm and pushed inside her again, she stopped giggling and gasped, opening her thighs a little more.

I remember my awe as her cunt clasped me and started to welcome me in. I held my breath, expecting at any moment to meet the tight, tense ring of muscle that had always before, with my other lovers, meant that I wasn't going any farther, that I was locked outside. But she was elastic, forgiving, her muscles strong but yielding, stretching to open around me.

Still I hesitated, pushing gently against that tighter spot but going no deeper, unwilling to hurt her. Until Andy reached down, grasped my wrist and pulled me inside her, silently making it abundantly clear that I was being sweet but kind of dense. My heart skipping madly, I leaned a little more firmly into my next thrust and suddenly, shockingly, the widest part of my hand slipped past the tightest spot inside her, and she swallowed me to the wrist with a rush, with an ease that I will never forget.

She made a little groaning noise like a cat's purr, arched back in the chair, and her lovely, welcoming cunt pulsed strongly around my hand. I'd never felt like this, never felt so honored with someone's sex and vulnerability. Touched beyond measure, I wanted to sink to my knees, but didn't, and wanted to cry, but didn't, and wanted to kiss her, and did. And I realized the happy groaning noise was coming from my throat as well.

What I remember thinking with the scrap of thinking mind I had left was that this must be how people felt when they found religion, and how ironic it was that my personal religious ecstasy was waiting in here, all along, inside the snug, wet and welcoming cunt of the hottest woman I'd ever seen.

sugar daddy

●

I. elise bland

By the time I hit thirty, I had performed many lewd acts, yet had never done a strip tease. It's not that I hadn't thought about stripping. The chintzy glamour of the strip club sounded like fun—flashy costumes, cool shoes, seduction, and the worship of countless adoring fans. Even the thought of money turned me on. However, stripping was only one of my many role-play fantasies. Always in search of an escape from my drab life as a graduate student and teacher, I got myself into plenty of trouble on the weekends with the local leather women. Although I had spent much time naked at parties with my wild friends, it was a long time before I found someone to strip for.

My first "customer" was my girlfriend, Alex. She was a fancy butch with porcelain skin and chic black hair that she sculpted into a retro ducktail. Alex and I first met at a women's BDSM seminar. She stared me down with her dark blue eyes. Without even knowing what she would ask of me, I immediately said "yes," so we dated and played for a couple of months. Before long, she had even talked me into submitting to her in public, but in a challenging new way.

"There's a party coming up," she told me one afternoon. "Do you want to play?"

"Sure. What do you have in mind this time?" I asked.

"I want you to strip for me," she said, tugging the edges of my tank top upwards to reveal the border of my ragged old jog bra. "I know how you like to show off."

It was true. In spite of my occasional shyness, I loved to flaunt my wares when coaxed properly. Play parties (BDSM parties at which safe, consensual power exchange takes place) proved to be a great escape from my mundane scholastic life. I soon found I could do whatever I wanted under the guise of "kink." I had been a bondage slut in black latex, a dominant bitch with a penchant for clothespins, a rebellious Catholic schoolgirl, a sadistic schoolmarm, and even a damsel in distress kidnapped by roving lady pirates.

"So, what do you say?" Alex asked, fiddling with the elastic of my jog bra to release my breasts. "Will you strip for me?"

"I don't know," I stuttered. "I can't dance."

"Of course you can. I've seen you out grinding around on the dance floor. Believe me, you know exactly what you're doing."

"But I'd be too embarrassed," I pleaded.

"It's never stopped you before," she told me. "You can be my private dancer and I'll be your sugar daddy."

It was hard to say no to Alex. She was scorching hot, and there was never a doubt that I would have a good time playing with her, no matter how intimidating the game. However, I wasn't kidding about my dance skills. I really didn't know how to dance, but if I was going to be performing in public for my new sugar daddy, I had to learn. Luckily, years of academic training had taught me to tackle all problems with research and practicum, so I rushed to the nearest video store and rented some educational dance films: *Flashdance, Striptease,* and *Showgirls.* For an entire week, I gyrated alone in my bedroom wearing nothing but a thong and painfully high heels. After a glass of wine or two, I started to look pretty good to myself in the mirror, but once I was clear-headed, the charm wore off. I was left to face one tragic fact; as an exotic dancer, I sucked. I was not a smooth-moving vixen, but rather, a limp-legged newborn calf staggering around on its hooves for the very first time.

There was simply no getting out of my dance date, though. Alex was beside herself with excitement. All week long, she had been bombarding me with crude, yet titillating, e-mails: "So, baby, are you going to show me your tits? Can I see your pussy? How about a blow job in the VIP room? What are you doing after work? Do you date customers? How much for a private dance at my place?"

The night of the party, Alex showed up at my door as a suave mafioso stud in a baggy zoot suit, pocket watch chain hanging down her leg, and exaggerated bulge in her slacks. She was the ultimate sugar daddy in both attitude and attire. I also dressed the part in extreme heels and a slinky black spandex number with a red thong. We headed off to the party to wow our friends with a kinky role-play scene: the desperate I'll-do-anything-for-a-dollar stripper bares all for the handsome, corrupt customer.

When we arrived at the party, not much was happening yet. We bypassed the snack table, avoiding an extremely dry discussion of electro play.

"I hate leather parties where people just stand around and eat," I complained. "Nobody's even naked yet!"

"Well, then let's get this party started," she said, leading me into the den.

Most of the partygoers were relaxing in the adjacent living room when Alex sneakily popped a CD into the player. She settled into a puffy reclining chair and waited for me to start my show. Soon, seductive melodies crept throughout the house, piquing the curiosity of the guests. The music was my signal to dance, or at least to make some attempt to move gracefully. Alex sat before me with her legs spread wide apart, her hand resting presumptuously on her crotch. I stepped nervously from side to side, swaying my hips and running my hands through my hair, hoping to look cool and seductive. Her dark, sculpted eyebrows followed my every awkward move.

Although I felt more gawky than sexy, Alex's intense gaze turned me on and kept me going. She was a total fantasy—too attractive to be a strip club customer. Where was the legendary beer belly? The tequila breath? The expensive yet tasteless golfwear? My beautiful sugar daddy had both class and style. Although she could almost pass as a real man from afar, up close Alex maintained a certain delicacy. Her face was devoid of prickly man hair, her lips firm and painted. I soon began to forget my stage fright.

I made a few turns, grinding my ass around and trying not to stumble in my new diva shoes. With one knee propped up on Alex's thigh, I lifted my skirt up to give her a peak at my new red thong. She pressed her long white teeth together and growled softly. She was trying to act tough, but I knew that she was really moaning out of hunger for me. Suddenly I had a moment of clarity; even though she was my "daddy," the one in control of the supposed money and power, I was the one who had the ability to tease, and to say no if the price wasn't right. With newfound confidence, I executed my trick once again. I lifted my skirt and, this time, ran one finger underneath my T-back and into my wet pussy. I leaned over her, only inches from her anxious mouth, and licked off all the juices.

"Hands off," she said, leaning up to grab the fabric covering my breasts. "That's mine." Alex pulled me into a kiss in an attempt to keep me in line.

"No, you take your hands of. This stuff is mine!" I shoved her back into the chair and she obeyed. From that moment on, I knew the erotic force was with me. I was riding on a power surge—both mine and hers.

I was still nervous because Alex wasn't the only one watching me. Women in various costumes and fetishwear had begun to bleed into the room to check out our scene. We had amassed quite an audience.

"Take it off!" yelled a tattooed dyke in a leather cowboy hat. My time had finally come. There was no getting out of it now. I pulled my top down, but with lingering hesitation. Even though everybody at the party had already seen me naked—hundreds of times, it seemed—I still felt self-conscious. Nudity was not the issue. Performing was. I was jittery, and the gawking audience was only making matters worse. I wished I were in a roomful of strangers because I would have been much more relaxed.

I tried moving my body more quickly so nobody would notice my trembling, but dancing faster only made me look convulsive. My large breasts flip-flopped with a mind of their own as I teetered around on my heels. I had definitely lost my groove. The fluid, decisive moves of the dancers I had seen in videos now seemed virtually impossible. My stripper power was slipping away from me before I even had time to bask in it.

"I dance so much better in private," I told Alex.

"What are you talking about? You're doing great," she reassured me, coming out of role for a second. "They're totally into it, and so am I." I looked around at the roomful of transfixed leather women. Alex was right. They were into it, and they were easy to please. I could do no wrong. After all, I was topless and in high heels, and I was making a perverse spectacle of myself. No one dared complain.

"Let's put on a show," Alex whispered to me as I arched my back onto her chest. I was becoming more comfortable, so I was ready to ham it up a little. I knelt down and ran my cheek along her open thigh. Her long, graceful legs flexed under my every touch. She was magnificent, masculine, yet ultimately feminine. From my spot on the floor, I eyed the harsh bulge framed by her muscular legs. Alex smirked at me from above and unzipped her pants. Out popped my very favorite dildo, the purple curved one with ridges that I loved to suck and ride.

"Big enough for you?" she asked loudly enough for the onlookers to hear. Then she grabbed the scruff of my neck and pulled my head into her crotch. The crowd went wild, bombarding us with catcalls. My ear pressed against the stiff rubber device. More hoots and hollers flew past us. When she released me, my dance truly began. I pulled out all the stops. I performed a butt grind on her cock, a body slide down her chest, and even teased her with a mini hand job. Every so often, I'd catch a glimpse of onlookers—a butch in a black motorcycle cap with stern, crossed arms or an ex-girlfriend in a shiny new collar. I flashed a giddy smile at my friends. Alex noticed right away that I was distracted.

"Get back to work," she said, blowing me a haughty kiss. "I'm paying good money for this dance." She pulled a twenty dollar bill out of her pocket and dangled it between her legs. The money floated magically above her oh-so-manly toy.

"Show me what you'll do for this, baby girl."

We hadn't negotiated exchanging money during our scene, but I wasn't complaining. In fact, the cash made the role play even more perverse. I loved it. She was my girlfriend. She fucked me, but she was going to pay me, too. It was sick and twisted, and maybe even a little too humiliating for everyday life, but I didn't care. I was a graduate student, swimming in student loans, and teaching spoiled brats at the university for mere pennies. That twenty-dollar bill would soon find a new home in my three-dollar Wal-Mart thong. Even more bizarre, the money turned me on. For once, I could have my sweet cake and eat it too. Maybe there really was something to the whole sugar daddy arrangement. Power exchange, money exchange, what did I have to lose?

I dropped to my hands and knees and targeted her with my eyes. Suddenly, I wasn't trembling anymore. I knew exactly what to do. Channeling the slick moves of a famished feline, I crawled towards the prize between Alex's legs. The smell of green freedom filled my flaring nostrils. To get closer the prey, I inched up her thighs and straight to the source. It was mine. I opened my mouth, ran my tongue up the shaft of her cock, and prepared to take in a mouthful of silicone. She moaned in anticipation and foolishly relaxed the hand holding the money. Before the cash could escape, my flashing canines nabbed it. With the money hanging out of my mouth like a wounded duck, I leapt into Alex's lap, straddled her hips, and dry-humped her bare toy for the grand finale. The partygoers broke into applause as Alex spanked my butt to the beat of the music. I shook my head around in exaggerated sexual frenzy to finish off the show.

Once the song was over and the ruckus had died down, Alex held out her hand towards me. "OK, I need my twenty back," she said blankly.

"Hey, no fair!" I protested. "I earned that money fair and square."

"Honey, I'm broke, too. You know that," she said as she loosened her necktie. "This was all a game." She kissed me to make up for my disappointment, smearing her red butch lipstick across my sweaty chin. She was right. It was a game, and a very exciting one at that. Nevertheless, I wanted that money. It had come and gone all too quickly.

"Alright, Daddy Warbucks," I said, grabbing her tie. "You want your measly twenty back so bad? You're going to have to work for it, extra hard." With that, I pulled her on top of me in the recliner and yanked my cheap red thong to one side. "It's my turn to be the sugar daddy." I guided her head down in between my legs and felt her hot, strong mouth pressing deep into my pussy. She knew all the tricks to getting me off fast, sometimes even too fast. I held her hair with one hand, and with the other I gripped my twenty dollar bill with all my might. She had only been sucking my clit for a minute and I was already on the verge of orgasm.

"You're cheating!" I squealed. "I don't want to come yet! Stop!" But it was too late. My heels dug into the floor as she worked every last bit of cum out of my body. This time, my twenty dollars was gone for good.

For a moment, I wished I were a millionaire, but at least I had my kinky sugar daddy to entertain me.

"Okay," Alex said, leaning back, stroking her cock, which was still out of her trousers. "Give me that twenty and maybe I'll find another way for you to earn it back."

The games had officially begun and I sure wasn't going to lose. I pounced on her and got to "work" immediately. That money bought us hours of stripping, role play, oral services, shoe worship, and raunchy sex. We passed the twenty dollars back and forth for a year until our relationship dwindled down and Alex moved away. I still have the bill, and she is welcome to come back and get it anytime, so long as she provides me with some more of that good sugar daddy sugar.

my modern history

●

devon black

Nothing that happened in high school could have prepared me for my college experience. I was your average midwestern girl with good grades and big dreams for the perfect future. My football-player boyfriend and I were going to marry and have three little boys. We were in love and would be forever. Then we started college. My first class was History 3150. It was a 9:30 a.m. class, and I was seventeen.

I would not normally have been in Modern American History as a freshman biology major, but taking AP history in high school had allowed me to choose whichever history class I could hope might be interesting. Having taken a blind, crossed-finger stab at 3150, I had fully expected to endure the monotonous droning of a sixty-something, balding, professorish man with small glasses and a distaste for freshman. What I got instead was Ms. Klein, tall, slender and fortyish, with long blonde hair and fake eyelashes that loomed an inch past her unnaturally blue eyes. Even more surprising than her pleasant appearance were her apparent joy of teaching and her soft but bold voice; her lectures were populated by poignant, concise sentences spoken in a decidedly un-American accent. Having never traveled overseas, or anywhere really, I couldn't decipher the exact origin of her melodious accent—probably European, perhaps German, but definitely not American, and definitely not what I had anticipated. I didn't know what to make of Ms. Klein. Of course, what could I really know as a seventeen-year-old college freshman?

Steven, my eighteen-year-old high school boyfriend, had already learned quite a bit about college by the time I got there. Somewhere between tryouts and preseason practice he had discovered college cheerleaders, while I was stuck with my parents at the lake house for the summer. I had gathered from one of his few phone calls that he spent most of his time on the bench, which gave him ample opportunity to watch the activity on the sidelines—namely Chrissy Buck. He found Chrissy Buck interesting enough to sleep with just three months after I had so vulnerably laid before him my sweet, adolescent virginity. Fortunately, Steven's cruel betrayal opened my mind to the previously unimaginable.

Young, dumped, and disenchanted with the present, I dove into history with an enthusiasm unmatched by my mostly third-year classmates. Everything in History 3150 seemed, unlike my own life, real and vivid. The demonstrations, the sit-ins, the moving speeches—the world in my history class was going places, and I was eager to become a part of it. Soon I was asking Ms. Klein how I could get personally involved. How could I make a difference in this unjust world? Well, I could give a special report on one of the college shootings, if that would interest me? Sure it would. And I would even get extra credit (like I was going to improve on my standing A with extra extra credit). Zeal does wonders for grades.

Looking back, I know that it wasn't the history that compelled me toward Ms. Klein's house that Friday evening. It could have been her long legs and high heels that stood on display two days a week underneath her terribly short black skirts. It could have been her shiny blonde hair or lucid blue eyes. It could have been her sonorous voice. But I think it was the faint scent of spice that had ignited an unexpected heat in my body the morning before, when she had bent down toward me to point out a photograph in my text. I learned then that Ms. Klein's expertise lay in the area of antiwar demonstrations. She explained that she had some original footage of some of these events; one clip included the very scene she indicated in my textbook.

After class I waited for the last student to rush out the door, then I begged Ms. Klein to let me come by and watch her films; I could use them for my report. She lived only a mile off campus—I knew how to get there, I jogged by her house every day. A little taken aback by my gusto, Ms. Klein was reluctant but finally agreed. I could stop in tomorrow night around eight.

I barely slept that night.

Ms. Klein greeted me at her door in her school clothes. For some reason I pictured her in something more comfortable, but I never saw her wearing anything other than the silky button-up blouses and short black skirts she donned in class. Her legs were beautiful; they looked so strong. I often caught myself staring at them rather than the chalkboard. They seized my attention again, because they were the closest thing to the ground, and I couldn't bring myself to look her in the eyes. I felt silly and nervous at Ms. Klein's front door—me, a freshman, standing blankly like a deer in headlights before this beautiful, older, stronger woman who could teach me about the world.

Enraptured by the film clips, I listened intently as Ms. Klein explained the circumstances surrounding each one. When the last reel spun free from the projector's clutch, she offered me tea, but I was bold and asked for a glass of wine instead. She hesitated, and I thought I saw her smirk, but she brought me a half-full glass of sweet white wine.

"You seem so taken by these images. I'm not used to students wanting to learn about my work. Why are you so interested?"

I didn't have a good answer for her.

"It's you," I wanted to say. "It's something about you." But instead I shrugged and gulped down my wine.

Ms. Klein laughed lightly, then her eyes narrowed, and she appeared to scrutinize me before inquiring, "When can you be ready to present on these films?"

I had forgotten that I was actually supposed to write a paper on what I had just seen.

"I could do it Tuesday, next class."

"So soon?" She asked.

"Sure."

Ms. Klein took my empty glass. "Then you better be off and get started!"

Crushed, I was ushered out the door.

The following Tuesday I stood in front of our apathetic class and poured my heart out to the only woman listening. Ms. Klein gave me an A for the semester.

I turned eighteen that winter, and since my declared major was biology, I had no other history to take. In the spring I searched for something Ms. Klein was teaching that I could sneak in as a legitimate credit, but anatomy, physiology, and zoology took precedence. Still, I read her books and attended as many of her outside lectures as I could, fascinated by her vivid stories punctuated by her Austrian (I had learned) accent. She would smile when she noticed me, pale beneath the fluorescent auditorium lights, but that was all I could gleam from her blue eyes and long lashes—nothing more than a smile. There was no glimpse of that half glass of wine shared in her cozy living room.

I found myself thinking about her more and more until I was desperate to get her attention. The school year was threatening to end before I finally I got up the nerve to go to her office.

When she opened the door, I balked.

"Miss Brinkley. What a surprise. How can I help you today?"

Struck dumb, I stammered something unintelligible, stopped myself, then finally spit out, "I just wanted to tell you that I read your last book, and it was wonderful. Are you doing a signing anytime soon?"

She chuckled. "Well, you are more than welcome to bring a copy by here anytime, and I'll sign it for you personally." Awaiting a reply, Ms. Klein batted her lustrous lashes. "Is there anything else?"

What could I say? I want to…? What did I want exactly?

"I, uh, could I stop by your house tomorrow with a copy?"

Ms. Klein paused midbreath. She tilted her head, thought for a moment, and then after an eternity of staring deep into my soul asked, "How old are you Miss Brinkley?"

"I'm eighteen," I answered confidently. Did that mean I could come over?

She searched my face a minute longer before she finally replied, "Alright, I'll be home around nine o'clock tomorrow, if you'd like to come by then."

I must have looked sixteen the way I grinned.

"Great, I'll see you then." Holding my breath, I walked as calmly as I could down the hall and out of her sight, before I exploded around the corner. I didn't even know why I was so excited.

I arrived outside her door at 8:54, but I waited until 9:01 to knock. She answered in a blue button-up blouse, short black skirt, and black heels, as though she had just left the classroom. Only her smile was different; its usual slightly aloof character was replaced by a warm, inviting aura.

Ms. Klein offered me a chair at her kitchen table. Taking a seat, I guarded the book carefully, keeping it tucked under my arm lest my reason for staying disappear too soon. I gazed around the room, at the table, and at the floor while she examined me.

"Would you like a glass of wine?" she asked with reservation.

"That would be great, thanks."

I watched her move slowly, easily around the quaint kitchen. Glancing occasionally back over at me, she poured two glasses then took a seat at the table. I had sucked down half my wine before she spoke again.

"So, Miss Brinkley…"

"Lara," I corrected her.

"Lara then." She sipped from her glass. "Tell me again why you're so interested in my writing."

"Well," I began my well-practiced spiel. "I find it so sad how we take for granted the rights and privileges we lacked just twenty years ago, and I want to understand more about what's happening *now* that we're neglecting or taking for granted or just not really aware of."

Silence loomed.

"I'm impressed, I must say. Not many people your age are in tune with the world around them." She paused. "So, I'll sign your book, and you can go."

Her hand stretched across the table and opened, awaiting the book that was hidden in my lap.

I was devastated. I wanted to cry. I wanted to run. I didn't know what to do or say, but I couldn't hand her that book or it was all over. I would have no other legitimate opportunity to see her or come to her house again. Focusing on her open hand, I gulped.

She continued to glare at me. I didn't move. Finally my eyes met hers, but the book remained in my lap.

"What did you really come here for Lara?"

I shivered. I blinked. I opened my mouth, but I couldn't explain how I felt.

Her hand came to rest on the table.

I reached for my glass of wine and swallowed as much as I could.

"Ms. Klein…"

I waited for her to say something, anything to make it easier—something to show that she understood. But she gave me nothing.

I mowed ahead. "I just want to…I mean…"

At last she interrupted my stuttering. "Have you ever been with a woman, Lara?"

My heart jumped into my throat. The words bounced wildly around in my head—*been with a woman.* I almost panicked. Been with a woman. I couldn't breathe. Is that what I was there for? I wanted to touch her? I did. I wanted her to touch me. I wanted to kiss her; somehow I hadn't been able to grasp it before.

"No," I stammered. Then I shook my head just in case I hadn't made myself clear.

Ms. Klein reached for my glass, but I managed to grab it and quaff the final gulp. She stood, took another sip from her own then put the glasses in the sink.

Clinging to the back of the chair to support my weak legs, I set the book aside and rose to meet her as she approached.

She touched my face and smiled affectionately as she brushed my hair away. Then Ms. Klein kissed me.

I would have died there in her kitchen, but she led me to her bedroom.

Ms. Klein's magnificent boudoir: it was painted a deep sienna and accented with beige. The windows were open; the curtains and candle flames fluttered slightly in the warm spring breeze. (Ever since college my fantasies sport fluttering curtains and candle flames.) I couldn't feel my legs as they transported me into her arms. She wrapped me with her body and kissed me like no high school boy could imagine. Her lips were full and bold, hungry for my guiltless desire. Somehow I managed to keep from collapsing into a puddle on the floor while she consumed my mouth.

At last she let me gasp for breath. Her stereo on the other side of the small room came alive at the touch of a button. Ms. Klein liked contemporary jazz; contemporary jazz would forever play as the soundtrack to my orgasms. As I stood stiff, she began to unbutton her blouse.

"Is this what you want?" she asked sincerely, pausing between buttons three and four.

I nodded furiously. I couldn't speak, but I knew I wanted what was happening. I wanted it so badly, that I didn't bother to think that it might just make me a lesbian for life. I didn't think at all, but, God, I felt like heaven.

I watched intently as Ms. Klein dropped her blue blouse to the floor, unclasped her bra and revealed to me her gorgeous breasts. I had been struck with a sudden fear of inadequacy. What if she looked like Steven's magazine bunnies? I didn't look like that. But her chest looked just like mine. I wanted to show her, but she had other plans.

"Come here," Ms. Klein demanded.

I obeyed.

With quivering hands, I cupped her breasts. They filled my palms while their nipples poked through the space between my fingers. Bending a little, I positioned the hard nipple of her left breast between my front teeth. I bit just enough to feel the pleasure in my own nipples. When I looked up, her head was tilted, her blonde hair sweeping the muscles of her back. Pressing my lips to her delicious neck, I licked and kissed and basked in her moans, filling my ears like warm liquid.

Tenderly, she grasped my shoulders and pushed me away. Ms. Klein had things to teach me, and the lesson was beginning. I was so incredibly excited, so wet and hot and dizzy with lust, that I feared I might come with my clothes on, but she didn't give me the chance.

She tossed me down, and as my head dropped into her pillows, her delicate fingers yanked loose the button on my jeans. She had them off before I could prop myself up to help. Holding me down with a hand on each thigh, she placed her mouth fully over my mound and breathed heat through the thin material of my panties. My clit was already swollen and throbbing; her touch created a gush of moist warmth that engorged it completely and sent sharp tingles through my thighs.

When she set me free, I pulled off my shirt with haste and removed my bra. I was on Ms. Klein's bed (candles glowing against the red walls, curtains slow dancing in the thick night air of spring) wearing nothing but my socks and underwear. Her eyes were on fire; I thought she might devour me in that very instant. But no, she made me wait, she made it last.

"Turn over," she told me.

I was nervous, but I lay on my stomach. I felt her nails slide beneath the elastic of my socks until they slipped from my feet. Then she lay over me. She pulled my hair to one side and applied a beautiful hickey to the other. Meanwhile, her warm body pressed against mine, her pubic bone grinding my cotton panties into my flesh.

"Are you sure?" she whispered into my exposed ear.

"Yes, yes please." I had never been so turned on in my short life.

I lifted my bottom enough for her to pull off my wet panties, but before I could flatten myself against the covers, she slid her hand beneath me. Her fingers scooped just low enough to gather some of the gooey liquid from my pussy before they settled on my clit in slow circles. I was grateful she couldn't see me, because my eyes rolled back into my head surely leaving me looking like a zombie under her command.

The heat, the pleasure, the intensity was mind-blowing. My breath came in quick pulls. I pressed my head back until I felt her hot mouth on my neck. Squirming and gasping I fought the severe pleasure in my clit until I had to bite the pillow to keep from crying.

"Stop please," I pleaded. I didn't want to come yet. I didn't want it to end. I worried that she would make me leave if I came too soon. Maybe I wouldn't pass her test, and I would be forever forbidden from her lair—her lusty, sienna bedroom.

Her fingers quit their torturing. For a moment I felt as if they still circled, rubbing slowly, tickling my soul. Finally the tingling lessened and began to spread outward. I turned to face her.

"I want to touch you."

She grinned then lay back on the bed beside me.

I straddled her slender form and surveyed my available territory. Her short skirt was hiked up around her hips. I ran my hands along her legs, up and around her waist until she lifted enough for me to fumble with the button and zipper. Making as brave a move as I could muster,

I stared into her eyes while I slid her skirt down her thighs and, as she readjusted, off her feet. Her pantyhose came off next, and there was nothing to remove beneath them.

When I bent my head to her short, blonde curls, I could smell her excitement. It was verification, even after all this, that she wanted me. Her scent was strong, and her lips bulged around her clit. She wanted me as badly as I wanted her.

"Wait," she said and led me up to her mouth. Ms. Klein kissed me deeply then held my face close to hers. "You don't have to do that."

I zeroed in on the candlelight reflection glinting off the pupils of her eyes. "Let me."

Relinquishing her gentle hold on my jaw, she rested her head on the pillow and allowed me to lie between her legs.

Piqued and tumid, her clit was easy to find. I probed uncertainly at first, then gave up trying to imitate what I had seen in Steven's porn and just licked and sucked as I had always dreamed of being licked and sucked.

"Your instincts are amazing," she moaned as she struggled to keep her mound still enough for me to minister. Her movements encouraged my slurping and lapping, searching for the right spot, rhythm, and pressure, until Ms. Klein sat up abruptly and closed her legs. "No, not yet."

I had been so busy with my task, that I had ceased to think about the goal, but I was thrilled to realize that she must have been close to coming.

She beckoned me to her mouth and kissed the juices from my face.

"Let me show you what it can be like." She pushed me over and down to the bed. "I have toys, but tonight you should feel it like it's real."

It was real; it was more real than high school or History 3150 or college cheerleaders, and it was like nothing I had ever experienced. Steven had never done that to me, not like Ms. Klein. Her tongue melted into my clit until its every movement drew me closer to orgasm.

Then I felt something new for me during oral sex. Her fingers probed around the entrance to my vagina, then began to slip into the wet hole, and when one coaxing fingertip stroked inside me, a sudden, powerful bolt of pleasure ravaged my entire body. I exploded with her tongue on my clit and her middle finger just inside between my shaking legs.

I stayed the night.

In the morning I didn't know what to say, and I was afraid of what Ms. Klein might say. But when she opened her eyes and saw me in her bed, she giggled.

"Well, I'll give you a C for last night. You certainly need more practice."

I was saved; a C was a passing grade.

"I'm sure you need to run off to class now, but I'll be available for private lessons every Monday, Wednesday, and Friday night for the rest of the semester."

Ms. Klein was the best class I ever took.

gabrielle's fountain

●

jean roberta

Her ketchup-red hair, her laughing blue eyes, and her healthy female curves gave off heat. Just being near her sent tingles up and down my spine.

Like animals craving each other's warmth, the crowd was packed onto the dance floor of the gay bar. It was after the legal cut-off time for serving alcohol, but no one wanted to brave the dark and the cold, to stagger over the ice in the parking lot to find cars which were mostly rusted, dented, and as unwilling to leave the premises as we were.

I liked to think I was a realist who could see what was under my nose. But I also liked to think I was a visionary who could see what was possible. I liked to visit the river town of Riel, Saskatchewan, because it seemed more fluid in several ways than my home town of Forgetville, the seat of a government which was officially and without sarcasm described as "provincial."

Riel was named for a wild, possibly insane French-speaking half-breed who had tried to establish his own nation on the Canadian prairie a hundred years before, and who had been hanged in Forgetville as a traitor to the federal government and the British Crown. What dyke wouldn't love the romance of that story? And what dyke could resist my wild, red-haired girlfriend in Riel, especially after she bragged to me and her other drinking buddies about being the great-great-granddaughter of Riel's second-in-command, Gabriel Dumont?

She called herself Gabrielle in the bar, although her large Catholic family knew her by a different name. Her parents had bought her a small house a block away from theirs when she was a twenty-one-year-old on welfare who refused to let them send her to college. By the time she was thirty, she had trained them to accept her parade of different jobs and different girlfriends, her tribe of Siamese cats who liked to fuck on the round oak table under her picture window facing a major bus route, her vegetarian cooking, her trade in marijuana (grown in her backyard greenhouse), and even the naked revelers who attended her moonlit garden parties and Wiccan rituals in summer.

"Baby," she teased me in the bar, casually running a hand over my hip. "You want to get me another beer, don't you?"

"Gabe…" I started.

She wrapped an arm around my waist, giving me a raunchy grin. "I'm just getting started, girlfriend. You know me. Booze keeps me going, so I can give it to you later. Have I ever jammed out on you?" She leaned in to give me a slow, juicy kiss.

Gabrielle was my addiction, and I couldn't resist her. "Mm," I answered. "I shouldn't, but I will."

"You're such a horny chick," she told me approvingly. "You'd do anything to get laid. You need to move in with me."

On my way to the bar, I was aware of my breasts, held snugly in place by my B-cup underwire bra. Gabrielle had told me that such armor was pointless in my case. She wanted me to go braless, winter and summer, and to stay naked whenever I was in her house. But I liked feeling my breasts supported, as if by her knowing hands. I hoped my hard nipples couldn't be seen through my good cashmere sweater.

I ordered one beer from the thin young man behind the bar, and paid for it.

"Change," he told me, throwing down a handful of coins. For a split second, I thought he was advising me to change my ways or the company I kept.

Everyone in the queer community of Riel seemed to know that I often spent three hours on a bus to visit Gabrielle on weekends. As she told her friends, I came there to get laid. Their amused contempt for the bureaucratic flatness of Forgetville was only matched by their feeling that Gabrielle, with all her quirks, belonged to them.

I had no way of knowing how many of the barflies who watched me had partied with Gabrielle. I felt stripped naked by their eyes. It was embarrassing, arousing, degrading, perversely flattering, and there was nothing I could do about it.

In Forgetville, I was a divorcée trying to support an eight-year-old daughter on whatever I could earn when I wasn't working on my endless Master's thesis. In Riel, I seemed to be Gabrielle's imported slut.

When I returned to our table, she was laughing at something told to her by Violet, the only MTF I had ever met. I fought down my fear that they were laughing at me, and took a swig from my own half-finished bottle of beer.

"Violet has the hardest time finding shoes to fit," Gabrielle told me. "Show her how small your shoes are, honey."

I didn't think my feet were unusually small for a woman's, and I didn't think the challenge of finding the right shoes sounded especially funny, but I wanted to be agreeable. I unlaced one of my black leather indoor boots and slipped it off.

To my amazement, Violet raised it to her nose, inhaled deeply, lowered her eyelashes, and smiled at me before releasing it. "As dainty as a glass slipper," she told me in a husky tenor voice. "I wish I had feet like that," she told Gabrielle.

Before I could guess her intention, Violet reached for my sock-covered foot again and held it in both her big hands. "Pretty little foot," she remarked.

"It's all right, honey," Gabrielle told me. "Violet and I go way back. She's into feet."

Violet held my toes firmly for a long moment, and the warmth of her hands was hypnotizing. "You don't want me to take your sock off, do you?" she asked. "You probably don't want to get cold."

"No," I managed to answer. Gabrielle snickered. Violet used her knuckles to massage the sole of my foot, and I felt it all the way up my legs and into my crotch. Gabrielle kept one hand on my thigh while holding her beer with the other. I couldn't keep my breathing under control.

The DJ put on a slow song by a popular girl-band. As an English major, I believed in listening to the lyrics. The song was about losing a lover to a rival, and I fought off my sense that the words were a warning.

"Sorry, Violet," said Gabrielle, pulling my foot out of her hands. "I want to dance with my woman. Come dance with me, babe."

"I'll do your other foot later, girlfriend," promised Violet. She winked at me, licking her burgundy lips.

Gabrielle pulled me close by my butt cheeks. As we swayed to the music, she grazed my cheek and kissed my neck. She pressed her soft, full, swinging breasts against mine.

At the wailing climax of the song, she teased me with her hips and her crotch, pushing her pussy as close to mine as she could. The layers of denim and corduroy between us grew so hot and damp that I could imagine steam rising off us. "You want something?" she taunted me.

"You," I confessed in her ear. "Hot thing."

"So do you still think I'm not your type?" She ran one hand up my back and stroked my neck. She wouldn't let me forget what I had said to discourage her when we had met at a women's retreat on a farm near Riel the previous summer.

But you're not! I screamed silently. You just appeal to my animal nature.

"Tonight you are," I told her.

"You'll let me do whatever I want, won't you?" she asked.

"If it doesn't cause damage," I admitted.

Gabrielle guffawed. "So what happened to the proper schoolteacher?" She emphasized "proper." We had been through this before. I didn't bother to answer.

She answered herself. "You've been loosening up since I met you, honey. Come on, we need to go home."

We agreed fully on that point. We said goodbye to Violet and a dozen of Gabrielle's other smirking friends, picked up our coats, scarves, toques, mittens, and winter boots from the coat check, and dressed ourselves for the outdoors.

By a miracle, Gabrielle's old Ford started at the first try. As we watched our breath in the fragile shelter of the car, I kept wiping fog off the passenger-side window. I felt as if I were nurturing my own lust like a flame between cupped hands. It was the basis of my relationship with Gabrielle, and it had to be worth whatever it would cost me.

"I hope Emma isn't driving Caroline crazy," I worried aloud. My daughter Emma was spending the night with one of Gabrielle's younger sisters.

"Caroline loves Emma," said Gabrielle. "She's one of the family." Getting her siblings to take care of my daughter was part of Gabrielle's campaign to convince me to move to Riel, get a teaching job in the university, and support the three of us. Gabrielle lived within sight of the ivy-covered institution she would never attend.

I had made her cry more than once by refusing to pack up all my belongings to move to her town, to live in a house that was really too small for three people and a family of territorial cats, or to support an alcoholic. I wasn't willing to think about that now.

The trees in Gabrielle's neighborhood glittered with frost, and the empty street gleamed darkly with ice under a cold white moon. The gnarled crabapple tree in Gabrielle's front yard was biding its time until it could burst forth with fruit that would attract birds. The tree had so much presence that I almost expected it to beckon us in. Her little house with the pointed roof looked like the cottage of a good witch in a fairy tale.

Gabrielle parked the car crookedly, and gave me a wicked grin. "Here we are, woman. You can plug in, then come inside." Knowing my role, I pulled the extension cord out from the glove compartment and brought it over to the electrical outlet on the side of the house. The prongs buzzed when I plugged them in, and a blue spark appeared. It seemed fitting.

We rushed into the warm house together. Without turning on the light, she pulled off my toque and scarf and unbuttoned my coat. She pulled me roughly to her panting chest with both arms, grunting like a bear. She kissed me with surprising gentleness, and slipped a sly tongue into my mouth. I wiggled against her, and she laughed before she withdrew from me. "We have to get these clothes off," she told me.

We shed our coats and boots in the hallway, left our sweaters in the front room, our pants in the kitchen, and our underwear in the bedroom before diving into bed in the dark, like naked swimmers jumping into a welcoming pool. Gabrielle knew where to find what she needed.

Lady, the matriarch of the Siamese tribe, ran into the bedroom with one of my fur-lined mittens in her mouth. She dragged it under the bed, and I was too distracted to stop her.

"Ohh, baby," commented Gabrielle, running a hot hand down my back as we lay side-by-side. She brushed my shoulder-length brown hair away from her mouth, and static crackled between us.

I slid down to hold her big, soft, generous breasts close to my face. I sucked one of her nipples into puckered hardness, making her squeal. "Mm, tits," I told her. She let me squeeze them, bounce them, pinch them, and flick them with my tongue.

Gabrielle grabbed my head to hold me in place. "Drink my milk, sweet thing," she told me. She had never fed a baby from her breasts, and probably never would. I was the one who had done that, but when we were together, it seemed natural for her to play the role of Mother, while I played the Spoiled Brat. I suckled her generous tits, feeling her heartbeat and the rhythm of her breathing.

I knew she was drunk because she had more energy and focus than at other times, just as she had promised. In my own way, I had faith in her.

"Get up here," she told me, rising up to a sitting position. She held me by the waist and I wiggled in several directions, trying to figure out what she wanted. "Up on your knees," she ordered impatiently. "No, not like that. Get your knees under you, and stretch out like a cat."

I did as she told me, and she rewarded me with a smart slap on my ass, which was sticking up as if asking for attention. She slapped one cheek, then the other. Just as her slaps began to sting, she stopped. I couldn't stop moving my hips, either to shake off the sting or to increase the sensation.

Gabrielle slid a hand thoughtfully over my sensitive butt cheeks as if searching out my reactions. "Don't move, honey," she told me. The bed bounced slightly as she changed position, and I heard a drawer opening. She stroked the crack between my cheeks, then probed my smaller opening with a finger coated in something cool and slippery. Knowing Gabrielle, it was probably an herbal concoction.

I moaned as she pressed on, sinking into my ass beyond the first knuckle. "Greedy pig," she snickered, letting out a deep breath. "You love to get fucked, don't you?"

She seemed to think she had won the argument between us, or at least the current round. I was in no condition to explain that I had never denied wanting her, and never disagreed with her reminders that I was as natural and unrefined a slut as she was, if not worse.

I probably was worse. I knew that my most honest reactions contributed to the credibility gap that had sprung up between us. I felt ridden, lashed, pricked, and stung by my own implacable conscience, which only spurred me on. "Oh yes," I answered.

Gabrielle's specialty was playing with several parts of my body at once, like a musician trying to find out all the different chords she could play on her instrument. As her finger sank steadily deeper into me, moving in small spirals, her other hand was exploring the outer folds of my cunt and my swollen clit. She tickled and stroked it persistently, snickering under her breath.

As she intended, I bucked and wiggled shamelessly, moaning and begging without words. "Come on, baby," she told me. "I want to watch you come."

"Oh! Gabe!" I yelled. All my muscles tried to pull her in as my clit erupted in spasm after spasm.

"That was good," she told me, easing her finger out of my ass. "You're wet."

As intense as my orgasm had been, I knew it was nothing special. For months, Gabrielle had been courting my G-spot by touching it with fingers and fucking me with various dildos. Every inch of my pussy loved her attention, and I came hard in response, but I still wasn't convinced that I had a real G-spot, let alone an orgasm that came from there.

According to Gabrielle's book on the subject, women who were capable of that could spurt like fountains as they screamed to heaven. Later, when we rented a porn video that showed a whole group of gorgeous babes coming like that, I thought they looked like supernatural beings with magical powers. Gabrielle had more faith than I did that we could both learn to come like that if we worked hard enough at it

She seized one of my nipples between her teeth and shook it gently, like a dog with a bone. I knew that she wanted to break down my walls, one brick at a time. I wanted to let her try.

"You need some dick, don't you, little woman?" she taunted.

"Yep," I confessed, blushing. This time, she pressed her mouth against mine and slipped me her tongue as she stretched her length on me, letting me feel her weight. When my breathing changed, she raised herself up to reach into her bedside drawer and pull out her plastic dong and its harness. During pot harvest season, she had gone to the store that carried specialty porn videos to buy the new toy just for me.

She slid down my belly to my wet, matted bush. I watched as her pink tongue poked delicately out of her mouth, like that of Lady when she was petted. The tongue tasted and tickled me while I squirmed, trying to get more of it inside me.

Gabrielle used two hands to part my outer lips, and lapped at my wetness until I was sure the roots of her tongue must be sore.

"Spread wide," she told me, pushing my legs apart. She hopped out of bed to gird her loins with her harness and the pale salmon colored cock which came complete with two hard balls. She shimmied and bucked like the star performer in a butch fertility dance.

Her eyes shone with boozy lust as she crawled over me. She grinned as she held her cock with one hand, and I reached out to help her guide it into me. I was so wet that it slid in to the balls in one thrust.

"Good girl," she told me. I moaned, feeling as if she had appropriated the man parts of a life-size Ken doll so she could take possession of all my nooks and crannies. She worked up to a galloping rhythm, and I answered by pumping back.

The smell of my own cunt mixed with the smells of our sweaty armpits, necks, and scalps, and it all rose to my nose like incense. She played with my nipples while riding me to a frenzy. I loved everything she did, but I couldn't focus on any one sensation.

Before long, I felt an explosion coming up from my depths. "Come on, woman," she urged me, and I did. I wailed like an animal, which must have been one of the effects she had in mind.

As she pulled out of me and touched the wet spot on the sheet, I wondered if my G-spot reacted differently from other women's. I seemed to have leaked enough fluid to drown any little crawly things that might have been hibernating in Gabrielle's bed, but I knew that I hadn't spurted. I just didn't seem to have that kind of a fountain.

We rested in each other's arms for long, dreamy minutes. I felt tired in a good way, but Gabrielle was still vibrating, ready to go again. I felt paws walking gingerly up my legs, and then I looked into the cool green eyes of Lady's oldest son. In the dim light from the window, I could have sworn that he was smiling.

Gabrielle was lying slightly under me, holding my hips between her thighs. I scratched her lightly with my fingernails, making her squirm. I reached her pungent crotch and burrowed into her slit with my nose and tongue. I wished I could shrink small enough to crawl up inside her and explore the terrain.

"Let me, baby," I told her, hoping I sounded sexy. I lay between her legs and reached into her hot cave with my index finger. I found the place inside her where her cunt-walls felt like hard goose bumps, and where they ballooned open to give me room.

My middle finger joined my first, and then my ring finger found room beside them. I tap danced on her hard bumps, and stroked them as if telling them to come closer.

"What?" yelled Gabrielle. I felt a spurt under my fingers as though the fire in her had set off a sprinkler in her ceiling. Clear fluid gushed out of her, soaking the bed.

"Ohh," she moaned. "Baby, what did you do?"

"I did it," I bragged. I felt more loving toward her than I had before, or ever would again. "I found it, Gabe. I played with your G-spot, and you squirted."

"It felt different. I didn't know it would feel like that. Honey, you can't tell me I don't mean anything to you."

I waited several heartbeats before answering. "You never know how something will feel before it happens. But now you know. It'll probably be easier for you to get there next time."

I was tempted to baptize myself by rolling around in the holy water from her secret fountain, her witchy well, but I knew better. I had shared a bed with a child who sometimes peed in her sleep, and I knew how quickly warm body fluids turn cold when exposed to the air. I climbed out of bed and went to the bathroom to find an old towel to soak up the puddle.

Gabrielle rolled over for me, stretching as proudly as a big cat. "Up," I told her, forcing her out of bed so I could change the bottom sheet. In such cases, change is good.

When the bed was covered with comfortable cotton, we snuggled together under the quilt. Gabrielle had several matched sets of bedding for her queen-size bed, and she always kept them clean and folded when they weren't in use. She was a very domestic witch, and I suspected that she would still be like that long after we had gone our separate ways.

As we fell asleep in each other's arms, I savored the knowledge that I had done something to her for the first time. Our experience gave us fresh, energizing dreams until we woke up to the clear light of a winter morning.

runway blues

●

radclyffe

I woke to the sound of the sea, the gentle swaying of the bed, and a soft moan. Swaying bed? Soft moan? What the hell?

The night outside the adjacent window, which was cracked open an inch to allow a whiff of cool salt air to float in, was still dense with fog. I was lying on my back in an unfamiliar room in a bed I didn't recognize. Even more disconcerting was the fact that a near stranger was lying next to me, and I was pretty certain she was masturbating.

I should probably start at the beginning, which was approximately twelve hours ago. I arrived at the airport in Philadelphia the requisite two hours before my scheduled flight to Boston. I've never liked to fly, and ever since the new security regulations were instituted, I like it even less. I should've known that it was going to be one of those trips when I pulled into the economy parking lot, which is about the size of a small state, and saw the signs saying Lot Full. I prepared myself for even more inconvenience but was pleasantly surprised when I was given an economy-rate voucher to park in the short-term parking garage adjoining the terminal. Amazing. A savings of both time and money.

I made the mistake of taking this as a good omen.

It was Friday of the long Fourth of July weekend, and I hadn't been able to leave the lab any earlier. I'd been waiting for a protein sample to make its way through the filtration column, and that's a process that just can't be rushed. Still, I'd arrive in Provincetown in the early evening and be able to enjoy a good start on the weekend. The line for the US Airways ticket counter wound its way through the path mapped out by steel poles and black nylon straps and overflowed into the main thoroughfare. I, however, had my Visa Preferred card, which allowed me, even though I was traveling coach, to check in at first class, where there were only two people waiting. I was checked in, had my boarding pass, and made it through security in forty-five minutes. Right on schedule for my four thirty flight.

Two minutes before boarding, the US Airways agent at the gate announced that all flights into Boston were being delayed because of severe weather—there'd been intermittent thunderstorms throughout the Northeast for the last two days. I settled back into my seat in the crowded waiting area, glad that I had scheduled over an hour between my arrival in Boston and the departure on Cape Air to Provincetown.

Unfortunately, my flight out of Philadelphia was an hour late, and by the time the airspace over Boston was cleared from the earlier delays, I had missed my connecting flight. The agent at the Cape Air counter couldn't have been nicer.

"Hi there," he said with a smile.

I tried not to snarl. "I just missed my flight to Provincetown."

"Well," he said jauntily, his smile still in place, "the next scheduled flight is in an hour and it's full, but I think…" His fingers danced on the keyboard and he made little humming sounds that made me want to choke him, "they're adding another plane on that route because of the backlog. Hmm. Yes. Here it is." He looked up, proud of himself. "I got you on that flight."

"Thanks," I said, embarrassed by my earlier surliness. I took my new boarding card and hurried toward yet another security checkpoint. My luggage had been checked through from Philadelphia to Provincetown, and I only had a small carry-on with my computer and the newest Claire McNab. The tiny waiting area at gate 33, the only gate servicing all of Cape Cod, was chaos. The last three flights to Martha's Vineyard and Nantucket had been canceled because of fog over the cape. The earlier storms had drifted off the mainland and now shrouded the narrow ninety-mile finger of sand that was the vacation destination of tens of thousands of people this weekend. And it looked as if all of us were stranded in Boston.

Feeling secretly grateful and a tiny bit superior, I worked my way through the crowd to the check-in counter for Provincetown, the last hurdle before I could complete my journey. I'd be in town by ten thirty, with plenty of night left. As soon as I deposited my luggage at the Provincetown Inn, I planned to head out to the Pied, one of the hot dance spots for women. Stress always makes me horny. And it was turning out to be a very stressful evening.

I passed my boarding ticket across the counter triumphantly. The young woman on the other side looked up sympathetically. Uh-oh.

"Hi," she said with a slightly less brilliant smile than the previous agent. "We just heard that the last two flights to Provincetown were diverted because of fog. We're canceling the rest of tonight's flights."

I heard a mournful groan and turned to see a blond about my age with a backpack slung over her shoulder and a frantic expression in her eyes.

"Sucks, huh?" I muttered. "You headed to Provincetown?"

"Yes, and I'm beginning to think I'm cursed. I've been trying to get three hundred miles for what feels like three days. God, I just should've driven."

"Me, too. I would've been there by now." I laughed and held out my hand and told her my name.

"Kiera Jones." She closed long, warm fingers around mine. Her hand, I noticed, was strong and very soft. A musician's hands, or at least what I imagined a musician's hands would feel like. I probably thought of that because a guitar case leaned against her blue-jean–clad leg.

"Vacation?" I asked.

She shook her head. "No, a weekend gig at the Crown and Anchor."

I knew the place in the center of town. It was best known for its drag shows and men's bars, but there was also a small lounge in the front. "Playing tonight?"

"No, thank God, or I'd really be crazy. Tomorrow and Sunday."

I turned back to the ticket agent. "Can I get on the first flight tomorrow?"

"I've got three hundred passengers from the other canceled flights to reroute. I might be able to get you on a flight late tomorrow afternoon."

"Thanks, but forget it. I'll rent a car and drive."

A man standing next to me at the Nantucket counter snorted. "Good luck. They've been canceling flights out of here all day. The last I heard, all the rental agencies were out of cars."

I glanced at the clock. Nine forty. The last ferry had already left for Provincetown. That left buses or limo services. I didn't care if I had to walk, I wasn't spending the night in Boston.

"I have to get to Provincetown tonight," Kiera muttered from behind me. "I've got sound checks and a run-through of the set first thing in the morning, and I've never played with these guys before. If I don't show up, they're going to think I blew them off."

I turned. "I'm going to see if I can get a private car. You want to share the cost?"

Her eyes lit up fleetingly, but then she shook her head. "Thanks, but—"

"Look," I said. "I'm going to do it anyway. Why don't you come along and just handle the tip."

"That's not fair."

"If you don't come, I'll be out the cost of the tip. Besides, I'd like the company."

She gave me an appraising glance, and it wasn't hard to figure out why. It sounded like a come-on, and I suppose on some level it was. She was easy on the eyes, with shoulder-length, sun-kissed hair, luminous green eyes, and a wide expressive mouth. Beneath a short Levi's jacket, she wore one of those tight white tops with the thin straps that look like you should be sleeping in it and not wearing it outside on the streets. It barely reached the top of her low-rider jeans, and a small strip of tanned skin showed between the two. That narrow band of smooth belly begged for a touch, or at least that was the opinion held by all ten of my fingers.

"No strings," I said, too quietly for anyone else to hear. She had to know from looking at me in the Dockers and polo shirt I'd worn to work where my interests lay. Stereotypes come from somewhere, and I knew that my short dark hair and rangy build, along with my debonair style, spelled dyke. "Just a little friendly companionship."

"We can start there." She grinned and hefted her guitar case. "Let's go to P-town."

It wasn't all that difficult to find a limo. The airport was crawling with drivers hawking private rides to just about anywhere at exorbitant prices. The trick was finding someone who looked reputable and who wasn't going to charge me my entire budget for the weekend. I could afford to rent a limo, but I couldn't afford to buy one. We finally connected with someone who fit the bill, and as we followed him outside into the steamy, overcast night, juggling our bags, I glanced at Kiera. "Things are looking up."

"Things are definitely looking up," she noted with a tilt of her chin.

I followed the direction of her gaze and whistled. "He didn't say it was a stretch limo. Well. Let's ride in style." I put down my luggage and beat the driver to the rear door, opened it, and gestured to the interior. "Ms. Jones. If you please."

She laughed in a wholly unselfconscious way, which made her appear even more youthful than she was. I'd said no strings, but I hadn't anticipated the little zing that my heartstrings gave at that moment. I climbed in after her and looked around. Wide leather seats, a minibar, and an honest-to-God live rose in a small glass vase tucked into a recessed niche in the door. Even better was the opaque Plexiglas that completely separated the driver's compartment from ours. I'd been in one of these limos before, and I knew that he could not, in fact, see us. Suddenly, as I settled next to Kiera, that seemed very important.

"This is wild," she said, leaning forward to examine the contents of the minibar. She cast me a mischievous look over her shoulder. "Do you think we can drink any of this?"

"Why not?"

She settled back with a bottle of fairly good champagne in her lap. "Now what?"

I opened a small compartment next to the minibar and took out two glasses while Kiera popped the cork. As we headed out of Boston, we touched glasses and sipped champagne. I was definitely looking forward to the two-and-a-half-hour trip. We finished off the champagne at a leisurely pace and talked a little bit about the things that people do when they first meet. Then, on impulse, I asked, "Would you play something for me?"

Once again, Kiera regarded me with a mixture of curiosity and caution. Whatever she was looking to find, or not find, must've been there. Wordlessly she nodded and opened her guitar case. I said nothing. There were times when the only answers came from listening, not asking.

I watched her hands as they moved on the strings. I've always been fascinated by hands that create. Music, art, passion. Hers made much more than music, they made promises—or so I wished. But I contented myself with the beauty that filled the air. Sad, poignant notes, rich with stories of love and loss.

"You play the blues."

She looked up, her eyes dark and deep. "Surprised?"

"You hide it well."

"Everywhere but here," she observed, glancing down at her guitar.

"Beautiful." And I meant more than the music.

She must've known, because she carefully set the guitar aside and edged closer on the seat. I sat perfectly still and let her choose the song. She slid under the arm I had placed along the back of the seat and turned against my side, her arm coming around my waist. I dipped my chin so she could have my mouth if that was her desire, and she explored my lips with the moist tip of her tongue and the soft brush of her lips. Her breasts were pressed against mine, her nipples hard. I slid my hand up to rest my cupped fingers just below the swell of her breasts. If she wanted me to touch her there, she had only to shift the slightest bit into my palm. She didn't, and I contented myself with what she offered. Her kisses were a feast unto themselves, long and languid and hot. She nibbled my lips, sucked my tongue, and teased the inside of my mouth with possessive strokes. She kissed me until I was dizzy and then some. At some point I felt her leg curl onto my thigh, and I felt the heat of her center where she pressed ever so gently against me in time to the thrusts of her tongue. I was going to soak right through my pants, I was so turned on, and she still hadn't moved her hand from my waist. I groaned softly, imagining I would die if her hand found my skin, or if it didn't, and heard her laugh.

"Excuse me," a mechanical voice said from a speaker behind us.

I groaned again, long and low, as Kiera moved away.

"Yes," I said hoarsely.

"I can't see."

"What?"

"The fog is so thick I can't see the road. I'm gonna have to stop soon."

"Jesus," I muttered, trying to get my brain to function as Kiera repacked her guitar. "Where are we?"

"I haven't made very good time," Mr. Mechano said. "Somewhere on the Cape."

"What do you suggest?"

Silence.

I blew out a breath as I felt the car slow to a halt. I looked at Kiera. "We'll have to get a room and wait this out."

"On the Friday of Fourth of July weekend? Good luck finding a vacancy." She smiled ruefully and traced a finger along my jaw. "But I guess we've been lucky so far."

I nodded and spoke to the voice. "Hello?"

"Yeah?"

"Go ahead and find us someplace to stay. Will you take us the rest of the way in the morning?"

"I'll sleep in the car. As soon as it clears, we'll go."

"Okay."

The limo moved on and, miraculously, the driver did find us a place. We were too far from the bigger tourist attractions for the myriad little motels dotting the Cape to be full. When we got to the room, whatever confluence of heart and harmony brought us together in the limo had drifted away on the fog. I could tell by the efficient way she went about stowing her gear and avoiding my eyes.

"What now?" I asked, unable to hide my regret or to think of anything else to say that wouldn't sound ridiculous after what we'd just been doing.

"I'm beat," she said quietly, meeting my gaze. "I've been on the road since five this morning."

I nodded, standing on the far side of the bed.

"And," she added, "I don't usually have sex with strangers."

"Kissing isn't sex," I pointed out.

"No, it isn't. Technically." She glanced at the bed. "But this would be."

"I can sleep..." I glanced around. No sofa. There wasn't even a bathtub. "...really far away."

Kiera laughed. "Let's just go to sleep."

We stripped down, or at least I did. I didn't look in her direction. There was no way I was going to be able to sleep, not with the way my body felt after the crazy day and the miraculous kisses.

I crawled under the stiff cotton sheets, murmured, "Night, Kiera," and closed my eyes. The next thing I knew I was awake again, and so, it seemed, was Kiera.

I had no idea the time, or how long I'd been asleep. It might have been three hours or thirty seconds. Her breathing was shallow and fast, and I sensed, rather than felt, the sheet gently brush over my arm where it lay across my stomach as hers stroked rhythmically between her legs. She moaned again, very quietly, and I felt her leg tremble against mine. I didn't even stop to consider proper etiquette in this situation.

"Kiera, I'm awake," I whispered.

"I couldn't sleep." Her voice was thick and breathy. "Your kisses kept me awake. And I really need...to sleep."

"I can go for a walk," I offered, since standing in the shower with the water running seemed stupid. "Or you can just finish now." My own breathing had gotten a little short and my stomach was in knots. I hadn't been sleeping long enough for the blood that had pooled in my pelvis to move out. I was still hard. Knowing that she was too only made me more so.

"I'd...like that."

She turned on her side to face me, her eyes a mere glimmer in the dark room. "Would you kiss me again while I do?"

I answered with my mouth on hers, and her tongue instantly filled me. Her leg came over my thigh again, this time with skin on skin, and she moaned softly. As I bit her bottom lip and tugged it with my teeth, I felt the back of her arm slide down my abdomen in the sliver of space between us and I knew where her hand had gone. Her body jerked, my head got light, and I realized I'd stopped breathing. I didn't want any sound to compete with her song now. I touched her bare breast very lightly and she arched, pushing into my hand. I rolled her nipple under my thumb, and she rocked against me. I could tell from her frenzied kisses and the rapid, rolling motion of her arm that she was getting close. My ears began to buzz, and I was afraid I'd pass out from holding my breath, but her staccato cries tore through me like sweet daggers, and I didn't want to miss a single note. I squeezed her nipple, hard.

Back bowing, she tore her mouth away and screamed, "Oh, God!"

"Oh, yes," I murmured, straining to see her face. She trembled and kept touching herself, keening softly, and I wanted to weep from the beauty of it. At last she lay quiet and spent in my arms while my heart thundered and my blood raced.

"You make such beautiful music," I whispered, stroking her face. I kissed her forehead, and she laughed quietly.

"I don't usually perform that one in public."

"I'm honored." I shivered, so aroused I was nearly sick with need.

She pressed closer and I felt fingers circle over my belly.

"Kiera," I whispered. "What—"

"Time for the encore," she murmured just before the applause began.

an incredible, amazing really true story

●

isabelle gray

It's a great story, really, the one about the first time I had sex with a woman. It's the kind of story that's almost too good to be true, and over the years it has acquired its own mythology among my friends and me. It could also be called the story of how I accidentally became a lesbian. I was nineteen, going on thirty, in my own mind at any rate. I was on sabbatical from college after two years spent doing most anything but attending classes and acting collegial. I was in the midst of a Western adventure from San Francisco to Phoenix, the likes of which I blush to recall. Eleven years removed from My First Time, I realize that my personal history is quaint and charming only to myself, but I still hold the memories fondly.

The story begins with a party—the kind where a bunch of kinky people get together with their favorite toys and use them on one another into the wee hours of the night. I had recently been introduced to the group, and it was made quite clear that I was the Flavor of the Month and a good decade younger than most of the other partygoers. I had no problem with that. It was nice to be the center of attention. I acted as worldly as possible, while biting my tongue and hoping that no one discovered that I had no idea what I was doing there. Don't get me wrong—I knew how to use my toys, but I had no clue how to get physically intimate with another woman. In fact, up until that point, I had never even considered being with a woman. It wasn't something I opposed. It was simply an option that had not theretofore been available to me until now. In the early hours of the party, I did my stroll through the three rooms where the party was taking place. I flogged an acquaintance I had met at a potluck a few weeks earlier. I let a boi shine my boots with hir tongue. I was seeing and being seen.

The peacocking was an act. I was painfully shy and found it far easier to get to know people with the kiss of a whip or the tease of a paddle than to attempt a conversation. If any of the women at the party had known me well, they would have realized that there was a fraud in their midst. Throughout the night I had my eye on one woman, Billy, a round, gorgeous lesbian in her forties with long black hair and green eyes. She wore jeans and a corset that barely covered her breasts, and her fingers were covered with intricate silver jewelry. We made eye contact several times throughout the evening. I would catch her, now and again, staring at me, and I pretended that I didn't notice. Slowly but surely, I drifted closer and closer to her, until I was sitting behind her, chatting with her as I dragged my fingers back and forth across the exposed expanse of her upper back. The light scratching evolved into massage, and soon Billy was moaning and leaning further and further into my body.

I can admit that I had no idea what I was doing. I wasn't quite sure how to proceed. While I'd had plenty of experience with men, making love to a woman was uncharted territory. The fact that we were surrounded by other women who were taking an increasing interest in what we were doing didn't help matters. Exhibition had never been my forte. After twenty minutes or so of manually manipulating Billy's upper back, she turned, grabbed my chin between her fingers, and pressed her lips against mine, her tongue darting between my lips as I gasped, then kissed her back. My lips were tingling. My fingertips were tingling. My cunt was throbbing. I placed one hand at the base of Billy's neck, and slowly slid it until my fingers were tucked between her breasts.

Carefully, I began to unfasten the corset until it fell back revealing the most beautiful pair of breasts I had ever seen—full, heavy in my hands, with erect, dark brown nipples surrounded by a few freckles. I brushed my lips across the upper curves of Billy's breasts and she smiled down at me, sliding her hand around to clasp the back of my neck. One by one I pulled her nipples into my mouth, enjoying the way they felt against my tongue and how they swelled as I began flicking the tip of my tongue over them. The room had gotten quiet as the people around us began to close in, forming a tighter circle around us.

"Do y'all have any preferences for music?" one of the women asked. Billy and I shook our heads, and soon the twang of Willie Nelson filled the air.

I could have lavished my attention on Billy's breasts for an indefinite amount of time, but her body was insistent, and her hand on the back of my neck urged me lower. I kissed my way down her belly, around her navel, to her waist. Slipping my hands beneath the waistband of her jeans, I quickly had them unbuttoned and Billy did her part by wriggling away from them. She wasn't wearing any underwear, and the first thing I saw was the dark, silky hair covering her mound. My lips moved lower, over the soft, sweet hair and down to her pussy lips. Billy sighed and lay back, pulling her knees up and apart. In the dim light of the room, I could see that she was already wet, though beyond that I was somewhat unclear about what I was looking at. Praying that no one would discover that this was all foreign territory, I pulled her pussy lips apart with my fingers and dragged my tongue along the length of her moist slit. The taste was tangy at first, and then, as I slid my tongue inside her cunt, I found the unexpected flavor of strawberries.

A Johnny Cash album started playing. Billy's thigh muscles tensed and she placed both of her hands atop my head, curling my hair between her fingers, tugging slightly as I slid my tongue lower still, then back toward her clit. When my tongue finally reached her clit and I began to lick in slow, steady circles, Billy hissed and whispered, "Yes, that's it, right there." I smiled into her pussy, determined to do whatever it took to keep Billy, and her pussy, as happy as I could. I slid one hand up Billy's body, enjoying the sensation of our skin coming together until I reached her breasts. As I teased her clit with my tongue, I rolled her nipples between my fingers until Billy gasped and sat up. "You're driving me crazy," she said. My heart fell but I wasn't going to let my disappointment in myself show. "Is that a good thing?" I asked. "Without a doubt," Billy answered.

My confidence renewed, I slid my tongue back to her cunt and began thrusting it in and out, slowly at first, but then faster and then slower again enjoying how Billy's body responded. Past the crowd watching us, I could hear the stereo switching to a new album—Tina Turner. I

117

propped myself up on my elbows, trying to push myself deeper into Billy, rocking my hips against the floor. I couldn't believe how turned on I was. Billy's pussy became wetter. Her fingers gripped my hair tighter. I was getting the hang of this, I told myself. I shifted slightly so I'd have a bit more room and began teasing the edges of Billy's cunt with two fingers while my tongue flicked around the edges of Billy's clit, darting away each time Billy tried to adjust her hips to put her clit on my tongue. I was being a tease and I knew it. I slid two fingers inside Billy's cunt and shivered as I felt the warm, slick tight flesh gripping me. The deeper I slid my fingers, the wider Billy's legs spread. Once I was as deep as I could go, I flipped my wrist and began pressing my fingers upward against something soft and spongy. "Fuck me, hard," Billy muttered through clenched teeth. I wrapped my lips around her clit, sucking insistently, while I thrust my fingers in and out of her pussy to the rhythm of "Private Dancer."

Then, Billy decided it was time to take charge. She pushed me away and said, "I want you on your back." I quickly complied and Billy straddled me, facing my feet. She inched backward until her pussy was pressed against my mouth. My jaw was beginning to ache, but I opened my mouth wider, and resumed with licking and sucking and sliding my tongue over every inch of her pussy. Billy began to rock, her body pressing into mine. The tender wail of Miles Davis filtered through the other sounds around us. Then she began to thrust, and her thighs started to shake. I grabbed hold of her ass, slapping the firm cheeks. A gush of wetness hit the back of my throat. "I'm going to come," Billy shouted. I stopped. She grabbed hold of my ankle. "Don't fucking stop, kid." I resumed my efforts, struggling for air. Billy began to grunt in loud, guttural tones as if she was releasing something deep and dark. I was certain of the moment she came—the very crescendo of her climax, when her cunt juice was thick and smeared across my face and her body shuddered above and around me.

Afterward, Billy rolled off and we lay there, side by side, facing opposite directions. I reached for her hand and entwined my fingers with hers. As sweat began to slide down my face and my neck I realized that I was exhausted. And suddenly I heard a smattering of applause that got louder and louder. When I opened my eyes and looked up, the entire party was standing over us with a range of expressions on their faces.

The woman who had started the music shook her head and said, "You guys went through four albums—that's more than three hours of pussy eating." I didn't quite understand the relevance, having no point of reference. Billy sat up, wrapping her arm around my shoulders. She kissed my forehead and said, "Either you're a sadist or you really enjoy eating pussy."

I smiled with what I hoped was a coy expression on my face. "Both," I answered.

questioning youth

●

gina de vries

i

I'm sixteen years old, and it's a Friday night in San Francisco. My curls are tinged with red, and I'm wearing dancing clothes—a sparkly pink spaghetti-strap top that hugs my breasts and shows my belly button, tight jeans that fit low on my hips, and platform boots. But Elise and I don't have fake IDs, so we go to CineClub instead. CineClub screens free films for teenagers and hosts discussions over expensive cheese and sparkling cider afterwards. It's held at the Randall Museum in the Castro. You meander up an elegant, snaking road and get a view of the whole city from the top of the hill—the Randall feels secluded, almost otherworldly.

CineClub is organized by a somewhat batty gay man in his fifties. Most of the movies are culled from his extensive personal collection. He's gray and slender, smartly dressed. He looks like he should be wearing a monocle. He flits around like a butterfly, talks way too much about the movies, and dominates the discussions that are supposed to be ours. But he means well, and any adult who cares enough about teenagers to show them material that's supposedly inappropriate for their age has my respect. He tells us that *The Decalogue* was originally a television miniseries on the Polish broadcast networks. Each episode is the director's take on one of the Ten Commandments. We watch "Decalogue IX: Thou Shalt Not Covet Thy Neighbor's Wife."

A young postal worker is obsessed with his beautiful older neighbor. He trains a telescope on her window and watches her at night while other men fuck her. She discovers that he is "peeping," as she calls it. She's disgusted, but something else intrigues her. She confronts him, and afterwards stripteases in the window when she knows he is watching. Soon after, they meet supposedly by chance on the street, go to a café, and have a bittersweet talk about linguistics and art, voyeurism and exhibitionism, fear and desire. The next night they go out to dinner, then back to her apartment. The boy is in a drab gray suit, the best outfit he can pull together, and his dark shaggy hair frames his sweet teenage face. She wears a black silk robe with nothing underneath. He sits on her bed and she crouches, facing him. Her robe falls open. She asks if he has ever been with a woman before, and he answers meekly, "No." He tries hard not to look away. She tells him she is wet, takes his hand and leads it to the space between her thighs, and the boy closes his eyes and comes right then, shuddering and sobbing. He looks like he has been slapped across the face and is waiting for the next blow. She gives him a tired look, says, "Oh, so quick?" and he leaps up, grabs his drab gray coat, and runs crying from the apartment.

My first thought is, "Was that sex?" I think about how after I came with Eva, she pulled away while I lay floating. When I finally looked at her she seemed scared, angry with herself. She looked at me, eyes filled with regret, and apologized. "I shouldn't have done that, I should have asked you if you wanted it."

I said, "But I did want it. If I didn't want it I would have stopped you. I was ready." She still looked devastated. I wondered for a moment if maybe she was the one who hadn't been ready for it to happen. She was two years younger than I was, a fact that I knew existed between us but that wasn't a problem, until now. I felt guilty, being the older one, and I think she felt guilty, being the experienced one, having had far more girlfriends than I had.

She'd told me she was a virgin, that what we'd done wasn't sex so it didn't count, didn't fall under that category, did it?

I asked, after a moment, "Has…that…ever happened to you before?"

She responded, in a stilted voice, "Once—when I lived in Chicago—there was this girl—and I was lonely, and she knew that, and she was

121

selfish, and she got what she wanted from me, and—then she left…"

I blinked.

"How did it…I mean, what exactly happened…?"

"I really don't want to talk about it."

"I…Okay…" I bit my lip, studied the way my hands curled over my stomach.

"Anyway, I'm sorry. That shouldn't have happened. I'm sorry."

Whatever it was we were doing got easier after that. We could touch each other through clothes, come with each other. Curious, I said to her once, "I thought you weren't okay with this…"

"Um, I am now, I changed my mind," and she pinned my hands above my head, giggled like a schoolboy who'd just heard a dirty joke, and kissed me long and hard.

I am trying to remember the good parts as I watch the boy on the screen slit his wrists, trying not to remember that the first time I did—whatever it was—that I did to her, her first words to me afterwards were, "This is one of my bad days. I wish, for your sake, you weren't here."

Elise is sitting next to me in the dark museum theater, gasping with the rest of the audience at the movie, at all the blood on the screen and the poor boy being rushed away in the ambulance. I'm gasping, too, but for different reasons. It takes all my strength not to start crying, not to turn to Elise and say, "You know, I don't know if I'm a virgin any more. I think I might have had sex with Eva. I don't know if you would consider it sex because some of our clothes were on and there wasn't any penetration or anything, but it felt good, it felt like sex, I mean, not that I would know what sex feels like, exactly, but…"

Elise and her friends and I go out to Sparky's diner after the movie. We get curly fries and milkshakes, and talk about the film away from our motor-mouthed host. One of the boys we're with, Sebastian, mentions a movie he's seen about two young queer girls. He says that the characters are twelve and thirteen, and I laugh. "Oh, I'm so glad they made that, I came out when I was eleven and…" and then I stop talking because he looks absolutely crestfallen. I realize that when we were having a conversation earlier, about Thelonious Monk, he was flirting with me in his own awkward nerd-boy way. A part of me wants to tell him that

I like boys, too, because his eyes are blue and his skin looks soft and kissing someone could be nice tonight. But there's too much in my head already. I don't want to hurt anyone.

ii

Six years ago this summer I had sex for the first time. I was sixteen, I was going to *Rocky Horror* every weekend, I was a stellar student, I was a queer youth community activist. I was trying to look femme goth and act brooding punk sexpot and still be respectable enough to give Homo 101 lectures to hapless straight people twice my age. I wanted to fuck badly, I wanted to know more about my body than I actually did, but I was too ashamed to ask anyone the questions that were constantly rattling around in my brain. This being queer thing had to do with sexuality, of course—how could it not?—but I straddled the party line, talked a lot about queerness being all about "who you love" and "respecting difference." I resented the idea that you had to be having sex to be queer—because I hadn't been having sex when I'd come out as a dyke five years before, and I still knew what I liked.

But then, what I liked was part of the problem. The things I thought about in bed at night—the parts of me that wanted to be fucked, hit, tied down, pissed on—well, queer youth activists didn't talk about those things, not to the community at large, not to other community members. I was supposed to be a good queer, a good feminist, and above all, I was supposed to be respectable. Being sexual meant being vulnerable, it meant being dirty. Being a pervert meant being even more on the fringes than I was already. And anyway, what if all these things were connected to my childhood sexual abuse? S/M felt so tied up in my survivor issues, I just couldn't bring myself to go there. But god, I wanted to.

The day after I ended my sophomore year of high school, I skulked around in the feminist section of Forrest Books in North Beach. I was too scared and ashamed to buy actual porn. I worried what my feminist friends would think of me, I worried what my intellectual friends would think of me, and I worried what the cashier would think of me—even though we were, in fact, in North Beach, and the bookstore was flanked on all sides by strip clubs. So I bought a book of essays by Susie Bright instead. The book is from the mid-eighties, Susie's wearing a latex dress on the cover and grinning wildly. This book seemed more respectable, somehow, more literary than the erotica anthology I'd also been eyeing. These were essays, after all—despite the fact that the title of the book included the word *Sexpert*.

I still don't quite know how to describe the intense effect Susie's work had on my sixteen-year-old self. My transition from being scared of sex to sex-positivity seems very quick—but I think I'd just been waiting for a catalyst. I started using the word *sex-positive* to describe myself. I became much less ashamed of my own perversity, even though I still didn't talk about it with anyone. And within a month, I started having sex.

I fell in love with a butch dyke with Buddy Holly glasses and a tendency to brood. The relationship was dramatic and short-lived. We didn't actually acknowledge that we were fucking—it was "that, um, stuff" that we did, stuff that wasn't terribly naked or terribly penetrative but that still left puddles of sweat in her bedclothes, stuff that made me feel fucked even though my jeans never came off, stuff that made me feel *bottom*, made me feel *girl* and *little* and open even though she didn't call me those things, even though I didn't think of myself as those things, yet. We rubbed each other off through layers of clothing and silence. When I came, stars shot around under my closed eyelids and she'd ask, tentatively, Was that…really okay? the same way I asked if it was really okay when I touched her tits.

My survivor body, her butch body, my girl body, they were all scared of anything closer. It's where we were at; we made do.

iii

The few times I hung out with the popular kids at my high school—a side effect of being involved in the theater department—I ended up at cast parties, drinking and smoking pot on redwood decks with girls much richer and skinnier than me, while I answered questions about sex. I went to a private, hippie high school in the middle of San Francisco's Haight-Ashbury district. I was a scholarship student who bussed in everyday from Ingleside, a mostly black and Asian working-class neighborhood. I'd gone to the neighborhood Catholic middle school with students whose single mothers worked at Kentucky Fried Chicken to support families of five, while my still-married Bohemian parents with master's degrees in literature and unionized social-service jobs fed me marinated chicken from the grill on our porch.

But when I started attending the private hippie high school, I was considered "one of the poor kids." The students at my high school were mostly white—a drastic change from a middle school where I was one of maybe fifteen white kids in a school of two hundred. Kids at the high school drove expensive cars as soon as they turned sixteen. They bought lunch on Haight Street every day, and they prided themselves on being good San Francisco liberals who liked gay people, as long as they weren't too flamboyant. Going to high school with people who held this attitude was admittedly worlds better than getting basketballs thrown at my head for being queer (which is what had happened to me during the three years I spent as an out baby-dyke in middle school). But being a young, politicized queer girl surrounded by a group of sheltered teenagers trying to hide their collective sexual anxiety was not without its problems.

Most of the kids in high school thought I was a lesbian, so they just assumed I was having sex, right off the bat. ("You can't really say you're gay if you haven't had gay sex," a student once told me, very matter-of-fact.) Pale, dark-haired, skinny girls with perfectly shaped B-cup breasts and jeans that fit like a second skin would corner me at the cast parties. They waved their drinks in my face as they interrogated me.

So, like, are you a lesbian or what? Oh, so you consider yourself bisexual? Pansexual? What does pansexual mean? I've never heard of that before. Hm, I still don't get it, but you must know some really interesting people. What do you mean there's more than two genders? So what is this transgender thing, exactly? You know, I saw this special on *20/20* about those people, I feel totally sorry for them! Why do you keep saying queer, isn't that supposed to be offensive? Hey, since you like boys too, are you and Neil (my male best friend) sleeping together? So, how many girls have you dated, anyway? What kind of girls do you like? You don't look hella gay, you know, like, butch, or whatever. Have you had sex with a guy, ever? But you have with a girl? Are you dating anyone right now? Hey, do you like anyone at this party?

Those last questions were always asked salaciously—new gossip, queer or otherwise, was something everyone thrived on.

Most of the time, being the token queer annoyed me. Other times, with particular people—the girl in my theater class who chalked up her chattiness to being drunk, but who whispered after a conspicuous silence "I think I was really in love with her"; or the boy who was so drunk that he couldn't stand up straight, who choked out that he liked having sex with guys before he misquoted my own poetry to me—I was glad I was there. I had this sinking feeling that I was one of the only people these kids were talking to.

Girls would tell me in drunken giggles that they had given numerous blowjobs or been fingered x number of times, but that they were still virgins. Some of them said that they'd had crushes on girls, or fantasized about girls, or made out with girls—at parties when they were drunk, or maybe when they were sober but with someone else equally "straight." Some of them had done more with girls, "experimented" with girls. But they weren't "queer." A few girls said they were bisexual in a casual but still very guarded way—the unspoken insinuation being that I couldn't tell other people at school, which of course I never did. Most people didn't say anything about their own identities at all. Many of the girls I talked to had had sex, but if they were still virgins, it was because they hadn't had intercourse with a boy. Oral or manual "stuff" with other girls could be considered sex, I learned, but doing the exact same things with boys was just "foreplay" or "fooling around."

All of the different definitions and limits and qualifiers made my head swim. It seemed like each girl had a different list of rules about what it was that made her technically pure and virginal, despite countless nights of debauchery. I listened to inebriated confessions and tried to respond as gently and thoughtfully as possible—a difficult thing to do when you are four foot eleven and have had a few bong hits, a rum and coke, and a white Russian. These girls were "virgins" who, to my mind, had had much more sex than I had—me, who had only slept with one person, and a butch dyke top at that. I knew that their definitions of sex and gender had very little to do with what Eva and I had done late at night on her bunk bed.

I thought, more than once, midconversation, What's wrong with saying that you've had sex if you have, anyway? Why are these rules so fucking arbitrary? If she knew the exact things I've done to people and had done to me, would she think I was still a virgin, even though I don't think I am? Why am I the one who gets asked all these questions?

iv

It's been two months since you started testosterone. We haven't talked for years, but I hear about you through mutual friends. You're one of the exes I always had that hunch about. I remember a conversation we had once, after we broke up but before we lost contact, when you told me customers at the movie theater where you worked kept calling you "young man," that "gender issues" had been coming up a lot. "So, what's going on for you with that, exactly? I began to ask. Are you…?"

"No, I don't, I'm not, I'm a girl, it's just annoying to have their definitions of what a girl is be so limiting. I don't mind getting 'young manned,' I don't mind at all, but it's aggravating…"

You don't mind at all, but it's aggravating, I wanted to repeat. Listen to what you're saying, dear. I'd seen my first trans boyfriend, Jeremy, through his own transition, listened to countless friends talk about their too complex, too dangerous, too "both/and" identities. I knew what was coming. I didn't say a word.

v

I don't want to see you or talk to you, but I do want to take a good long look at you, give you a lingering hug hello, kiss you a little too long on the cheek, tell you you're gorgeous, that I love you, that I'm proud of you, my sweet boy. (Can I say that? Can I say mine anymore?) It's been years since I've spoken to you, years since we've fucked, and I still have dreams that wake me up in short breaths and starts, my body shaking, my cunt spasming. In dreams I feel your dick in my mouth, pushing past my lips and back to the base of my throat, dangerously close to my gag reflex. My stockings aren't enough to protect my legs, they're cold on the cement, but I don't care, I just want your cock in my mouth, I just want to make you feel something, finally, make you lose control long enough to show me some semblance of emotion. I can make you feel like something's really there, I can make you come just from looking into your eyes, I can make you come just from my mouth on this thing hanging between your legs, this thing we can forget isn't technically your flesh.

You pull my hair, hard, pull my head to your hips and push your cock further into my mouth. The tip hits the base of my throat and I pull away to keep myself from gagging. I feel you start to spasm and shudder, your legs are shaking over me and I grab the base of your dick for balance and push you hard up against the brick wall, move my lips down the length of you as you gasp for air. Your hands are relentless at the back of my head. You're trying not to make noise, and you're failing. If I could smirk at this moment, I would. I feel slightly absurd as I pull you out of my mouth, try not to laugh at myself, on my knees, holding onto you for balance. Try not to laugh at you, more clothed, but far more flustered than I am. You can barely look at me, and I don't know why I let you get away with averting my eyes.

I help you tuck your dick back into your briefs. My eyes are on you and your eyes are on the ground. I'm careful not to touch the rings and straps that hold your cock in place, careful not to touch you otherwise, careful not to make you aware of my body. I wait for you to look up at me.

The things I noticed about you and waited for you to tell me, the things that you would never admit to me—Is this why you didn't want to talk about it, whatever it was we were doing in your bed while your father and step-mother slept upstairs? Is this why you could lose control enough to come, lose control enough to fuck me (yes, you did fuck me, you might not have penetrated me but you most certainly did fuck me), but couldn't bring yourself to speak about it?

What scared you, boy? Was it your body? Was it the pleasure you got from it and the sinking feeling that something still wasn't right? Was it me? Was it my lack of experience and your wealth of it? (I was nervous to talk about how I liked it when you sucked my nipples, how no one had ever done that before and it felt good. You finally laughed at me and told me jokingly, sweetly, that I could say the word "breast," that it wouldn't kill me, because I kept referring to "doing that." But I wasn't like that with the other people I'd made out with. I wasn't scared to name things as they were, and I only kissed them, maybe had my breasts touched lightly with cautious fingers. What made me so scared to talk about it with you? Why did I have to have sex with you and not the others, why did I have to be scared to talk about sex with you, but not the others?)

Did you think you were corrupting me with that mouth of yours, those hands of yours? Did you?

I have no idea how you feel about the parts I used to rub up against with my thigh. I could make you come just by rubbing up against you, and I'm curious sometimes if that's all you really needed, all you really wanted. How do you feel about the parts I never touched? Did you like them? Hate them? Accept their existence and figure you might as well make the best of them? I don't even touch those parts in my dreams. I stick with what my subconscious remembers, with what my subconscious thinks you'd want. I'm waiting for you, still, to tell me what's really there. I've never dared to ask before.

"What, boy, so quick?" My voice is low, my gaze scrutinizing. You look up, your eyes are wide with confusion and—is that fear I see flash across your face? But you're not going anywhere. You're still watching me. I move my body closer to yours, slowly. Your eyes get bigger. I let my mouth break into a smile.

the organic orgasm

●

jen cross

I was somewhat obsessed with carrots as a kid—I ate them constantly (okay, often), truly convinced they'd improve my eyesight. All these years later (after innumerable nights spent squinting in weak light to finish "just one more page") and I'm still the only one in my family who doesn't wear glasses. Go figure.

Anyway, in high school, when I packed my lunch, along with a thermos-full of mushy ramen noodles or a turkey-and-lettuce on wheat bread, I'd usually bring a great big carrot—the biggest one in the bag, often just washing it off and wrapping it up in damp paper towels and aluminum foil to keep it moist. Now, to my mind, I was more provocative than the average hypersexualized teenager, given my stepfather's ongoing sexual abuse. So at lunchtime, armed with this phallic vegetable, I had an object with which to not only make sexual innuendo but also to display some latent, shall we say, irritation with men and the male member. I'd joke about the dildo-like qualities of the vegetable, then bite it's head off. Loudly. You know. And I was as serious about the innuendo, the sexual possibilities, as I was about the consumption and destruction. I just didn't know how to untangle it all—who does as a sixteen-year-old?

This is all to say that the stage was set for my vegetable deflowering long before I met D. Little did she know how my memory of our short tryst would be anchored. Rooted, as it were.

In 1994, I was young, out, and often in Boston for some political organizing event or another. Because why? I wanted to meet girls—and the dyke community at my little northern college was just too insular. During one of these ostensibly activist outings, I met D., upon whom

I became obsessively crushed for a good long time—like six months. After I met her, I found a whole lot more reasons to visit Boston. Organizing, of course.

D. was somewhat shorter than I am, with fair skin and dark, dark hair, and her half-closed eyes burned through me when she slid, snake-like, up and down in front of me on the dance floor. She was, to me, the epitome of queer womanhood (of course, every queer woman I met at the time became the epitome of queer womanhood, so take this statement for what it's worth): bold, confident, and seductive. She moved so smoothly through her life that I constantly felt like an ox around her.

I can't remember how I came to be staying at her home that night, but I remember that we fell asleep without having sex, just stretched out against each other in her twin bed in the small narrow bedroom of her shared Jamaica Plain apartment—I remember wondering if her roommates were around, aware of us, able to hear us. I probably fell asleep trembling with desire. Seriously. You know how coming out brings on a whole second adolescence. D. made me feel like a teenage boy with a constant, looming hard-on tenting his pants. It's amazing I slept at all.

We woke—well, I woke and didn't know if she was awake or not. Carefully, I traced my fingertips over her skin: on her arms, along the dark hairs shading her there, along her back, her shoulders, her neck, as far as I could reach without moving any part of my body besides my arm. I wanted to make her feel good. I hadn't been with that many women and I remember how she (and ever other woman I had sex with at the time) seemed very worldly and experienced, as compared to my incest-inflected perception of desire, need, and fear when it came to sex—I'd overcompensate by being somewhat forward. She just lay there for awhile, feeling my fingers. Then she reached back for me, grabbing my hip with her hand and grinding her ass back into my crotch. Oh, yeah. Now we were getting somewhere. Soon I was kissing down the length of her body, running lips and tongue (and palms of hands) over her flat belly, her strong thighs, everything but the most erogenous of zones—I wanted to build her lust, so we'd both be shaking with desire. This is what happens with memory: I don't remember if I fucked her or not, but I think I must have. Soon enough, though, there I was with my crush, in a tiny J.P. bedroom, not getting fucked because we were out of gloves. It was the mid-90s and we, the queer girls of the Northeast, at least the handful I knew, were incredibly attentive (at least verbally, intellectually, politically) to safer sex. We educated, we compared dams and lube types, we proselytized. It was kind of obnoxiously self-important, but we were righteous in our desire to have lots of sex while not also contracting HIV. More than that, there was a sense (for me) of showing solidarity with the gay boys. Those pockets full of gloves and squares of latex and little plastic bulbs of lube became a kinky badge of honor—they were testaments to our queerness, 'cause god knows straight people didn't proclaim their sex-protective readiness that way. We were here, queer, and ready to bag it up and take it in.

Now, I didn't like the latex any more than anyone else—and wearing a glove the first time I fisted someone, I learned why so many guys didn't want to wear condoms: it was an object lesson in sensation loss. But I was nothing if not somebody who'd go along with the crowd, if it seemed like the crowd could offer me home—and the sex-radical queer community gave me that. So I preached the important joys of latex, and was careful that morning to only touch D. on mucous-membrane–less skin when my hand was naked, lest I engage in some untoward bodily-fluid exchange. Later, I understood her not touching, or more to the point, fucking, me once we'd run out of gloves.

Here was the strange thing, though—here's why all that matters: I'd gotten so turned on, touching her, that I wanted to come after she did, and said so. This was unusual, as, at the time, I rarely asked long-term lovers to take the time to get me off, and never even considered putting the possibility before a casual fuck. Getting me off is only slightly more complicated than, say, putting the space shuttle into orbit, requiring the proper placement (and extended stay) of hands, mouth, toes, utensils, office supplies, and so on. I'm only sort of exaggerating. For whatever reason, though, I felt comfortable enough with D. to ask for this attention, and she was game. So we got her mouth here, that hand there, the other hand there, her body just right against me and things were going pretty good for awhile. However, as I got closer, the one hand was, ideally, supposed to move right up inside me. But, as I've already said, we were out of gloves, so this became a problem. We did have condoms, but they were a bit large on her small fingers, and…

Wait! Now I remember. I was bleeding at the time. Thus the overcaution. I was ready to give up (being used to doing so), but (goddess bless her) D. was tenacious. We did some quick sex brainstorming. She said, what about a substitute? and went off to root through her fridge. Now, I liked this idea—I was all about adding new experiences to my sexual repertoire at the time, and, like I said, I'd never been fucked with a vegetable before. It wasn't like I hadn't already fantasized about crudités: not only is it standard, if cliché, girl-on-girl porn fodder, but there was the aforementioned large-carrot fetish/fascination. I was getting all ready for a nice fat organic something.

You know how when you buy a bag of carrots, you use some of them right away and then most of the rest soon after for soup or something cooked, but there's always one left over, the one standing still in the bag, the smallest one? You planned to eat it one day after work but you never got to it, and then it got kind of old and reddish and a little soft and bendy and covered with little white hair-like roots. You know that carrot in a wet, broken-down bag in the crisper of your fridge right now?

That's exactly the carrot she brought into the bedroom to show me after making noises of frustration and frantic searching for anything else. Now, by this time, I was pretty fucking worked up. My body'd had a whole lot of attention, and I was right there on that fat edge of plateau that promises to slam into a good hard orgasm if only you can just get things right.

I said yes to the sad, wrinkled carrot.

The condom fit even less well over the carrot than it would have over her fingers, although there was more length to work with. D. had to pinch the condom closed so it wouldn't slip off in me, and she had to hold the carrot stiff, so she could move it in and out of me. I remember thinking it was ridiculous, that carrot, and us there working so hard for my orgasm. But I didn't tell her to stop. She held on as tightly, as gingerly, as she could, given she was trying to fuck me through to a very wet place without getting a whole lot of danger on her fingertips.

Today, I can't really tell you how it felt to have that wilted vegetable inside of me. All I really needed was something to push against those nerves and tightening muscles inside my cunt. Really, a finger or two would've been fine, and too much bigger would have been a distraction from coming—probably if she'd found a Japanese eggplant or something in her fridge, I would've just wanted to get fucked blind (not that that would have been a bad thing). As it was, the little-carrot-that-turned-out-it-could felt, you know, like something sort of stiff, loosely bagged in a condom. Combined with all the rest of the stimulation she was giving me (and I was helping with), plus a little bit of humiliation and embarrassment as an added bonus, my face flushed hot and every muscle in my body tensed, and I raced off the plateau and smack into a solid, exploding wall of stars that was my orgasm.

Okay, it probably wasn't that big. At the time, I was still regulating my orgasms, trying to keep them tight to my body. I didn't want to go too crazy; who knew how that would look? But it was good anyway, and then there we were on her bed, a little bloody and wet but mostly clean and uncontaminated by one another's fluids. She carefully carried the carrot, tucked up in latex that was now covered with stringy threads of bloody cum, to the trash in the kitchen. Yeah, it definitely wasn't the hot, big-fat-carrot-up-the-pussy scene I'd been vaguely envisioning all those years. It was much, much simpler, and a whole lot more real.

I don't remember if we had sex again after that time—so much work, only to be left with the sad, bloody beginnings of a salad. And I was embarrassed by my need, what I'd done to have it met. And, at the time, coming didn't even really feel all that good to me—so much residue still ran over my body after every contraction. But here was something, anyway, something it would take me years to properly integrate: I could want to come, and someone, a lover, would care enough—be turned on enough, even—to help me do just that. You know? For a girl just one or two years out of an incestuous, controlling situation, that realization is pretty fucking big stuff.

What did I see that morning? I'd thank D. for the gift of this memory, if I knew where she was. Something that was a hysterical party story told at my own expense for years has transformed in my consideration into something less ridiculous and humiliating and more truly beautiful. If I remove the protective blinders of shame and visit what I gave me then, I find it was a *yes* sheltered in anonymity, something I didn't have to (couldn't, really) take home with me. She held my risk in her hands, in the bloody condom, in the empty crisper. She held it when I couldn't. It's why, probably, we didn't talk much longer. Unless you're ready for the slippery weight of your joy, yes is a hard thing to hold onto.

thank you, frannie, wherever you are

●

lynne jamneck

For the sake of making her feel at ease, I'll call her Lola. I'll call myself Kate. I've always wanted to be a Kate, but I ain't got the freckles. Or the gun. Girls called Kate should carry big firearms.

You know, when you're young you have balls the size of Montana and simply no clue. Of course, you'd never admit it, because that would go beyond the Code of Butch, and that, well…that's just tantamount to being spiked and skewered, really. Can you see I'm a Stephen King fan?

But I digress.

The first time I saw Lola, her ex was in the backseat of her car. I saw the ex, but I noticed Lola. She was wispy, and seemed sweet, and she was fucking sexy as hell. My butch cojones fluttered. I had no style back then, Lola told me later. It was she who taught me not to stick my shirts way down my jeans like that. Dorky.

Lola would surprise me.

Our first date was having respectable drinks at a place overlooking the ocean. Our second date three days later was at her house. She slept upstairs in the loft. The high-ceilinged acoustics were tremendous.

We were going to watch a movie. She rented one she'd already seen. Clever minx. She was not as innocent as she seemed.

Our first kiss on her single bed was already a fight for supremacy. Almost immediately, she had me underneath her when I knew I wanted to be on top. It was because of those outdated issues of *Spare Rib* I'd read at seventeen. Those feminist journals all carried contradictory messages. The personal is not political as they liked to tell you, it's fucking personal! Feminism brings out the sailormouth in me.

But I digress again.

I wanted to fuck Lola all right, but I had no idea how. When last did you hear a butch dyke say that?

Sitting in my room, crunched into a tight ball on my bed, I knew I wanted to do several things to her. Those "unnatural things" you hear about on Sunday mornings. (And by the way, side note: the more you tell someone not to do something, the more they want to. It's ironic, but encouraging.)

I smoked one cigarette after another, but their influence offered no answers. They just made me feel cool and suave and debonair and started the whole libidinous puzzle all over again. Because smoking will do that. Make you feel cool. And when a butch starts to feel cool, she gets cocky, and all she wants to do is conquer. Take my word for it. Overcome, overpower, surmount.

Lola was my first femme. She gave new meaning to Bruce Springsteen songs. She was a puzzle because she acted all shy and demure when I looked in her eyes, but when it came to sex the boy in her awoke. I started to realize very soon that there was something Lola wanted to do to me, something no one else had ever done. Like the song goes—I had a little secret.

I was in poised confusion. On one hand, I was entertaining myself with fantasies of fucking Lola, and on the flipside I had to figure out how I was going to give myself over to her. Her intentions were becoming clearer by the day.

She used to drive us around town. Expensive sunglasses gleaming on her nose, my hand on the inside of her thigh, and the African sun bleeding on her hair. We'd get takeout and eat it parked by the graveyard. I found it mildly stirring that we'd want all those dead people to know there were dykes eating KFC outside the gates.

Lola had a brother. He was as queer as the idea of democracy and lived with his boyfriend in the same house as Lola, downstairs, while she had the loft upstairs. He was a whiz with computers and made music using a mouse and a keyboard. Every fag is a DJ, whether they prescribe to the stereotype or not. Somehow it's just special when a gay man plays Gloria Gaynor instead of hearing it from the turntable of a thirty-five-year-old straight divorcée, you know?

Upstairs. That's where Lola and I would be. On her bed, bodies touching, talking in short sentences. Talking slow and long, and making out the same way, trying, trying to be quiet. And Lola, trying, trying to get her hand inside me.

What was I to do? I spoke to myself from inside the bathroom mirror, black hair cut to a buzz, wearing protective flannel armor.

Lola was my second.

Right at the beginning there was Francesca. I'll call her that because she won't like it. My revenge in words, ha. Even better—Frannie.

Frannie had issues. She wanted me to do all sorts of things to her, except put my fingers in her cunt, which is what I wanted to do.

When I was twenty, Frannie's bartender hands initially revealed to me that I was indeed most definitely a dyke, down to my budding Daddy complex, which would slowly start to assert itself over the next ten years. Hey, fuck off—I'm a late bloomer.

After I fell for Frannie, she went away and wrote me a letter and said thanks for the support, but she's not the committing type. Two months later, Lola rose out of her little car in front of me like a vision and I was in deep trouble.

I was a virgin.

Sex, you know.

It's a curious thing to think about because most butch dykes will never admit to ever being intact. There's this magnificent fallacy that they emerge from the womb already strapped in and knowing how to swing that thang and how to make a woman come in three strokes flat. It's not true, of course. The fact that they'll convince you of the opposite is just part of their charm.

Lola used to get this wicked grin when I listened to my Indigo Girls CDs. She saw the latent talent in me. She always said I was a diamond in the rough. Nonetheless, first it was time to surrender myself to her. Or I'd never know her the way I'd want to.

Kate and Lola, turning up the heat, F.U.C…K.I.N…G.

That bed of hers was small but, shit, it was worked in good. She said she'd had it since she was a teenager, which was a sexy sort of affirmation, if you know what I mean. She was skilled, Lola the femme. Wasn't it supposed to be the other way around? Hadn't it been *Spare Rib* and *Ms. Magazine*'s job to prepare me for this? To boldly go where Kate had never gone before?

I was nervous, so I got off the bed. Lola was undeterred. She was a woman on a mission. We were kissing, standing up and scrambled, a hand touching warm skin. My head was starting to swim. I was afraid that Lola would think me inept. That's a short word but it encompasses so much.

I wanted to get Lola's clothes off because her body was…so exquisite.

But Lola wasn't bothered. She just pressed me flat against the wall. She had these two tall wrought-iron candelabras. I crashed into one and sent it tumbling onto the wood floor. Downstairs they must have heard it. "Oh fuck," I said. Lola said "Shhhh," and stuck her hand down the front of my pants.

I may have been reticent but I was hot for her. Hot, tight, and hard. She had me against the wall so hard I couldn't move, her one hand at my fly while the other pressed hard against my hipbone. Her brother was downstairs making his club-music. I think his bedroom door was open.

I felt Lola's hand break past the barrier of my panties—white cotton, because I'm a sensible sort of girl. Her fingers played with me, teased me. Without words she affirmed what I'd wanted all along even if I'd been trying to bullshit myself into believing the contrary. Just because I knew my phantom dick was throbbing enough to be heard didn't mean that I couldn't let Lola show me what it was hurting to do in the first place.

She planted her hand on my mouth because she knew that I would make a noise. Like I said, she was experienced.

It only took one smooth but forceful thrust and Lola broke me, forever. Tore away the last restriction between my insecure, protestant, feminist-repressed shadow and the cocky, self-assured dyke I was destined to be. Sensible, but cocky.

It did make a noise, but only into the palm of Lola's hand. It only hurt for a moment, and I bled only a little, which I was grateful for. Blood makes me feel vulnerable. And when the momentary sting was gone, something completely different began to happen.

Suddenly I began to give Lola instructions. As if I was a goddamned pro! I believe *harder* was the most popular direction of the hour.

This was what I'd been afraid of for so long. Of feeling Lola, of knowing what it was she could do to me. Scared of the thought that it was what she wanted to do to me, because the pleasure of getting fucked brings up all sorts of questions, doesn't it? What exactly is it that will make a person want to do such an intimate thing to you? Is it because you have good hips, long legs, a fucked-up mind, or the ability to name all the states of the U.S.A.?

Damned if I know, but I let Lola do it to me anyway. I let her enter me, and in more ways than one. Her hand inside me felt like it filled all my questions with mouth-watering answers.

Lola, Lola, you wench of a masquerading lass—you knew all along what this girl wanted, didn't you? How could I ever hope to give a woman what she needed when I myself had never experienced it? In the end, it's not about being vulnerable. It's just about getting to know your own needs.

Frannie ended up losing out big time. She was the type who chased infamy and controversy. She just chose to refer to it as not being tied down. Today Lola has all the infamy she can handle.

I'm always trying to kiss her in public and upset those queer little people who choose to live in boxes. And I write about her. With words I commit her to infamy. Billy Joel was right. He didn't start the fire. Lola did.

learning it at her knee

●

sacchi green

"Spanking," the girl in the scarlet shirt told me firmly. "Spanking, all spanking, and nothing but. That's what I'm interested in. Strictly spanking."

The bright color became her, setting off her vivid face and curly dark hair. Two months later, in the form of a thong leotard, it would set off even more of her, but at the moment I was too pleased and bemused by the possibility that she had an interest in being spanked by me to envision the moment when I would have her over my lap.

"Very strict spanking, I presume?"

"Very strict indeed," she agreed, laughing. Her wide mouth inspired considerable regret that her tastes were apparently so narrow, but her expressive face and sturdy, compact body appealed to me enough to make expanding my boundaries seem more than worthwhile, even with limitations.

"And the more unfair and undeserved it is, the better," she added. "I'm not a submissive bottom; I just like to be punished and feel righteously angry about it."

"A real connoisseur," I observed, hoping my own knee-jerk aversion to displays of anger didn't show. Research, I told myself. Gotta research my smut-writing craft. We'd already established our mutual interest in writing both erotica and science fiction, and I was beginning to hope that my publishing history and editing prospects might get me somewhere I hadn't been. Not, it appeared, quite as far as I might like to go, but somewhere.

The other members of the women's BDSM club had got well ahead of us on the way to the restaurant where they always convened after meetings. V and I were new here, both introduced to the group by friends met in other circumstances.

In front of us, a cluster of cute young baby-dykes and femmes thronged so thickly around my old friend Q's tall, impressive form that only her brush-cut gray head showed above them. V, to my delight, seemed happy enough to keep me company, though her gaze did stray toward Q from time to time. What the heck, so did mine, and always would, no matter how profoundly I understood that the friendship she needed from me had nothing to do with sex.

"I guess you could call me a connoisseur," V agreed. "It's not that I have a one-track mind, it's just that all the tracks seem to lead to the same place."

I hung back a little to get a view of the seat of her jeans. "And a very nice place it is, too," I said, or at least I might have said it, if the comeback line hadn't waited until a day later to occur to me, as they so often do.

Maybe that was just as well. In later e-mail conversations, whenever I steered the topic toward the sexual aspects of her favorite pastime, she steered it firmly away. I'd managed to ask her, as we left the restaurant's restroom just before I had to make the three-hour drive home, whether she'd be interested in sharing her expertise with an inexperienced top, and she'd seemed enthusiastic. Clearly, though, we'd be playing by her rules. Just as clearly, there was no way she could prevent me from getting a good deal of erotic pleasure out of the whole affair.

When Q e-mailed to ask how I'd liked the group and whether I'd seen anybody I was dying to play with, I was overjoyed to be able to report an intriguing prospect. My forbidden, gut-level impulse was to point out that of course I had, since she'd been there, but it didn't take much effort to suppress under the circumstances. I confided my doubts about being able to concentrate purely on sadism and not sex, and she tried to share the philosophical underpinnings of the attitude and role she'd mastered, but the fact remained that the masochistic girls lining up for punishment at her hands wanted those hands to go on to thoroughly fuck them. And I doubt that they felt much need to philosophize about it.

V did need to. It made some sense, I knew, to "process" for a while, since she didn't know much about me except that I was Q's friend, a published writer, and very new to the BDSM scene. She needed to be sure that I was neither too crazy to be safe, nor too safe to be just as crazy as she needed.

I struggled to understand why the sadism I wasn't sure I had in me was supposed to be its own reward. Maybe it was a matter of semantics. How could you call it *sadism,* I wondered, if your "victim" wanted the pain? But the more I thought about it, the more arousing the prospect became. Her body wriggling across my lap—her naked, rounded flesh feeling the full force of my strikes—the sounds of her cries punctuating the sharp slap of hand against reddening ass cheeks—yes, I wanted it, and labels be damned.

She sent me fantasies she'd written, which went a long way toward helping me understand what she wanted, especially the one involving a boy, a belt, and the principal's office. In return I described the painful experience I'd had when a confirmed bottom friend I lusted after teased me into writing an s/m fantasy letter to her; it turned out to give her flashbacks to her abusive mother, and she hadn't been able to finish it. She'd freaked out at the very idea of submitting to an older female, although she swore she hadn't thought of me that way before.

So where the hell do you go from there?

If you're lucky, you go with someone who does want, quite cheerfully, to be spanked by a female authority figure. And you wring every transgressive drop of sensual stimulation from it.

V and I had met in November, and, since I make my living in retail, there was no way I could take time for erotic adventures in the city until after the holidays. January, though, brought Boston's annual Fetish Fair Flea Market. Besides all the Fair's other attractions (including the opportunity for me to moderate a seminar on publishing erotica), our club would hold a women-only play party for members, guests, and others interested in joining.

The huge old hotel was bursting at its figurative seams with occasions for sensual stimulation. A good many literal seams seemed in danger of bursting, too, especially on corsets laced so tightly that the flesh confined within strained to join the luscious mounds allowed to overflow. However tantalizing the scenery on the mezzanine and in halls and ballrooms and even the exceedingly close quarters of the elevators, though, my mind fizzed with anticipation of the party to come. I'd been to a couple of smaller play parties, as an observer, but this time V was coming, and we had plans. Or at least, I hoped we did.

Just down the hall from the party suite and around a corner was my own room, palatial with two big beds, two bathrooms, even a relatively elegant sofa, but seeming hollow and dreary with only me to occupy it. I'd reserved the double room long ago when friends from a distance had planned to come, but the stretch of bitter January cold and snow gripping the whole region had forced them to change their plans and stay home to take care of ranch animals. I'd immediately offered the extra space to V, but she'd only responded that she wasn't even sure she'd make it herself. She'd have to travel by bus and subway and on foot a long way to get there, and did not intend to stay the night. My offer of picking her up at home brought no response at all.

I arranged a dinner date with another friend of Q's, whom I'd met a few times when she'd come to readings and been touchingly enthusiastic about my writing. A virtuoso with all kinds of whips, she would miss the play party due to being a featured entertainer at the official Fetish Fair Ball Extravaganza with her human percussion program, after which she had to rush home to check on frozen pipes. She was as strictly focused on whips as V was on spanking, and as firmly positioned as a top as V was as a bottom.

Dinner was pleasant, with good food and conversation, in the course of which we discovered that her mother had graduated from college the same year I had. Oh, great. Mothers again. It was just as well, I thought, that I'd never worked up any particular desire to be whipped, and doubted that I ever would; certainly not by someone a generation younger.

Spanking, though, could be another matter, although the generational differential would still be a sticking point. It's hard to comtemplate the full force of your hand striking someone's quivering buttocks without a certain sympathetic tingling creeping warmly across your own.

In my lonely room, getting ready for the party, I stood naked in front of the full-length mirror, trying to see my backside. I don't suppose any amount of craning your neck to see over your shoulder can give you a realistic idea of how your ass would appear to observers, assuming you ever decided to impose such a view on them, but it did seem to me that mine had held up remarkably well, and was certainly spankable.

Like V, though, at least as she claimed, I didn't have a submissive attitude, and unlike her, the only time I could indulge wholeheartedy in recreational anger was in a political context. It was a moot question, anyway. The one person I'd ever allow to spank me would never do it.

The party suite wasn't all that crowded yet when I got there, but it was getting warm enough that my burgundy flocked-velvet poet's shirt with the cascade of ruffles down the front might turn out to have been a mistake. It was such a perfect blend of tactile elegance and whorehouse-upholstery tackiness, though, without being definitively either femme or butch, that I didn't want to change.

V wasn't there yet. Q, engrossed in her first full-fledged official Daddy/girl relationship, cuddled on a couch with her sweetly voluptuous young blonde. Someone had set up a sturdy sling on a rack in a corner, and its naked, sighing occupant was being stroked with ostrich plumes as a prelude to more demanding exercises. I wandered a bit, chatted briefly with the few people I'd met, peeked into a connected room where a cluster of high-femmes seemed to be comparing the merits of their various corsets, and wandered off again through the halls. Was V coming?

The Fetish Fair Ball Extravaganza producer, who owed me a big favor (which is another story entirely, one I won't tell here), had given me a volunteer's armband so I could get in free. I visited the ballroom to see whether my young whip-virtuoso friend would be on stage soon. No one seemed to know the schedule, so I took note of the most outrageously creative costumes and master/slave pairings, then went back upstairs to the party.

No V. The sling-occupant's sighs had grown strained and erratic, as various clips and clamps were applied to her tender parts. I wouldn't have minded watching, but in a wide space cleared of furniture nearby, my friend with the abusive-mother trauma crouched submissively while her young, feminine mistress lashed her back with a force and unerring rhythm worthy of the Extravaganza stage. With strangers, I'd have admired the artistry and intensity. Under the circumstances, when the domme switched to caning, I left again.

By my third approach the party had become so crowded that it seemed impossible to find anyone. I was both keyed up, without anywhere for the energy to go. The back of Q's familiar steel-gray head rose visibly across the room, so I edged my way toward her. Maybe she'd seen V.

And then I saw V myself, gazing up at Q, face animated and lips moving quickly in a conversation that clearly went beyond asking where I might be. The scarlet leotard rising out of black jeans accentuated her body in ways the cotton shirt had only hinted at. I knew very well how much Q was enjoying the view.

Before I had time to work up a good head of jealous steam, though, V saw me and waved. "Guess what!" she called, when I was close enough to hear. "Q is willing to help us out with some spanking instruction, if that's okay with you."

"Sort of a master class?" I asked. "Sure, that would be great." I meant it, too. Working with both of them would provide double the fuel for fantasy.

"I can't do it quite yet, though," Q said, looking longingly toward the door where her girl waited. "I had something else planned just now. Maybe in an hour or so. You two could find some space and get in some practice."

"Space is going to be a problem." V peered around through the crowd. "We need a good chair, at least, and a couch would be even better, but they're all occupied."

That was an understatement. Two of the three couches supported activities that vied with the sling for the status of center ring in a kinky three-ring circus, while the third was packed with avid voyeurs.

"My room is just down the hall," I said, "and there's a couch in there just going to waste." V looked hesitant until I added, "the air conditioning is top-notch, too," which could no longer be said of the party suite. No system yet invented could cope with that many people breathing that heavily in a space that size.

"Great idea," Q said with urgent enthusiasm, and I gave her broad shoulder a swift pat and slight shove in the direction of her girl. She forged her way through the crowd with her own unique blend of power and grace.

"I suppose I could leave my book bag in your room," V said a bit shyly, bending to pick up the heavy pack at her feet.

"Books?" I asked, edging her toward the door. "I thought it must be your toy bag."

"Well, there are a few toys, too," she confided as we went down the hall. "But it's mostly books I'd loaned to a friend and picked up on the way. That's why I was late."

What else had she been doing with that friend? I already knew she had a wide range of "spanker" connections, both male and female. I didn't ask.

Once in my room, she looked around with approval at the space and the couch set with its back to the beds, creating a separate sitting area at one end. I asked her to show me the contents of her bag. Exploring toy bags was, I knew, a time-honored ice-breaker on occasions like this, and besides, I was genuinely curious about what books she was carrying.

A hairbrush (of course), several wooden paddles, a braided leather belt—and half-a-dozen children's and young adult fantasy books, some of them classics that I had loved in my long-ago youth.

"The books just happen to be there," V said, somewhat flustered, but it seemed to me that they were the perfect accessories for the age-play she had a taste for. I managed to infuse a mock-stern note into my voice.

"'Just happen to be there'? That was careless, wasn't it! Seems to me that a girl who carries Joan Aiken and Madeleine L'Engle in the bag with her kinky toys deserves some pretty severe punishment!"

She ducked her head, but couldn't conceal a grin. "Yes, Ma'am," she murmured, stripping off her shoes and black pants with practiced speed. Her leotard ended in a thong disappearing between her very available butt cheeks.

I sat down heavily on the couch. "Come here," I ordered, patting my lap, and she obeyed immediately, wriggling herself into optimum position across my knees. I gave her ass an experimental slap, and then a harder one.

"Go ahead, as hard as you want," she said, "just not too high, not too near the tailbone. You could damage something that way."

So I hit harder, open-handed, over and over, not minding that my "authority" was necessarily somewhat diluted by the fact that she was the expert and I the beginner. "Hold me tight with your .left hand," she panted after a while, "so I can't get away. It's okay to be rough!" So I gripped her right hip sharply and found that I gained the leverage to put more force into my spanking hand. A little rocking motion let me swing all the way from my shoulder and even put my back into it, besides intensifying the sensual pleasures of her body writhing and pressing into my lap. I wondered whether the invisible thong was forced harder against her clit and lips as I spanked her. My own parts were certainly feeling some pressure.

I'd worried about getting tired, but once I got into a rhythm that I could control and vary enough to startle V from time to time, it felt like I could go on forever. V wasn't giving directions any longer, just moaning and grunting and occasionally gasping sharply when I surprised her with a syncopation of the pace.

Finally she began to murmur a few indistinguishable words. I remembered guiltily that I was supposed to be scolding her enough to arouse her righteous indignation, but I was too immersed in the flow of physical sensations to think of words. Her voice strengthened, though, until I could clearly hear her low chant of "Thank you! Thank you! Thank you!" at every stroke.

It was clearly a ritual familiar to her. I hoped it meant that I was taking her deeply into the space she really wanted to find, even if it wasn't the one she had claimed to be looking for. I spanked even harder, tirelessly, until her ass glowed nearly as red as her leotard and she was running out of breath. "Do you need a break?" I asked softly, not knowing where to go from there. My natural urge to progress toward other sensory stimulation was, I knew, forbidden. Strictly spanking. She had trusted me, and I wouldn't betray that trust.

"Yes…" V said breathlessly, "…we'd better rest some before going back to the party." Then, when she'd rolled sideways on my lap and I was gently stroking her inflamed thighs and buttocks, she added, "I had no idea you'd have so much endurance!"

Maybe she said that to all her first-time spankers. I didn't mind. I'd nearly forgotten about the party, but I didn't mind her eagerness to get there, either. She wanted the public aspect, and so, I realized, did I.

Even the fleeting paranoid thought that she might be using me to get Q's attention didn't bother me. The prospect of getting Q's attention in a context I wouldn't usually manage was almost as appealing to me as the chance to spank V.

We rested and talked for a while, and resumed our play briefly to take advantage of the couch's upholstered back. I tried her leather belt, wrapping around my hand enough to leave just the right length to strike with, and admired the texture of the marks it left on her, but still preferred the sound and feel of my hand on naked flesh and her body across my lap.

We rested a bit longer, this time with V sitting quietly on my lap and leaning her head against my shoulder. The comfort-after-punishment stage, I decided. Very pleasant. When she finally asked, tentatively, whether I though Q would be ready yet, I cheerfully agreed that it was time to go and see.

"Q certainly has…well…presence, doesn't she?" V said as we gathered up her toys, leaving the books behind.

"She certainly does," I said, with only a little envy, and ushered V out the door.

Q was not only ready, she'd staked a claim to a chair between the sling (in use, but only languidly now) and a tall sideboard bearing trays of safe-sex supplies. From the way a young redhead was coyly chatting her up, if we'd been five minutes later the spanking lesson would have started without us.

V sailed right in to claim her place. She showed Q the ebony hairbrush and a wooden paddle with one side finely ridged and the other padded with velour. "We've had a very nice session of basic spanking," she said, glancing at me with bright eyes and a warm smile. "Maybe you could start out by hand, and then switch to these other things. I don't like too much of the bristle side of the brush, but a little is good. And the soft side of the paddle once in a while gives me chance to come down and get ready for more."

She launched herself across Q's broad lap with no hesitation and wiggled and squirmed until they were both satisfied with the balance and leverage. I missed holding her myself. On the other hand, I could press close to Q's side and imagine what it would feel like to lie across her thighs with my ass exposed. I was quickly distracted from this pleasant reverie, though, when Q kneaded V's upturned buttocks lightly and speculatively, then gave the right one a sharp, resounding slap.

"That's what a full flat-handed stroke sounds like," she told me, and lay a swift, staccato series of them across both sides. "Where you strike varies the sound…," she said as she moved down the thighs and then back up to the curve of the ass, "…and so does how you shape your hand." She demonstrated this principle, too. A curved hand produced a more hollow, drumlike tone. I'd already discovered some of this myself, but watching her large, strong hand in action held a fascination all its own.

I was eager, though, for my hands-on turn. "Go ahead now," Q said, holding V firmly by the waist and shoulders. "Just be sure to pay attention to her reactions."

Standing above V like this gave me a longer, more forceful stroke. I could swing from the hips, and got into a rhythm that stirred my whole body as much as it impacted hers. In minutes, or maybe seconds—I lost track of time—my shirt became unbearably hot. I slowed only slightly while my left hand fumbled at buttons and sleeves until I could toss the flowing velvet aside. I was briefly aware of an audience, but V's moans and whimpers reclaimed my full attention.

Harder…on and on…even without the shirt I was sweating, but I was determined to give her everything she wanted. And then her moaning chant of "Thank you! Thank you! Thank you!" began, making me wet in ways beyond sweating. I couldn't stop then, couldn't slow, until finally her voice faded and her legs began to rise, heels twitching.

"Watch her feet!" Q directed. "Ease off now. When the feet come up, she's had all she can take for a while."

V mumbled some kind of assent. Q handed me the paddle, and I stroked the velour side across V's rosy ass and thighs lightly for a while, until she said she was ready for the hairbrush.

Where spanking could conceivably be taken as an extreme caress, beating with a hairbrush had to be pure punishment. V seemed to take it that way, too, but still to want it, even though it brought tears and sharp cries and made her feet bob up after a dozen strokes. She urged me on, but it wasn't long before I saw traces of blood on her skin and had to stop. Drawing blood was against the party rules.

I searched in the supplies for disinfectant, but by the time I found it the slight bleeding had stopped. Q applied the ointment to V's skin anyway, and told me that above all else, a top was responsible for her partner's well-being, including aftercare. The top had to know when to stop, even if the bottom didn't want to.

V, when she stood up, was visibly shaky. I brought her a drink and led her to a place on a crowded couch. "You sit there," she told me faintly, "and I'll sit on the floor at your feet."

"No," I told her firmly, "I appreciate the thought, but it's your ass that needs a soft spot. I'll even bring you some fluffier pillows." So I did, and then spent the waning hour of the party leaning against her knees, not as a slave but a guardian, while she stroked my hair and whispered an occasional "Thank you" into my ear. I hadn't realized how pleasant this aftercare business could be.

Q came by with her girl before leaving. "Are you staying for the night?" she asked V. "You really shouldn't be going out into the cold."

"You saw how big my room is," I told V. "There's even an extra bathroom. You don't have to worry about anything."

"Well..." she said shyly, "I do have to go back there for my books, anyway..."

"It's settled, then," I assured Q. "She won't want to let Joan Aiken and Madeleine L'Engle catch a chill. Don't worry, I'll take good care of her." I got up to help V to her feet; and, much as I usually like to watch Q from behind, I didn't even glance that way as she departed.

In my room we wound down from the tension of the party. I was reassuringly low-key, and her wariness faded until she was willing to cuddle innocuously on the couch for a while as we exchanged bits of our life histories. It was my turn to thank her for giving me a chance to prove to my friends that I could do more than merely observe the kinky world I'd ventured into.

"I'll take you to breakfast," I said, as I climbed into bed at last. My spanking hand was tender and throbbing just a bit. It was a wonderful feeling. "The hotel buffet is supposed to be great." V was already safely between the covers of the other bed, after showering and brushing her teeth—I noticed that she'd brought her toothbrush, anyway—in the other bathroom. She still wore the red thong leotard; I tried not to speculate on whether it was still comfortable after all this time.

"That would be nice," V said sleepily; and then, when my eyes were beginning to close, her voice came again, softly. "You know, you could tell your friends anything you wanted to about tonight. I don't mind what you say."

"Stretch the truth?" I asked. "How far?"

Her mattress sighed softly, and then, in a moment or two, so did mine. "Not all that far," she breathed into my ear. "I do think…I would like…to be held."

It was nobody else's business, though, I thought. Not even Q's.

"Let them wonder," I said, as my arms went around her.

snow dancing

●

laren lebran

As I stood in the middle of my driveway and slowly turned three hundred and sixty degrees, I understood what inspired the title *Pure as the Driven Snow*.

There was no question that everywhere I looked the view was painfully beautiful and hauntingly chaste. A pristine, sparkling blanket covered everything: overhead, tree branches bowed beneath the feathery weight; the road narrowed to nothing more than a path between encroaching drifts; and all around me, swirling white nymphs floated on the air. Not a single footprint or errant noise suggested that I was anyone other than the last survivor in a world where sound and fury had succumbed to the inexorable march of millions, trillions of falling flakes.

I have always loved to shovel snow. It's always so very quiet, and the steady scrape of metal on stone is like another heartbeat keeping me company as I work. I'm an orderly shoveler. I outline boxes, starting first along the edges of the drive and then connecting the trenches at intervals with perfectly perpendicular ones, exactly the width of my shovel. Once the area is mapped, I clear the box closest to the house, then make another and move forward. If I'm feeling particularly adventurous, I might on occasion make a diagonal through the box. I'm careful about how I pile the snow, being certain to leave enough room on the top for later accumulations. Bend, extend, lift, and throw. A rhythmic cadence, an endpoint in sight, a job accomplished. When I reach the end of the driveway and look behind me, noting the perfectly squared edges and the even mounds of snow lining both sides, I have a sense of satisfaction and even pride. My secret pleasure.

Unfortunately, today promised to be an instance of delayed gratification. There were fourteen inches of powdery white stuff covering my eighty-foot driveway. There was going to be a lot of bending, extending, lifting, and throwing going on before I reached the street. And it was still snowing. Steadily. I could barely see to the end of the driveway. With one last reverent glance and a whispered apology, I broke the surface of tranquility with my shovel.

Time to begin my assault on nature.

Thirty minutes later, it was clear to me that nature was winning. I wasn't even a third of the way done, and when I looked behind me, the area that I'd already shoveled was blanketed again in a substantial coat of snow. I was reminded of a story I'd heard: it takes so long to paint the Golden Gate Bridge that once the crew reaches the end of the bridge, it's time to go back to the opposite end and start over.

Bend, extend, lift, and…

"Need some help?"

I could just barely see the figure at the end of my driveway, looking pretty much the way I did, I figured. That is to say, shapeless. Large, snow-covered, and shapeless.

"That's okay. Thanks. I've got it."

The form trundled forward through the mists of snow, slowly emerging as a recognizable human figure ten feet away. Blue woolen watch cap pulled low over straight dark brows, a few strands of dark hair escaping from the back and curling on the jacket collar, slightly above average height, blue nylon jacket, blue jeans, blue gloves. A study in blue with eyes I was willing to bet were the same color, but I couldn't tell through the curtain of falling flakes.

"My driveway is about a third the length of yours. I'm done with it, and I don't mind lending a hand."

Lovely voice, melodious and deep. Second alto or countertenor, depending on the gender. Which for the life of me, I could not discern.

I lifted a hand to shield my eyes, blinking as the crystals caked on my lashes. We were standing in the middle of a blizzard. "Yes. Thank you."

With a brisk nod, my new accomplice in this losing battle strode purposefully back to the opposite end of the driveway. As I watched, he—or she—made a neat square ten by ten feet wide and began to shovel it clear. Oddly comforted, I rededicated myself to the task. When I reached the midpoint of the driveway, I finally looked up again in time to see her toss her parka onto the top of a towering snow bank. And there was no question about the "her" part—the swell of breasts beneath the tight, blue, silk thermal top put all doubt to rest.

"You'll freeze," I called.

"No," her voice carried back to me. "I'm naturally hot-blooded. This feels great."

From where I was standing, it certainly looked great. Her jeans molded to her firm ass and solid thighs as if the material had grown there. She moved—bend, extend, lift, and throw—with an economy of motion and a precise rhythm that was mesmerizing. I was slowly becoming a snow statue as I stood unmoving, watching her work. I could almost imagine the muscles in her strong shoulders bunching as she thrust the blade into the snow, could almost feel her powerful thighs flexing, then lifting, as she threw the load clear. Oddly, I wasn't cold. If anything, I was pleasantly warm, and the heat escalated the longer I watched. Taking care to follow a path already shoveled so as not to pack down the snow beneath my boots, making it more difficult to remove later, I made my way to her.

"We've been out here quite a while. Can I offer you something hot? Coffee, cocoa, soup?"

She leaned on her shovel, her arm bent at the elbow and her legs casually crossed. She did have blue eyes. Blue blue, sky blue eyes. And they were appraising me in a way I hadn't seen for quite some time, but still recognized. I met her gaze so that she would know that I knew she was looking, and she smiled.

"Cocoa and soup?"

I laughed and extended my hand to introduce myself. "Fin Brewster."

"Jules Howard," she replied. "I'm new to the neighborhood."

"Ah, you arrived just in time for our annual snowfall." I turned and started back toward the house with Jules beside me.

"This is all there is, huh?"

I'd left the garage door open, and led her through to the small mud room that adjoined my kitchen. "You can take your boots off and leave them out here. Your jacket and things as well." I was busy shedding my own outerwear as I spoke. "Actually, we probably get two or three substantial snows, and it's always an event."

"It is pretty," she remarked.

As we shuffled about in the small space, we bumped shoulders and thighs several times. When I nearly knocked her over as she stood on one foot to pull off her boot, I grabbed her around the waist to steady her, laughing.

"Sorry. You first."

Unexpectedly, her weight settled into my arms, her back to my chest, and I found myself holding her in a loose embrace as she lifted first one foot, then the other, to untie her laces. Her hips rolled gently in the curve of my pelvis as she bent forward to pull off her boots. My arms were wrapped around her middle, fingers splayed on her stomach. When the muscles contracted beneath the single thin layer of silky material, I had the sudden, nearly overpowering urge to slide my hands up and cup her breasts. I stood completely still, barely breathing.

"I'm warm deep inside, but everything else is cold," she whispered. "The heat from your hands feels so good."

When she straightened I didn't let go, but merely leaned my shoulders against the wall, braced my legs, and took her weight once more against the front of my body. My mouth was very close to the back of her neck. A few snowflakes still lingered, the edges blurring and melting before my eyes. I have no idea what I was thinking, but I touched the tip of my tongue to a single shimmering droplet that clung to her skin, and when I did, she sighed. A long, shuddering sigh of pleasure.

"It's warmer in the kitchen," I said, my mouth against the shell of her ear.

"You're just what I need."

She reached between us and placed her palms flat against my thighs. I looked past her shoulder to a small mirror on the opposite wall and saw us reflected there. Her eyes were closed, her head tipped back slightly, her neck exposed above the crescent of navy blue. In the mirror, I watched my fingers curve around the column of her neck and dance along the taut muscles until I cupped her chin. When I pressed ever so slightly, she turned her face until I could brush my lips over the corner of her mouth. Her skin was soft and cool.

"You're going to get chilled," I murmured, skimming my lips along the angle of her jaw until my mouth was against her ear. "The snow is melting, and your jeans are soaked."

"You're right," she said, her voice husky and low.

She moved one hand from my thigh, and I heard the unmistakable sound of a zipper sliding open. "I should take these off."

"I'll do it." Watching her face in the mirror, I smoothed my hands down her abdomen to the waistband of her jeans, slid my fingers underneath, and pushed the material downward. She never opened her eyes, smiling gently as she shifted her hips from side to side to help me. The undulating pressure of her body rolling between my thighs made my stomach clench, and my hands trembled on her bare flesh.

She was shaking, too, and from the heat of her body reaching me even through my T-shirt and jeans, I knew it wasn't from the cold. With one arm around her hips, clasping her to me, I found the bottom of her shirt with my free hand and slipped underneath. I heard her murmur what sounded like a yes. She stretched against me, letting her head rest in the angle between my neck and shoulder, her hands braced against my thighs again, as I cupped her above and below. Her nipple hardened in my palm even as the silky evidence of her passion slicked my skin through the whisper of cotton between her thighs. I squeezed gently, then rolled my hand over her flesh, massaging her until her cool pale skin glowed red with the burn of desire.

"Jules," I whispered.

"Mmm?"

"It's supposed to snow again tomorrow."

"Oh," she sighed, covering my fingers with hers and guiding me inside her panties, drawing my fingertips up and down over the spot where she needed me. "Did I mention…oh, do me hard…yes yes just like that…"

She was hot and slippery, her clit so hard I could barely stay on it. I rubbed and stroked and felt her knees buckle. "Mention what?"

"How much I love…"

She whimpered and I pushed inside, the heel of my hand crushing her clit. She slapped a hand over mine and ground against my palm.

"Tell me what you love," I urged, my throat tight, my heart hammering so loudly I feared I would not hear. She was close, her eyes tightly closed, her mouth a silent oh. I didn't expect an answer.

She pumped hard on my fingers and laughed. "How much I love…to shovel. Oh god…please, don't stop…"

"I won't," I murmured, watching her face in the mirror as she climaxed, the planes and angles blurring like a snowflake melting in my hand.

wet

●

tina simmons

Somebody once said sex is like pizza: even when it's bad it's pretty good. I guess I always felt that way about my own sex life—nothing spectacular, really, but it satisfied my hunger. Until I met Alice. Then my whole life, or at least my sex life, changed for the better. It seems fitting that I met her on a rainy day. Things have been pretty wet since I met Alice.

Alice moved in downstairs one soggy weekend in April. I live on the third floor of a sprawling three-story brownstone in Queens, so I'm used to my neighbors coming and going. I keep to myself, pay my bills on time, and don't play my music too loud, and for the most part my neighbors do the same. I'd never felt a compelling need to introduce myself to any of them until one rainy Sunday in April, when I looked out my window and saw a lean, athletic carrot-top in cutoffs and a SUNY sweatshirt, trying to unload a surfboard off the top of her VW bug in the rain. Suddenly, I wanted to get to know my neighbor in a bad way.

"Hey, let me help you," I said, a little breathless from running down three flights of stairs.

Alice gave me that wary look of all New Yorkers, the one that says, "Watch it, bitch, I've got pepper spray and a black belt in kick-your-ass." She took in my lime green Give Peas a Chance T-shirt and purple tie-dyed yoga pants. I guess I seemed harmless enough because she smiled. "Thanks. My friend Tom tied it down for me, but now I can't get the knots out because they've swollen up from the rain."

I bit my tongue on a suggestive comment about knot tying and worked diligently on getting the surfboard untied. Five minutes later, with her working on one side and me working on the other, we got the board down. She hefted it on her shoulder despite my offer to help and headed up the stairs to her apartment. I watched her go, thoroughly enraptured by the swing of her hips and the look of her short, wet hair curling on the nape of her neck. Then I did the only thing I could do—I grabbed a box marked "CDs, Books and Shit" and followed her, feeling a little bit like a lost puppy following her home. I had it bad.

By the time we had unpacked her car, it was raining in great windy sheets and we were both soaked. I invited Alice up to my place for a drink. If it were a Saturday night and I'd asked her to hit the clubs with me, it would have sounded like a come-on. But it was Sunday, it was raining, the rest of her stuff wouldn't get there until Monday morning, and she was new to the building, so I was just being neighborly. Okay, so it was still a come-on. But it was a good one.

I made a pot of green tea and poured two mugs. Alice had stripped off her wet sweatshirt and was wearing a tiny little white tank top. She flopped down on my futon by the window and watched the rain while I tried not to stare at the large nipples poking through that white tank. She shifted around, pulling her knees up under her chin and hiding her nipples from my view with long, lean legs that seemed more suited for the fifty-yard dash than the runway. She reminded me of a greyhound, lean and sharp with awkward limbs that wouldn't seem to do what she wanted while she was sitting still. A greyhound with amazing tits. I grinned.

"What's so funny?"

I shook my head. "Nothing."

"Mmm. This is just what I needed," she said, sipping from the mug I handed her. She looked up and narrowed her eyes at me, probably because I was still grinning like an idiot. "C'mon. tell me why you're laughing at me."

I sat on the corner of the futon, as far away from her as I could be and still be sharing the same piece of furniture. I would have sat someplace else, but the futon was the only cushioned thing I owned besides the bed that took up almost the entire alcove that the landlord called a bedroom. Some people are funny about having their personal space invaded by a stranger, so I was trying to be polite even though I didn't think Alice was like that. Or at least I was hoping she wasn't like that.

"I was just thinking that you look like a dog." I realized how bad that sounded as soon as the words were out of my mouth. My face flushed hotly. "I mean, you look like a runner, someone who is more comfortable in motion."

She laughed, no offense taken. "Yeah, that's about right. I ran in high school and college and played just about every sport they'd let a girl play." She wrinkled her nose. "I'm still pissed they wouldn't let me play baseball."

"And you surf," I said. I was just filled with witty, insightful comments. "I mean, you must have surfed at some point. Not a lot of surfing around here."

I wanted to bang my head on the hardwood floor so the word "surf" would stop falling out of my mouth.

Alice reached over and put her hand on my thigh. She had to lean toward me to do it, and her mug looked precariously close to spilling its contents all over my dry-clean-only futon, but I didn't give a damn. I stared at her hand on my leg, the long, tapered fingers with their short, neat nails, and I didn't care if she drenched the futon in tea. My entire body tensed at that gentle touch. It was ridiculous, I'd just met her, but my brain had become detached from my body, which was quivering with pent-up anticipation.

"Don't try so hard," she said softly.

"Huh? What?" It was as if my brain had not only shut down, but had completely left the room.

Alice laughed and I decided I really liked the sound, even if it was at my expense. "I like you, kid. You're cute."

"Um, thanks?"

She set her mug on the floor and scooted closer to me. I couldn't have moved if there had been a fire in my kitchen. Alice leaned over, and I thought she was going to kiss me, and I thought I was going to come in my panties if she did. Instead, she whispered in my ear, "I love rain storms. They make me horny."

That was all it took. I am not a dyke who lets an opportunity slide by. I turned toward her, nearly kneeing her in the groin in the process, and took her face in my hands. "Can I kiss you?"

"Yeah," she breathed into my mouth as I kissed her.

Kissing Alice was, in a word, in-fucking-credible. Her mouth was soft and warm and wet and she leaned into me as I kissed her deeper, her hands on my hips, bracing her weight so that I knew she was there, right there, practically in my lap, kissing me harder and deeper and wetter until I was panting raggedly into her mouth and we hadn't even undressed yet.

She yanked my T-shirt up, breaking our kiss only long enough to get my head through the neck hole. Then she was palming my bare breasts, kneading them almost as hard as she was kissing me, driving me to distraction so that I almost forgot she was still fully clothed. I quickly stripped her tank top off, admiring the nipples that had been teasing me before. Her areolas were a rich, chocolate brown and seemed too big for her small breasts, but the effect was incredibly sexy.

I nibbled my way down her collarbone to the swell of her breast, finding the edge of one areola and sucking until she whimpered and thrust her chest at my mouth. I kept sucking until I reached the center of her hard, rubbery nipple, taking it into my mouth and sucking rhythmically until she urged my head to the other nipple. I alternated like that, one nipple then the other, until she was thrashing and moaning against me. I would have been quite content to spend the rest of the afternoon sucking Alice's nipples if she hadn't gotten her hand down my yoga pants and found my cunt.

"God, you're wet," she gasped as I gently bit her nipple. "So fucking wet."

I tried to get my hand in her shorts, but they were damp from the rain and too constricting. "I bet you are, too," I mumbled around her nipple in my mouth. "Get these damn shorts off so I can find out."

We giggled and fumbled our way out of the rest of our clothing, a tangle of limbs and damp hair and wet cunts on my too-small futon. It never occurred to me to move to the bed. I didn't care about comfort or space or washable fabrics. I just wanted to get fucked. Fucked by Alice.

"Let me see how wet you are." I spread Alice's thighs with my hands and she lay back on the futon, open and exposed. She was stunning. I couldn't stop staring at her, from the sprinkle of freckles across her upper chest, to the too-large nipples that made my mouth water, to her flat, muscular stomach, to the neat, orangey-red triangle of hair above her glistening cunt. "God, you're stunning."

I didn't give her a chance to respond. I buried my face between those lean thighs and licked her, bottom to top, then worked my way back down. Slowly. So slowly. Until she was clutching at my hair and thrusting her cunt up to my mouth with the same ferocity she'd pushed her nipples into my face. The futon creaked as she thrashed and I had a moment's concern that we'd end up in a pile on the floor. Then she was coming, coming hard and wet in my mouth, and I couldn't think of anything else except how musky sweet she tasted and how her moans sounded like a Buddhist chant.

I teased her quivering clit gently, oh so gently, until she relaxed her grip on my head. I rested my head against her thigh, breathing her in. I'd never smelled anything quite as good as fresh rain and wet girl in my entire life.

Finally, Alice giggled and pulled me up between her thighs, wrapping those long arms and legs around me. "Come here," she said. "Come here and let me fuck you."

I went willingly. I expected her to flip me over and slide down between my legs. Instead, she reached down between us and slid two fingers into me. I gasped as her palm grazed my clit.

"Mmm, you're even wetter now," she said. "I wonder how wet you get?

I tried to say something witty, or at least coherent, but all I could manage was, "Don't know. Find out."

She angled her fingers up into me, cupping my cunt in her hand and squeezing on the outside while her fingers stroked me on the inside. It was an amazing sensation and I melted against her, my mouth instinctively going to her nipple. I sucked as she fucked me, finding the rhythm she used on my cunt. Steady, steady, milking her nipple the way she milked my cunt.

I was wet, wetter than I'd ever been. I could tell by the wet, squishy noises her fingers made as the slid in and out of me. I rode her fingers, fucking myself on them, wanting her to rub my clit harder and make me come. Instead, Alice rolled me off her and over onto the futon, flat on my back with her kneeling between my legs. She never took her fingers out of me. I closed my eyes and spread my legs wider, waiting for the feel of her tongue on my clit. It never came. I opened my eyes and watched her leaning over me, her hand angled between my legs, stroking deep in my cunt. I keep my crotch bare in the summertime and I could see my clit standing up, swollen and red and aching to be sucked. I whimpered, I moaned. I even tried to push her head down between my thighs. But Alice never touched my clit, she just kept fucking me.

I was starting to get annoyed. She felt good, so fucking good, but I couldn't come without her touching my clit. I leaned back on my elbows, watching her watch me. Or, rather, watching her watch her fingers go into me.

"I need your mouth," I finally gasped. "Please."

"No you don't," she muttered, though it appeared she was talking to my clit, not me. "You're going to come all over my hand in a minute. You're so fucking wet, baby. So wet. Just let it come."

I'd heard of what she was talking about, but I didn't have the heart to tell her I wasn't that kind of girl. I felt suddenly inadequate, an unliberated dyke who didn't have G-spot orgasms. I could feel my body tense, resisting her, rejecting the fingers stroking me so sweetly.

Alice looked up and the pure, naked lust on her face nearly made me groan. "Don't, baby. Relax. Let it come. Trust me." Then she leaned down and gently, oh so gently, licked my clit. "I'll make you come. I promise."

I don't know if it was her words, the look on her face or my clit anticipating her mouth, but I did relax. I lay back on the futon and closed my eyes and let her finger-fuck me with wet, squishy noises and soft, breathy words of encouragement.

"That's it, open for me," she whispered. "Your cunt is so wet and open. I've got three fingers in you now, did you know that?"

I shook my head. I couldn't speak. I kept my eyes closed and imagined her fingers, three of them, sliding deep into me. I was so wet, wetter than I'd ever been. I could feel it trickling down my ass. I was spread wide, opening to her, wanting more.

I didn't realize I'd verbalized my request until she asked, "More? You want more, baby?"

"Yes. Please. Yes."

I was so wet, so fucking wet, I wouldn't have known she had four fingers inside of me if she hadn't said, "That's four, baby."

I'd never felt so full and so open at the same time. My hips undulated against her thrusts without conscious thought. I raised myself up and fucked her fingers whenever she would go still inside me. I forgot about my clit and simply felt my cunt swell and grow wetter, wetter, until something released inside me. Then it felt as if my insides were gushing all over her hand.

"That's it, baby," she said, making shallow little thrusting motions in my cunt. "That's it, let go."

"Oh God, oh God, oh God," I gasped. I reached between my thighs and grasped her wrist tightly. Whether to pull her away or pull her closer, I wasn't sure. Thankfully, she wouldn't let me direct her. She just kept fucking me with quick, steady thrusts of her fingers.

I felt it again. A rise, a quiver, a gush. And again. She stroked me over and over as I came, wetness flowing out of me like a river. I arched my back and cried out, every muscle in my body taut, all my feeling centered on my cunt.

I opened my eyes and looked down at her, her fingers buried in my cunt, her gaze between my legs. My clit stood up as hard and red as before, but I was coming, coming, coming and it didn't matter how. She lowered her mouth to my cunt and flicked my clit with her tongue. It felt amazing, delicious, but just a part of the experience of being fucked by Alice, not the main course. I stroked her head softly, running my fingers through her hair that was now damp with perspiration and not just rain.

Alice eased her fingers out of me gently, leaving me feeling empty and open. She looked up into my eyes as she slowly licked her fingers, making my entire body quiver at the expression on her face.

"Told you," she said.

I wasn't going to argue. "You're incredible. I've never...wow."

"I think your futon is ruined, though."

I reached under my ass and felt the wetness that was spreading beneath me. "I think you're right."

"Sorry."

"Fuck it. I'll buy a new one."

I pulled her up until she stretched out on top of me. There wasn't enough room for us to lay side-by-side, but I didn't care. I liked the weight of her damp body on mine. Besides, it didn't seem fair to make her lay in the big, wet spot, even if she had caused me to make it.

"I have a confession to make," she said. She looked down at me, her hair falling forward to partially shield her face. "I don't surf."

I studied her, trying to keep the smile off my face and failing miserably. "Too bad. I only let you get into my pants because I thought you were a hot surfer girl."

She nuzzled my neck. "I'll learn to surf."

We laughed and held each other while the rain fell and the wet spot grew cold underneath me. Alice never did learn to surf, but I bought a new futon. With a washable cover.

don't call me ma'am

●

gun brooke

Deliza Acampora was as stunningly beautiful as her name was unusual. Short-cropped black hair framed a thin, angular face that was symmetric and elflike, with the largest blue eyes I'd ever seen. Her nose was short and slightly upturned, and the soft-looking pink lips made her mouth look innocent, only contradicted by the word she'd utter at the staff meetings. Her southern accent sounded sweet and dreamy, but that made it all the more scathing when she cut someone off by the knees for slacking off, or worse, lying about it.

I guessed my boss was five foot four, pretty average for a woman, but that was the only average thing about her. Nothing else, in her personality or her appearance, was standard issue. She wasn't like anybody I'd ever met, and, not to brag, but most people would agree that I'd been around. I tried to rely on my experience, on how I had learned to handle situations in the past, but there was something about her that pulled me in. I did my best to act professionally around her, but the sugarcoated voice, combined with her commanding presence, drew me toward her. "Brooke," her soft, yet unyielding, voice broke through my dreamy admiration of her perfect features. "Can you stay late tonight? I really need to finish this, and if you can help me, we can put it behind us and take the rest of the weekend off. How does that sound?" She leaned back in her chair behind the large mahogany desk, making more of her delicious body available for me to admire.

"Sound's great, ma'am," I managed. "Just put me to work." She could have asked me to sweep the vast parking lot and I would have used my toothbrush if it pleased her.

"Why don't you sit next to me, and I'll fill you in on how far I've come?"

Next to her. God. I pulled out the chair by her side, and sat down, adjusting my linen jacket to cover my rigid nipples that had been standing at attention since I entered her office.

"Why don't you take your jacket off? It's going to get hot in here."

What does she mean by hot? As in "my flesh on yours" kind of hot? I stared at her, momentarily dumbfounded.

"There's something wrong with the thermostat," she continued, sounding perfectly casual. "Maintenance has sent out for spare parts, but they won't get here until tomorrow." Ms. Acampora leaned her chin into her palm, smiling faintly as her eyes kept my gaze prisoner.

"I'm fine. Really." God, I sound like a complete moron. Nobody would think I'm a hard-boiled chick with a degree from Harvard Business School. "Well, perhaps it is a little warm in here," I relented when Liz quirked an eyebrow. It gave her a funny, endearing look that was just as sexy as her wide-eyed fairytale entity persona. I knew it was hard for most people to believe that this ethereal woman, looking barely seventeen, was the CEO of a multinational company and in charge of the entire North American branch. Her CV stated she was thirty-three, eight years my junior. But who's counting?

I, for one, had almost blown it the first time I met her. Her secretary had shown me into her office for a job interview, and the sign on her desk said D. Acampora. I had assumed the slender young woman standing by the window, obviously lost in thought, must be the boss's daughter or something. Dressed entirely in black, she had oozed dangerous sensuality. When she looked up, the expression in her eyes belied the fact that she looked way too young for a seasoned, slightly scarred corporate warrior like me.

If anyone had asked me, I would have estimated her age to be not a day over seventeen. Only the fact that I was tongue-tied by instant desire, which I suppose was pretty pathetic since I thought she was so young, saved my ass. Relieved that the object of my desire was over the age of consent, I was still mortified when Deliza Acampora seemed to read my mind and rolled her eyes in exasperation. I bet she gets the same reaction from people all the time. I've often wondered why I got the job despite my pitiful performance during that initial interview. Perhaps the other applicants made an even worse first impression? Either that, or they didn't have my reputation of intimidating the hell out of the opposition and getting the job done no matter what. Lucky for me, I did battle well in the corporate world, conquering the competition, and consequently was able to quickly redeem myself in my employer's eyes... and speaking of eyes...

"Brooke?"

"Sorry. Let's get to it." I would have preferred to get to something entirely different than contractual intricacies. I draped my jacket across the back of the chair, and persuaded myself that my aching nipples were not showing through my sleeveless black silk shirt.

To my horror, I felt her place an arm on top of my folded jacket as she leaned against me, pushing the documents closer for my inspection. "Here's where I'm not certain if we can accommodate their demands. As you know, I normally rely on my assistants to finish the last draft of a contract, but a deal of this magnitude...I just can't risk it."

She sounded tired. I knew she had worked two all-nighters this past week. A discreet yawn on her part created an unexpected protectiveness in me. It made her seem more human, but not any less perfect. I looked down at her hand, which held a pencil in a firm grip. Deliza had slender, long fingers, pink nail polish on manicured nails, and smooth, pale skin with clearly visible veins. Gorgeous. Every cell in her body oozes beauty.

"I understand," I said and forced myself to scan the three paragraphs that were bothering her. In the meantime she was beginning to roll the pencil between her fingers and it distracted me since it brought images of her doing that motion on my nipples. Chastising my overheated brain for bothering me this way, I was relieved to finally find something in the text that didn't make sense. "Here. I suggest we strike this, and put in our standard, mitigation clause. They're trying to pull a fast one on us. Written like that, it seems innocent enough, but I've seen their subsidiary companies try this approach as well. It didn't fly then, either. They should have told their mother company that they get slammed when they try stunts like these."

"Brooke, you're a godsend." To my astonishment Deliza leaned toward me and put her arm around my back, her left hand pulling me close as she gave me a quick squeeze. "What would I do without you?"

At least you wouldn't have me drool over you when you're trying to conduct serious business. Her close proximity made my thighs tremble and I grew hard and wet. Pressing my legs together, I attempted to stop the unwarranted physical reaction to her touch. "You'd be fine. You have many contract lawyers on your payroll."

"Not the same. I certainly wouldn't want to try running this circus without you. You've made yourself indispensable during these eighteen months."

Whoa. What did she mean by that? I stared at her, knowing that she looked even smaller next to me, dwarfed by my tall, well-toned frame. During business hours, I dressed similarly to Deliza, a navy power suit, good quality tops, and pumps, but my five-foot-ten frame made the outfit seem more austere. My hair was also black, but not with her bluish tint; instead it had gold highlights. My eyes, dark gray, almost black, were very different from her soft blue gaze. "What are you saying, ma'am?"

"God, you're so stubborn with that formal way of yours."

She obviously didn't realize it was a sure way for me to make sure I kept my head out of the gutter, when it came to her.

Deliza grinned. "Call me Deliza, like everyone else. You make me feel like an old tyrant otherwise. Bossy in the worst way."

She can boss me around anytime, anyway she wants. "I aim to please." Oh my God, where did that come from? Note to self—She's the freakin' CEO, you idiot!

Deliza let go of the pen and turned fully against me on her chair. "You do, huh? Sounds good to me." She reached out and her fingertips reached the front of my neck. A faint difference in the feel of the shirt made me realize she had unbuttoned it.

"Ma'am…" I was tongue-tied again. It was impossible to find the correct words. And it was beyond impossible to call her Deliza.

"Mmm…when you say it like that…I think I changed my mind. Say it again." She purred.

That was a purr! What the hell…? I wasn't sure what it was she wanted me to say, but I couldn't resist her. I couldn't even find it in my heart or mind to refuse. "Eh…ma'am…"

"Yes. Again."

I felt sweat break out on my forehead and it was the sorceress next to me who caused it. I couldn't believe my own reaction. "What are you up to…Ma'am?"

Suddenly she seemed taller, sitting on the chair. Her back straightened, and she let her left hand slide up along my naked arm, slowly, slowly, with enough contact to drive me right up the wall. Up against a wall. Oh, God, yes, with her pressed against me. I could picture her maneuvering me up against a wall, her smaller form challenging my superior muscle strength. Hey, I've always been the aggressor. Where was this coming from? The thought of her dominating me, seducing me…delicious. I swallowed hard, my mouth going from desert dry to salivating in seconds.

"I'll give you the opportunity to say no, Brooke," Deliza murmured huskily and unfastened another button in my shirt. "Truly, I wasn't prepared to address this tonight and if I've misread all your signals, I apologize. I certainly won't hold it against you in any way. If I'm right, and if you want me as much as I want you, all you have to do is say yes."

It felt as if my heart began to drill a hole up through my lungs and into my throat.

Deliza looked at me with a calm I sure didn't feel. "Well?"

"I…I…yes, ma'am?"

"You have to be a little more assertive than that." Deliza rose and walked behind me. She placed her hands on my shoulders, massaging lightly as she spoke. "I've tried to keep my hands off you ever since you stepped into my office the first time. You looked at me with those feral eyes of yours, and dismissed me right away."

"That's not true." I had to confess, because there was an honest pain hidden in her teasing words. "I…I thought you were young. Too young."

"That's a first," she said ironically. "So, what's not true, Brooke?"

"I didn't dismiss you right away. I harnessed my initial reaction when I realized who you were. And no matter what my rep suggests I don't make a habit of seducing my bosses.

Her hands were still on my shoulders, "Well then, your reputation remains intact since I'm the one seducing you. Tell me," she whispered seductively into my ear, "what reaction did you harness?"

There was no room for anything but honesty. In a way, it was a relief to not have to pretend around her. This might still be the biggest career mistake I would ever make, but her initiative had lowered every single one of my defenses. "Sexual attraction."

"I love how you always are so to the point," Deliza laughed. "I've come to depend on you, in your Argus eyes and your unyielding persona."

"So I'm a good warrior to set on the corporate sharks, huh?"

"Yes." She didn't deny the obvious.

I shrugged, but a cold spot grew in my stomach. Is that all I am?

"But that's not all." Deliza answered my unspoken question and pushed her hands forward, in under my collar. She flattened them against my chest, just above my breasts. My nipples hurt and needed human touch, preferably a voracious mouth. "You're so much more. You're an extraordinary person, and…gorgeous. Stunning."

Me? I had heard other compliments, such as strong, impressive, and even handsome. Nobody had called me gorgeous. Or stunning. Instead some of my femme lovers had seemed to find my "rugged good looks," combined with my "dangerous streak," attractive. I leaned my head back against her chest, and her hands slipped further down.

"You haven't quite answered my question," she murmured as her fingers brushed over my sensitive nipples. They twitched and ached like they were skinless under her hands.

"Yes. Yes to everything." There could be no holds barred, no resistance. She's in control. And I surrendered. I never surrender. Ever.

"Excellent." The single word came out in the sexiest whisper I had ever heard. "Let's get you naked then."

Wetness gushed between my legs at her casual remark. This also was a first. I couldn't remember that I'd ever gotten naked before my lover. Lover?

"Stand up." Deliza let go of my screaming nipples and stood to my right as I obeyed.

"Only for a second, little girl, and then I'll make you mine," she continued her seduction. It was erotic as hell to give in, give up, even, but I was pretty sure I'd be back in charge within minutes, but was content to go along with her commands for now.

"Here, let me do it. You obviously need assistance." Nimble fingers undid all the buttons in my shirt and tugged it off my shoulders. The air-conditioned breeze from the ventilation swept over me and made my nipples pulse with a profound ache.

Deliza unfastened my large, tin belt buckle. Stepping so close to me that my nipples inadvertently brushed against her shirt created a new set of beads on my forehead. "Deliza…"

"You know what to call me."

"Yes, ma'am."

She unzipped my fly and pulled the slacks down. I kicked off my pumps, fast, and was about to step out of the slacks when she instead pushed me forward. "Bend over the desk, Brooke. Remain there while I lock the door."

I winced at the idea of being interrupted and caught with my slacks around my ankles. I bent over the desk, pushing the contracts aside and felt the cool cherry-wood surface against my breasts and stomach. My ass exposed, I briefly closed my eyes. I was wet and I knew she'd find out the moment she stepped behind me again.

"Oh, my…look at this. So nice," Deliza whispered. She slid her fingers along my crack, making me shudder and give a soft moan as her fingers approached the drenched area further down. Damn her. Why do I obey like this? I'm normally the one pulling the strings.

Deliza grabbed both my butt cheeks in her small hands and kneaded them with just enough force to make them burn and tingle. "Mm, you feel good. You are almost too good to be true."

Nonplussed at her choice of words, all I could do was feel. I parted my legs, embarrassingly willing when she ploughed her fingertips through my folds. I wanted to spread myself more, but the trousers around my ankles hindered my movements. The desk was now warm against my naked front, and the discomfort of the hard surface somehow added to my climbing arousal.

"So, you're this wet, this wanton, for my touch?" Deliza said huskily. "You are making a mess of my desk. You are so out of control, aren't you?"

My desire, combined with her touch, was driving me insane. I wanted to hiss at her to stop. Her audacity unnerved me but the feelings, the way she touched me…Her fingers explored me without hesitation, as if she had a right to my reaction. Relinquishing control to someone I barely knew on a personal level was something I had never thought I'd ever do. And to her, someone I worked with, who also was my boss, who I had desired from the moment I saw her. I just had never pictured myself in this position, literally! My body reacted all of its own accord and paid no attention to my inner misgivings. I pressed my cheek to the desk and a moan escaped my lips when I suddenly felt pert, naked breasts with small nipples pressing like two little bullets into my back. "Oh, God."

"You like how I feel against you, Brooke?" Deliza whispered, her voice urgent, passionate. "I love how you feel, how you look, the way you're displayed to my touch, to my exploration. How about if I do…this?"

Pleasure stung me out of nowhere when her inquisitive fingers entered me, reaching depths I would have thought impossible for such small hands. My outcry muted to a low gurgle as she began move inside of me, unrelenting despite my pleas. "Ma'am, please…"

"Enough with the 'ma'am.' Call me by my name."

"Deliza." My body was already twitching in preorgasmic preparation. My head spun and the faint scent of furniture polish seemed to go to my head. Or to my sex. I'll go off like a firecracker. I'll embarrass myself by screaming when I come, spread over her freakin' desk like this.

I took a new hold of the edge of the desk. She must've seen my knuckles whitening, because she began moving in and out of me, building up a steady rhythm. "You…feel so good." Her voice was strained now, deeper and huskier. "Brooke…" Small gushes of air came from her pink mouth when she whispered my name, while pressing her head onto the back of my shoulder. "I've dreamed of this. I've dreamed of making you mine, of exploring your body and finding out every one of your secrets. Let me?"

What was she talking about? Any more and she'll hit my larynx, for crying out loud.

"Relax, Brooke. And turn around. I need to see your beautiful face."

With a groan, I pushed up from the desk and her fingers slipped out halfway. I ached for her touch, and didn't want her to pull out completely. Sweating profusely I kicked off my slacks and silk boxers all the way. I maneuvered carefully, turning on the desk and, not without feeling quite proud, managed to swing one leg over her and keep the touch between us.

She was right. It was something entirely different to be able to face her. Deliza's blue eyes had darkened, and this emphasized an otherwise undetectable bright yellow ring around her iris. Her shirt was open, displaying her small breasts with their light pink nipples. I wanted to feel her even more intimately and took hold of her petite waist to pull her closer. Her body remained rigid, eyes still aglow, until she slowly gave in and leaned against me.

"You trying to take charge?" Her voice was noncommittal, but there was an underlying tone of steel.

"No." I let my hands fall. This was her show and she made sure I knew she intended to run it.

"Good. Now, it was still a good idea." She slid her fingers deeper inside me and held onto my shoulder with the other. She nestled closer in between my thighs. "Get comfortable on the desk and then touch me."

I wiggled until the short end of the desk didn't cut into my buttocks anymore and raised both hands to her breasts. I don't know which one of us moaned the loudest when I touched them and felt the hard tips prod my palms. Wetness gushed between my legs when I rolled her nipples between my fingertips, every now and then chafing them slightly with my blunt, unpolished nails.

Her fingers began twisting inside me and when they curled up, finding that exact spot that made my heart thunder and my head spin, I arched against her, never letting go of her nipples for a second.

"Brooke..." Her husky voice rippled along my spine and traveled from my veins to every single small capillary. My hips began to roll to the rhythm drummed up by her fingers.

"My clit...please," I whispered.

"Not yet. Take my shirt off."

I slid both my hands up and pushed the shirt off her arms, letting it spill to the floor. Oh, my God. Perfection. There could never be another word to describe her. Tummy flat, breasts pert and crowned with those delicious nipples. The sight of her made me tremble even harder, and I drew a new breath too fast, too deep, and almost choked. Coughing, I blushed, embarrassed, but she merely leaned against me, and used her free hand to lower me onto the desk.

"Shh. It's okay. I have to have you." Her feverish tone was marginally calmer. There was a hunger, an ache, present that ignited every cell in my body, and perhaps the notion that someone found me that attractive was enough of an aphrodisiac to cause another flood of wetness to emerge between my legs.

Deliza pulled back and examined my eyes, and I wondered what she was looking for. Surely she knew she was in control, that I had surrendered?

"Brooke," she whispered. "I want you to see all of me." "Please…"

Deliza stepped back, slowly removing her fingers, leaving an aching, scorching need that I somehow knew only she could meet. "What…?"

Without answering, she removed her clothes, placing them carelessly on the chair before turning back to me.

I complied. I leaned on my elbows on the desk, not taking my eyes off her when she stood still for a short moment and allowed me to watch her. Soft, thin down cast a dark shadow at the junction between her slender thighs. Her scent was more evident, of citrus and something darker, reminding me of thick velvet. My mouth watered again and I licked my lips slowly.

Deliza grunted, sounding almost as if she was in pain. She placed her hands on my spread knees and pushed them up and further apart. "Spread your legs more for me. That's it."

Unexpectedly shy, I tipped my head back, closed my eyes, and pulled my knees up. Opening my eyes again I watched her stare at my sex for a few seconds and then lean to the side to kiss the inside of my right thigh. She nibbled, licked, and blew her way down to my sex, and I knew I wouldn't last long if she would place that skilled tongue of hers on me. *Oh, please, touch me. No, don't. But yes…*

I felt her soft fingers part my folds and spread them wide. Now I had no more secrets. She knew how wet I was, and I felt shivers come and go in my legs when I felt her breath against me.

"Delicious…"

I whimpered. Since when do I whimper? I make others whimper, damn it! Fuck, I'm putty in her hands. Literally. I couldn't fathom why, but for the first time I trusted another woman with my body. And there have been quite a few women. I refused to be ashamed of that, but I also knew that most of my affairs…had been just that. Affairs. Brooke Cabot just doesn't have time for relationships. And when you itch, you scratch, right? So Deliza Acampora wants to scratch? I wanted to persuade myself that this was all it was about. Rubbing where it ached, like so many times before. I knew even before I considered it further that it was as ridiculous as it sounded. Who in their right mind could only think of the physical aspect of it, when Deliza Acampora was about to place her mouth on their most intimate part?

I whimpered again, almost inaudibly, when I felt her agile tongue lap at me for the first time. Like a hot flame—the term *liquid fire* entered my mind—it slid along my folds, circled my clit without actually touching it. Slowly, slowly, she ran it up and down, from my dark curls to the origin of the copious moisture.

"De…li…za," I hissed, pulling my legs up, spreading myself almost painfully wide. "Take me, please."

"I'm going to do that. And more." Her breath was hot against my center as she spoke.

To hear that voice, dark with passion, almost a growl, coming from such a pretty mouth, was almost more than I could bear. My clit twitched, agonizing arrows of pleasure drilled through my stomach and down my thighs. Oh, God, I need to come. I have to. "Fuck me…"

"All right, babe. All right." Deliza placed her fingers at my entrance, never taking her tongue from me, and pushed inside without any other preliminaries. She filled me completely, with…how many…two, three fingers? I didn't care. All I knew was that she finally was claiming me again, driving me closer to the edge.

I grunted deep in my throat, by now beyond forming any coherent words. I felt her move, but didn't care since she didn't lose contact with my body. Her tongue was still pressed hard against my clit, and her hand pounded in and out of my body, urging me on. I knew I couldn't last much longer, that I would come in this extraordinary woman's presence.

My body wanted to scream in protest when Deliza suddenly moved her mouth from me. "Help me," she said.

My eyes snapped open, and to my surprise I saw that Deliza had somehow managed to climb onto the desk. Sitting on my left side, her hand was still performing its magic. I didn't understand at first, but when she raised her right leg, I knew what she wanted. Eagerly, I let go of my knees and pulled her toward me, across me. With her knees firmly in place on each side of my head, I was now trembling, and sweat trickled from my temples into my hair.

"You know...what to do," Deliza murmured as she leaned down between my legs, twisting her hand to keep up the thrusting motion.

And I did. Greedy for her, I grabbed her buttocks and pulled her down, opening my mouth in anticipations of that sweet nectar. I moved one hand in between her legs, and just as I parted her slick folds, she responded by taking my clit between her teeth, biting down on it, just enough to start my inevitable journey towards orgasmic bliss.

I flattened my tongue against her sex, quickly finding her clit, and devouring it. Instinctively I knew she didn't want to go slow. She needed me to obey, to do as she wished, with no hesitation. I massaged her with my tongue and lips, drank from her as she groaned out loud. The sound reverberated through my engorged sex, and vibrated farther into my body.

My legs began to ache and I hooked them around her, holding her with all my limbs. "Deliza," I managed, muffled against her moist tissues. "I'm going to come."

"Yes."

"It hurts..."

She renewed her efforts and I sucked her hard into my mouth. Small flutters began against my tongue and I realized she was just as close.

"Harder," she groaned.

"Harder..." I pulled her closer and opened my mouth wide, and took as much as I could of her inside.

"Now!"

She didn't have to tell me. Her sex pulsated and she trembled where she lay on top of me. This set me off, and I gave a sharp cry, bucking under her. I felt her other hand reach around my leg and slip into my crack, where she massaged my anus.

I grew rigid with an almost excruciating pleasure shooting from my clit and ass. Bucking wildly now, I still had my mouth locked on her, licking furiously.

"Brooke!" She jerked a few more times and then fell limp onto my body. Slowly, she withdrew her hands and merely cupped my hips, gently kissing my center. "Oh, damn, Brooke."

"Well put," I agreed, my head spinning as I gasped for air. "Damn, indeed."

Deliza managed to turn around and lie down on the desk next to me. "You are amazing."

Me? And this coming from a woman who turned me submissive with just one look, one word? I turned my head and looked at her. I had to smile. Her hair was standing on end and the look on her face was endearing, there was just no other word for it. She looked mischievous and happy at the same time. Her eyes, now returning to normal, searched mine, and I understood that she, despite her tough and take-charge personality, needed some reassuring after the fact.

"And you took everything." I tried to find the right words to describe how I felt. "You made me surrender, and you took me. Nobody's ever done that before, or given me such pleasure." I cringed as I confessed.

Her fairy-looking face brightened. "Never?"

"Nope."

"Well, I have to live up to my name."

"What do you mean?" She has a weird rep that I haven't heard of? Somehow I doubted that.

"My name. The Latin version of Deliza is Delicia. It means 'gives pleasure.'"

"You suit your name well." I finally began relaxing, little by little. "You made me forget my usual hang-ups. Perhaps you've figured out that I'm usually…in charge. This time it was, I mean, you were, very different."

"And so were you. You trusted me."

Boy, are you ever spot on with your observations, boss. You never say die, do you? "I guess. Yes."

"I want to level with you." Her eyes grew serious. "I don't mix business and pleasure."

"I think, in our case, they blend well." I tried a faint smile and pulled her close. I didn't want her to get cold, and since I was still hot from her touches, I was able to warm her.

"I think so, too." Deliza wrinkled her nose and smiled. "I wouldn't want this to be a one-night stand."

Same for me. This can't be over, can it? How could I walk away from this? "You have to make sure it isn't. As for me, I'm not going anywhere." I risked calling it as I saw it. "You need me to negotiate business…and you need me, to show me who's boss. Ma'am." I winked at her, holding my breath.

"You're right. I guess you've made yourself indispensable in more ways than one."

I liked the sound of that.

Deliza leaned over me and cupped my cheek. "Now to something more intimate that I feel one should ask permission to do."

What now? I swallowed. "Yes?"

"It's an act of incredible intimacy."

Really. What is she up to? I only nodded and watched her lean in closer. She pressed her lips onto mine, softly first and then with increasing passion and intensity. I opened my mouth and let her tongue in, caressing me over and over. I returned the kiss and raised my heavy arms to hold her head in place.

She was right. This was a very intimate moment.

"Mm. Now I know all I have to know," she said and pulled back a little.

"And what is that?" I could not take my eyes off her.

Deliza placed a quick kiss on the tip of my nose. Another first. "I made the correct decision when I hired you."

yolanda's sports bra

●

kate dominic

I live heteromonogamously. Happily so. But my spouse and I have agreed fantasy is not cheating. What happens in dreams is just that—dreaming.

I'm not sure where my fantasies about Yolanda fit in. I don't even know if that's her real name. Seeing her was very real, though, as was fantasizing about her while I watched her at the gym. I'd never done that before—fantasized about someone while I was looking at her. After, yes. But not while I watched a soccer game. Not two days later, while I dutifully trod along on a treadmill in the back row of the cardio room, ignoring my book and watching rounded feminine hips rocking side to side on the stair-stepper in front of me. I could almost see underneath the low-slung gray sweats, to where the tiny black thong dipping below her waistband pulled tight and rubbed hard between her bottom cheeks.

When I realized how fast I was "fast walking" while watching her, I made the executive decision that observational fantasies were also in the category of "it's hot, it really turns me on, and it doesn't hurt anybody—so it's damn well okay!" I'm certain Yolanda didn't even know I was there. She was busy playing and working out. I was busy watching her. Left, Right, Left, Right, my shoes hitting the treadmill as she climbed, my eyes blurring as I focused on an empty flagpole high up on the wall and discovered just how nice exercising could be while I watched the real "Yolanda" segue inside my head into the woman in my dreams.

I want to be Yolanda's sports bra. To the sounds of squeaking sneakers and a soccer ball slamming off the gym walls, I'd cup her heavy, rounded breasts in my hands. I'd cuddle her with firm, tender support as she raced up and down the shiny wooden floor. My Yolanda's a digger. As she kicked and ducked and slid under the defender's outstretched arms, I'd lick the sweat from her cleavage, burying my face in the lightly perfumed scent of her skin. Honeysuckle. Just a hint. From her soap. But as I licked and her sweat-warmed skin got hotter, the smell would intensify. I'd rub her nipples, allowing just the tiniest bit of friction when she was running hard. My soft lycra fibers would stroke her large, tender nipples, like the fingers of an insistent lover intent on bringing her pleasure each time her chest rose and fell when she yelled, "Here!"

As her sweat wet me, I'd tongue her nipples to hungry peaks. I'd put just enough scrape and salt in my kisses to make her shrug her shoulders, maybe make her run her hands unconsciously down the front of her shirt in silent acknowledgment that I was bringing her as much pleasure as the throbbing pump of blood and endorphins coursing through her veins.

I want to be Yolanda's hair scrunchie. When she runs up and down the court, I'd give her curvy butt a gentle love pat. Tap, tap, tap—each time the tip of her long brown braid swayed gently from one side of her ass to the other. Tap, tap, tap—to the rhythm of her shoes as she bounced from left to right, running hard. When she dug into a corner, I'd give her a quick snap, a spank that would leave just the lightest pink beneath the clinging knit of her gym shorts.

My mark would be gone by the time she climbed into the shower. Then I'd kiss her again, tenderly, on the same spot. Tap, tap, tap—on her naked bottom. Tap, tap, tap—spanking her just to make her shiver. Just because I liked it.

I want to be Yolanda's workout thong. I'd brush over her pubic hair, tugging her soft dark curls between her legs. I'd inch my way up the crack of her ass as she climbed the stair-stepper machine. Up, down. Up, down. Slipping up to kiss her pretty pink pucker with each step. Rub, kiss. Rub, kiss. I'd work my way up in front as well, into the sweat-dampened recesses of her sweet, musky pussy. I'd slide between her slippery wet lips, soaking up her pussy juice as my sweaty fibers rubbed her hooded nub. Up, down. Back and forth. Rub, kiss. Stroke, tease.

With each step, I'd ease my way tighter, further up into her slit. I'd rub like a relentless finger, like a determined lover with a girlfriend who's a hard come. I'd press against her clit whispering, "I'm not going to stop, sweetheart. Keep climbing. Higher. Let me make you shiver. Pump your legs. Up. Down. Up. Down. I'm rubbing your hood back and forth. I'm going to keep rubbing until your pretty clitty peeks out at me, until it pokes up hard and hungry. Oh, sweetheart, I'm going to make you come so hard. I promise."

I'd smear her juices over that exquisitely silky smooth nub of nerves, rubbing her slippery juices over her clit as she climbed the stairs, as her hair tapped against her rhythmically moving bottom. Up, down. Up, down. I'd rub her clit until it was almost too tender to be touched. Almost. I'd rub until her sweat and pussy juice flowed so freely the moisture wicked up in back to join the sweaty cloth still kissing her anus. Up, up, up, baby. Rub, rub. Lick, kiss. Up, down. Up, up, up.

And over.

My Yolanda's clear, sweet juice would squirt into me as she shuddered hard. She'd grab the bars of the stair-stepper machine, turning her hands so they were gripping backwards. The gold of her rings and bracelets would shimmer. She'd thrust her chest out, nipples pressing hard into her sports bra, then into the clinging, sweaty, ribbed white cotton of her exercise T. As she breathed hard, I'd once more work my magic on her nipples and between her legs and deep up into the crack of her bottom. I'd do her like we were the only ones in the crowded, sweat-thick room. I'd do her so she liked it so good, she couldn't help coming. Again.

I'd sigh with contentment when the machine finally hissed down to the floor. In the mirror, I'd watch Yolanda's back. I'd see the tiny black triangle of fabric outlined through the clinging gray knit of her sweatpants. The point of the triangle aimed down to where her now juice-soaked thong slid in between her cheeks. In the mirror the other people would see only damp gray sweatpants cuddling the strong, muscular, smoothly rounded orbs of my Yolanda's perfect ass. Only Yolanda would know how tightly I still rubbed up into her crotch—kissing, always kissing.

I want to be Yolanda's soap. The locker room would be quiet this time of night. When she stepped into the shower, the warm spray would pulse over her skin. Her fingers would slide over me. Strong and supple, her fingers would bring my juices and oils to the surface, drawing out the scent of honeysuckle, until her fingers were slick with me. She'd rub me over her neck and shoulders, over the top of her chest and down over luscious breasts. They'd be hanging freely now, swaying heavily and glistening in the tantalizing water. As the warmth drew her heat up, she'd rub me over her nipples. She'd smile as they perked to my laving tongue. She'd pause a moment to let me tease them, to let me get them slick and sweet-smelling so she could milk them in her tugging fingers, so her fingers could suckle them to hard, hungry peaks.

Yolanda would draw me down to where her scent was strongest—there, under the weight of her beautiful, heavy breasts. She'd slide me under her arms, then back over her nipples, smiling just because my kisses felt so good.

Then she'd let me glide down over her belly. I'd give her navel a quick bath, then move down between her legs. I'd shampoo her pubic hair with my sudsing bubbles. Not for long, though. My Yolanda would be antsy to slide me further down. When her pubic hair was lathered thick with the scent of my perfume, she'd draw me deep into her slit. She'd rub me between her cunt lips, and I'd be in heaven. I'd lick her clit and her labia, kissing first the outsides, then teasing inside. Teasing against the mouth of her pussy. I'd tongue her all over, kissing in delicate, ladylike licks, then swiping in great, hungry, slurps. I'd draw her taste onto my tongue until her pussy juices mingled with my swirling honeyed suds. I'd wash her like she was melting ice cream on a sweltering summer day and I did not want to miss a single drop of her sweetness.

I'd reach back, my tongue stretching for her wrinkled pink pucker, but I wouldn't reach it. I'd wonder why, then I would be back on the soap dish, alone and watching.

Oh, god, I want to be Yolanda's shaver. She'd stand with one foot on the shower chair, spreading her legs as she stroked my gleaming silver blade over her dark pussy curls. They'd fall away in clumps, swirling over the shower floor and into the drain as she stroked down and down and down. My bared blade would glide gently and ruthlessly over her soap-slippery pussy lips, peeling away the hair until she was smooth as peaches on a hot summer day, sweet as mangos and kumquats, juicy as passion fruit. My Yolanda would be so smooth and sweet and juicy. When her hand slipped, she'd jerk at my quick, biting sting. My tears would flow silently into the water as a single tiny red droplet washed away to the floor.

Yolanda's pussy lips would be hypersensitive now. She'd put down her razor and take my slippery, soapy body back into her hands. This time, she'd moan as she slid me between her legs. My honeysuckle oils would mingle with her pussy juices. Her fingers would rub fiercely, using my juices to moisten her slippery cunt even more, to tease her clit from its hood with her thumb as her fingers slid into her pussy. Spreading her legs wide, my Yolanda would squat back in the steaming spray, the shower beating on her chest and nipples. She'd take my soapy body in her other hand and reach in back of herself.

Yes! Oh, yes! With her fingers still fucking her pussy, with her thumb rubbing her clit and her fingers working her slit, my sweetheart would finally let me kiss her quivering pucker. She'd rub me hard against it. I'd tongue her pucker fiercely, laving its wrinkled pink lips with my slippery body, reaching for more of her heat as I slid further up. Yolanda would inhale deeply, slicking her finger quickly over me. And as she exhaled, she'd press the pad of her finger against her beautiful, shivering pucker. With a long, low groan, she'd slide her finger in.

I want to be Yolanda's fingernail polish. Cherry red and glistening on the tips of each short, well-manicured nail, I'd slip inside her pussy and her ass. I'd slide on honeysuckled soap deep into my lover's hidden pleasure zones. I'd ride her pussy walls and inside her ass, stroking her tender places, riding her thumb over her clit as she pressed and rubbed and fucked herself with her fingers. When she stiffened in the pulsing wet heat, I'd spur her fingers on, exhorting them to keep moving, moving, moving, as she bucked into the steaming streams of water.

"Oh, yes!" she'd moan, arching as she wiggled her fingers wildly. My Yolanda would pump and rub until suddenly her pussy and ass clamped hard around me. She'd cry out, her thumb grinding as she groaned and shuddered, as her taut, strong muscles squeezed me so hard I saw stars. As they squeezed and squeezed and squeezed and her slippery juices once more rolled down over me.

Yolanda would lean forward in the shower, her face resting against the wall. She'd laugh softly and draw her fingers from her still quivering holes. As I rode her trembling fingertips, she'd wash once more, this time quickly, and step from the shower.

I want to be Yolanda's towel. I'd rub her face and hair, down her arms and over her gently heaving breasts. I'd inhale the fresh-washed scent of her still-steaming and well-satisfied pussy and ass. I'd dry her trembling legs and feet.

I want to be Yolanda's panties as she pulls them up over her newly shaved pussy. I want to kiss her pussy with silky lips each time she walks. I want to be Yolanda's lacy bra and her crisp cotton T-shirt and the jeans she's worn so often they fit like they were molded to her skin. I want to be her leather boots and the shimmering band she slips into her still wet hair.

Tonight, I will go home to my spouse and my usual life. And I will be happy there. But sometime after the moon has set, when even the cats are quiet and just a hint of honeysuckle tickles my nose, I will dream I am Yolanda's membership card, resting comfortably in her hip pocket while I wait for the next time we slip into the gym to work out together, hard and long and sweet.

now arriving

●

therese szymanski

I raced through the parking lots of LAX, trying to figure out where to park. I glanced at my watch: 3 p.m. Her plane should have landed ten minutes ago. Shelly had given me screwed-up directions to the airport, and I had had to drive eighty miles an hour in my bright red Jeep Cherokee while simultaneously ripping through the glovebox and trying to read maps.

At times like these that I wish I was better with either directions or maps. Or that I at least had the appropriate maps, instead of Utah and Alabama and a road atlas that was far too generalized for such a thing as finding an airport.

At least I had looked up when the road signs announced the direction for LAX. Occasionally I get lucky.

Like the night I first met Heather. Well, we hadn't actually met. We wouldn't meet until I parked the car and found her in the myriad concourses of the airport, but the night we first typed to each other was about two months ago. I had just gotten home from a twelve-hour shift as a scrub nurse at my current assignment in Redondo Beach, California. I got home and decided that a cold beer and a bit of time online was just what I needed to calm down enough to sleep after a hard night of brains, guts and gore.

As a single female in a city far, far away from my hometown of Huntsville, Alabama, I was tempted to go out to West Hollywood to meet some women of my particular persuasion, but I was hesitant. I didn't know anybody out here, and I was still rather new to the entire lifestyle. After all, it wasn't quite a year since I broke up with my fiancé, and I'd only had two female lovers since then, one of whom was one of my best friends back home, in a short-lived affair. The other one was a woman I worked with at a prior assignment as a traveling medical specialist: that was an ill-fated relationship.

And so there I was, alone on a Saturday night with just my computer to keep me company. And whomever I might find on it.

I was playing around in a few different lesbian chatrooms, trying to find somebody who wasn't a horny guy, when suddenly there was a pinging noise and a little window opened up on my computer screen:

Hey honey!

I didn't recognize the screen name, but she was acting as if she knew me, and by quickly checking out her online profile, I realized she was a lesbian who lived in Atlanta, where I was hoping to have my next assignment. Because she didn't immediately give out her measurements or ask for cybersex, I decided to chat with her for a few minutes.

About fifteen minutes later we realized that it was a case of mistaken identity—she had a friend who had a screen name quite similar to my own, so when she saw me in a lesbian chatroom she thought I was a friend she hadn't spoken with in quite a while.

I got off the plane and looked around, excited to finally be meeting the woman with the soft and exciting Southern accent. Just thinking about that sultry voice sent shivers down my spine.

Back during my hour-long layover in Denver I had called her in a last-minute surge of fear. My heart was pounding the blood through my body, and I felt like I might throw up. I was having trouble breathing. What if she really wasn't who she said she was? What if the picture she e-mailed me, a pic supposedly of her and her ex, wasn't really her? What if she was some crazed psycho and this would all end up on the Jerry Springer show?

I really didn't want to throw chairs or have chairs thrown at me on national TV.

Calling from Denver, I suggested maybe it wasn't such a great idea to meet. I was almost there, and common sense was kicking in, telling me that I was going all the way across the country to meet some strange woman I really didn't know much at all about. Everyone knew how all these things turned out—you fly across the country, move to another state, and you end up either dead or dumped because she wasn't who she said she was.

That same fear spread through me now, coursing through my veins—but this time it was joined by a ripple of excitement. Hearing her voice again in Denver momentarily made everything seem so much better as she calmed me down and convinced me to continue my journey. It's amazing where your imagination can take you when you have a few hours up in the sky with only screaming babies, metallic voices over intercoms, and tired stewardesses to keep you company.

In the air, just hours away from the meeting that I had looked forward to since booking the flight a few weeks ago, it seemed that every magazine had a story about online romances gone wrong—where people weren't who they said they were, or kidnapped and killed their unsuspecting prey. I wondered just who I was going to meet. I could only hope it wasn't Jane the Ripper. Or some old, tired couple looking for a threesome.

I set aside the magazines and closed my eyes, remembering…and trying to imagine the voice I had heard, the woman I knew, as the one in the picture she had shown me.

But as I departed the airplane, I glanced around and didn't see the woman in the picture. Here I was, standing alone, after having flown across the country for her. My mind raced over the past two months. After the case of mistaken identity, we had talked for several hours online. Our online chatting became frequent, each of us planning on when we could chat next, until we finally began calling each other on the phone, running up exorbitant phone bills. The sound of her voice always sent chills running through my body now.

But there's something about talking on the computer, when you can't see each other, can't hear each other, and don't know each other. You feel safe and protected and know that all you need to do to cut off communication with this person is to hang up your modem. She's not a real person, so she's not a real part of your life, so there is nothing to lose if she suddenly drops out of your life.

Because of this layer of protection you can either pretend to be someone you're not, or else you can be yourself in all your dirty clothing and bad habits. It's an all-or-nothing game oftentimes in cyberspace.

Heather and I decided to play it on the "all" side of things, or so I thought, and kept on thinking even when we shared all of our secrets, all of our past and who we were, first on the computer and then on the telephone.

And all the while I had been slowly falling for this shy, soft-spoken, young Alabama blonde.

When she first told me she had blonde hair and green eyes, I didn't believe her. After all, 95 percent of all folks online are blonde with either green or blue eyes. Or so they say.

But as I glanced around me now, I didn't see the sexy little figure I had seen in the pic, nearly doubled-over in laughter in her now ex-girlfriend's arms.

I had been dissed by the woman who knew me better than anyone, by the woman I thought I knew best of all

I ran up to the gate, afraid she was upset with me, or maybe wasn't there, but then I saw her.

She hadn't had a pic to send me, but her description was accurate, even if it didn't do her justice. Her shoulder-length black hair shone with a glossy sheen, highlighting her softly cut features. Her rich skin was luscious and creamy, bespeaking her Asian heritage while giving her an exotic mystique. Her neat, dark skirt suit showed off her finely toned legs and slender dancer's figure. I could easily imagine that body on a stage in New York, dancing on Broadway. Her every movement told the story of her past, a past in which she was a classically trained ballerina, able to dance anything.

My mouth almost dropped open as I looked at her. My imagination quickly did its own thing, imagining this lithe, beautiful woman in bed with me, her slender body pressing against me, her flesh soft against mine. I tried to regain my composure as I met her deep brown eyes.

This was the woman who had flown across America for me, the woman who was supposed to drive back across the country with me as I relocated from L.A. to Atlanta. The woman I'd spent countless hours with online and on the phone, the woman I'd confessed so much of my past to, with whom I'd shared so many insecurities, doubts, fears, and finally so much love with. I had fallen in love with a woman I had never met.

And she was now standing just a few feet in front of me. I could now reach out and touch her, and not just in Ameritech's sterilized version of such.

I had been so excited to finally meet her that I hadn't slept in the past two nights. Regardless, I ran my hand down over the light dress I had specially chosen in dressing up for the occasion of our first meeting, making sure it was tidy and neat. I wished I had had a chance to double-check my makeup before rushing from the car into the airport.

"Heather?" she asked, meeting my eyes.

I dumbly nodded my response, moving forward into her embrace. It seemed somehow unreal, to finally be meeting her, though I had longed for this moment since we first decided that she would come out to California to meet me and help me drive back to my new home in Atlanta.

I couldn't pull my eyes from her. At the luggage carousel she caught me checking her out. All I could think was, "My God, what was Malibu Barbie doing online?" The woman was drop-dead gorgeous with long, sun-bleached blonde hair, deeply tanned skin, tantalizing green eyes, and a slim figure with teasing curves in all the right places.

I was almost tongue-tied. I felt like a complete dork. We had talked so much, so easily over the computer and then on the phone, and here I was without a thing to say. I was worried I didn't live up to her expectations—that one look at me had told her that I wasn't who she imagined I was.

But then I realized that she, too, was checking me out. And suddenly I felt warm all over. Especially between my legs.

She asked all the appropriate questions about my flight, and I gave the appropriate responses. She apologized for being late, and I said it was no problem. She helped me carry my luggage to the car, and I let her.

My fears had all but vanished, especially since there was no place in that dress of hers to fit anything even remotely lethal, but I did briefly wonder how this was going to work out because we were both so femme.

But when her looks warmed me to my core, I knew there really was nothing to worry about. Her looks warmed me the same way seeing her screen name appear on my buddy list had, the same way hearing her voice had. But now we were with each other and I ached to do what we had done on the computer and on the phone—I wanted to do those things that thus far we had only talked and typed about doing.

Heather had already given up her apartment in preparation for her move. She was staying her last few days with her coworker Shelly, who was also a lesbian. Because she didn't want to admit how we had met, she had told Shelly that I was an old friend, and that we had decided to date.

Introductions were made and Shelly quickly excused herself, saying she had some errands to run. I think she had just noticed the looks Heather and I were exchanging. I don't think anybody with a clue could've mistaken those looks. Even I was able to fully interpret the signs Heather was giving me, enough so that I was wondering who was going to make the first move, even as I worried that it might have to be me, and I had never been the one to make the first move before.

Being the proper Southern hostess, Heather started by giving me a tour of Shelly's house, but we only made it as far as Shelly's bedroom.

Heather opened the door, "And this is Shelly's bedroom." She started to close it, but she was standing so close to me that her perfume made my head swim. Earlier I couldn't keep my eyes off her legs, her full breasts, her slender waist, her beautiful face. Now I couldn't stay away from her lips. I just had to have them. I had to know if they really were as soft as I had always imagined they were.

We're about the same height, so it was easy to lean forward and press my lips against hers. She moaned softly and opened them, pulling me into her arms. All I could think about was how warm and inviting her mouth was, how soft her lips and tongue were against my own. But my hands had a mind of their own as they traversed across her body. I wanted all of her right now.

I don't think either of us led or followed, but the next thing I knew we were lying on Shelly's bed and I couldn't get Jade's clothes off fast enough. She tried to pull mine off, but I was intent on seeing all of that rich skin and finally tasting this woman.

I had fantasized about this moment so long and wanted it so much, it was like an explosion going off. My heart was beating hard and fast and my breath was jagged. I was in my body, but I wasn't in charge. I didn't think, I just experienced.

I didn't hear any doors open, but the next thing I knew Jade was gasping. Shelly had several mirrors in the room, and it just so happened that they were angled in such a way that when she walked into the bedroom, she had a front-row view of Jade spread out on her bed. And I mean that Jade was spread out with no secrets left. And Jade knew it, but I had her so close to the edge that she couldn't even think of doing anything but gasping.

I guess getting caught is a theme with us. The next morning we started on our cross-country drive with every intention in the world of behaving, but we couldn't seem to keep our hands off each other.

We stopped for lunch in Flagstaff, Arizona, on our first day out.

Throughout lunch we looked at maps and discussed timetables and routes and how the food and weather were, but all the while I'm sure Jade had more than a few other things on her mind. The same things that were on my mind. After so many months of wanting to touch her and be with her, I now had the chance, and I couldn't stop trying to make up for the lost time. Each time we touched it was like an explosion—the passion and sensuousness of each encounter was enough to about make me explode.

"I need to use the restroom," Jade said, giving me a suggestive look, teasing me with those brown eyes as I paid the bill. Because we're both femmes, it made perfect sense and didn't arouse any attention at all when I accompanied her.

Jade walked into the fluorescent-lit room and quickly peered under the doors to all the stalls before she turned toward me and, with one finger, gestured for me to follow her. She went into a stall, flushed the toilet, and turned back to me with the stall door open.

She grinned as her fingers danced over her shirt buttons, slowly opening her green silk blouse as the toilet flushed. I could almost hear striptease music in the background; it played in my head, at least, while she dropped the blouse down a bit, revealing her silky black bra. She licked her lips and ran her hands down over her hips, moving suggestively before she unsnapped her jeans and began to pull down the zipper, my eyes locked on her fingers for every inch of the long, torturous journey.

I longed to pull her forward into my arms, to feel that skin against my own, to slip my fingers into her silken wetness...

And still the toilet flushed.

"Sonofabitch!" a woman screamed. I glanced down toward the floor of Jade's stall and realized the water was overflowing from the toilet and onto the floor, a floor on which, just a few feet over, a woman was using the next stall. Her pants were close enough to the floor that they were probably getting soaked. Jesus, she must've been taking one helluva dump that she had been in there for so long!

But Jade really ought to learn to check things out better.

I couldn't stop wanting, stop touching Heather—even while we were doing eighty on the interstate, so that I had to slide up next to her and run my hand up and down her lusciously long thigh, play my tongue around her ear and delectable collarbone, slide my fingers down her bra to tease her already taut and wanting nipple, or to pull her shirt up out of her jeans so that I could feel the firm flesh of her abs before slowly pulling down her zipper, slipping my hands inside her pants, and then sliding them into her. I had my way with her in so many ways throughout the entire trip, sometimes to the amusement and voyeuristic fulfillment of the truck drivers who drove next to us on our long trip.

After Flagstaff we didn't stop with our restroom antics, even if it meant propping ourselves up against the door so that we could stop any unwelcome intruders, or at least have a heads-up when they tried to push their way into our little den of iniquity.

I don't know how many women we startled when we walked into highway rest stops along the route with our keys jangling, or when they heard our barely disguised moans coming from another stall in the bathroom. God knows we were sometimes spooked after dark when such things happened to us!

What I do know is just how sleep-deprived we were when we finally reached Atlanta, because every night we got to sleep late, and got back on the road later than planned the next day, and not because we had overslept.

I couldn't get enough of this extremely sexy woman. I couldn't taste her enough, with her sweet, intoxicating juices that were like nectar on my tongue, her musky scent that surrounded me and filled me like her fingers and tongue so often did. I loved her soft yet firm flesh with its teasing tan lines around the parts of her I especially enjoyed touching and tasting, loving the way whatever I did there caused her to writhe and moan. The way her soft Southern accent slid around silky words just after she came was enough to make me wet, but that was nothing compared to what that sultry voice raised in a moan could do to me.

And the way she touched me was nothing short of heaven. It was as if she could read my mind, knowing just what I wanted, what I needed, each step of the way—whether it be to have her tongue tease my nipples just a little longer, or maybe even lightly nibble on them with her teeth, or whether I needed her inside me right then, or just needed for her to taste me and to enjoy my taste and feel.

It was the most highly charged, incredibly erotic time of my life, and I enjoyed every moment of it.

But then one night we got a motel room along the way. We lay in bed, our naked bodies still hot and sweaty, sharing a single cigarette. The flashing of the highway motel sign was the only light besides the ember of our cigarette. And that was when I looked deeply into those emerald green eyes. For the first time I didn't just look at them or into them, but I looked into Heather herself.

I had touched her in so many ways, and she me, but this was by far the most intimate moment we had shared.

I knew I had been falling in love with her when we were still talking online, before I even knew what her voice sounded like, but here, in this motel by the interstate, I looked into her and knew I loved her.

And when she looked at me, I knew that she, too, was looking into me, and loving me as well.

I leaned forward and kissed her, my black hair brushing her blonde, our bodies tightly together, and our eyes wide open. I looked into her as we kissed, as our tongues met and danced, and I knew this was what I had been waiting for.

Heather gave a cute little chuckle and nudged Jade while winking at me. "These days we mostly fall asleep in bed with our books on our laps." They're now living, together, in Atlanta, and working full-time, together, while going to school full-time, together. They've adopted two dogs and one cat, together.

"I'd still like it twenty-four seven," Jade says, relaxing into Heather's arms. She still has her slender dancer's figure.

"One of my friends wonders what two femmes do in bed together, I mean, besides paint each other's toenails," I say, my ankle crossed over my knee as I sink into the deep couch, sipping my Miller Lite. The singer has quit for the night, and now low music is playing in the sports-bar atmosphere of My Sister's Room, voices of other women's conversations swell as they enjoy the mild Atlanta night.

The two women look at each other. "Pluck each other's eyebrows!" they say, together.

picture this

●

kristina wright

I don't know when I first realized I liked girls. I just always remember having crushes on my girlfriends, imagining what it would be like to kiss their soft lips and to touch their bodies the way I touched my own. It wasn't until I was nineteen that I got to experience my adolescent fantasies and discovered that reality was infinitely more fun than daydreaming.

I was working in a photo shop near the beach in Fort Lauderdale, going to college part-time in the evening and learning the sex secrets of Canadian tourists during the day. Honestly, I learned more from the tourists than I learned from my professors, so it's not surprising I dropped out of college a year later and spent another ten years figuring out what I wanted to do with my life.

Tina Marie was the tech chick who fixed our photo equipment when it broke down (as it seemed to do on a monthly basis). She was a few years older than me and had short dark hair, a compact, well-muscled body from daily runs on the beach, and a Cuban heritage that had bequeathed to her an olive complexion, a husky accent, and a determination to get what she wanted. Lucky for me, the summer after I turned nineteen she decided I was what she wanted. It took her long enough, that's for sure. I'd known her for over a year, and we'd gotten to be casual work friends, talking and teasing enough to know that we liked each other. I was too shy to make the first move, and she seemed to take great pleasure in driving me crazy.

I'd called Tina Marie to come take a look at our film processor because the thing was clanking and banging along, filling the air with the peculiar smell of smoking chemicals. She showed up within the hour, swaggering into the lab wearing battered jeans with the knees ripped out and a thin white T-shirt over a sports bra.

July in Florida is an incongruous blend of sticky humidity outside and chilly air conditioning inside. Every business and restaurant seems to keep the thermostat on frigid, and our lab was no different. It was impossible not to notice Tina Marie's nipples poking out in the icy cold room. I tried hard not to stare as I explained the equipment problem to her, but she noticed the direction of my gaze.

"I know, I should wear something heavier, but it's fucking hot out there."

I laughed. "Sorry."

She shrugged it off. "I'd rather have *you* looking at me than the assholes at the main lab. Those third-shifters are freaks."

I left Tina Marie to wrangle with the processor while I helped customers and printed photos and tried not to make a fool out of myself while I watched her work. Douglas, the guy who worked evenings, came in about an hour into Tina Marie's visit. He ogled her ass as she bent over to reconnect the processor and let out a low whistle. The hum of the machinery was loud enough to keep Tina Marie from hearing him, but I still poked him in the ribs.

"Knock it off, Douglas."

"Sorry. Hard not to admire the scenery," he said with a toothy grin.

Douglas was a geeky photo tech with raging hormones and an impressive collection of dirty pictures acquired after years of making duplicates of naughty tourists' exploits. In other words, he was an utterly harmless pervert.

"You're not her type," I whispered as Tina Marie finished reconnecting everything.

"I know. You are," he said.

I didn't bother to argue, because Tina Marie was standing there looking at us. "He's right," she said with a grin.

I blushed and fumbled a stack of honeymoon pictures, sending them fluttering to the floor. The three of us knelt to pick them up and Tina Marie handed me the last picture, which happened to be a close-up shot of the bride's bare breasts.

"Uh, thanks," I said, my face still burning as I took the photo from her and stood up.

"Yours are nicer."

Douglas wandered off, whistling softly under his breath as he gave me a "told you so" look.

"Well, thanks," I said again. She had me completely flustered. "Um, I'm going to lunch. Want to come with me?"

"Can't. I've got three more calls this afternoon, and if I don't leave now, I'll be at it all night."

"Oh." I felt like an idiot. I was just thankful Douglas wasn't standing there, making choking gestures. "Okay. Maybe another time."

"How about dinner when you get off work?"

That caught me by surprise. "Oh, um, yeah, that would be great."

"Cool. I'll meet you back here around five, okay?"

I nodded, unable to do anything but grin like a fool. I spent the rest of the afternoon in a daze. A happy, giddy, lustful daze. Even Douglas's teasing about making lesbo porn couldn't get to me.

I got tied up with a customer at four fifty-five and it was nearly twenty minutes after five before I could leave. Tina Marie was nowhere to be seen, and I could feel my good mood slipping away as I hung up my lab coat. It was Douglas who noticed the truck parked next to my car, and the hot-looking dyke leaning against it.

"Go get 'er, tiger," he said with a smack on my ass.

If I hadn't liked Douglas so much, and been so intent on getting to Tina Marie, I might have smacked him back. As it was, I just giggled and bounced out the door.

"Hey, thought I was going to have to come in and drag you out," she said.

"Sorry." There was no point in pretending to be cool because I was still grinning like an idiot. "But I'm here now."

She gave me the once over, slowly. "Yes, you are. Where to?"

"Whereever," I said. "I'm easy."

"Good." She grinned. "I know the perfect place."

The perfect place turned out to be a little diner with oyster shells on the floor and an open-air deck with an ocean view. We split a pitcher of beer and munched on fried clam strips as the dinner crowd came and went. It was well after nine by the time we were heading out to her truck at the far end of the parking lot. The temperature had dropped a few degrees, but the humidity was still high, making my shirt stick to my skin.

Tina Marie unlocked my door, and I thought she was leaning past me to open it, but instead she turned her head and kissed me. Her mouth was warm and tasted of beer, and I shivered when her tongue stroked my lips. She sucked my bottom lip into her mouth and I could swear I felt the sensation in my clit. I whimpered and pressed against her, feeling her nipples hard against mine in a way that had nothing to do with the air temperature.

We stood there, more or less plastered against the side of her truck, for several long, glorious minutes. I tucked my hands in her back pockets and held her close, reluctant to let her go now that I had her. My world shrunk to Tina Marie and her mouth on mine. I could feel myself getting wet, my cunt hot and swollen. I was barely conscious of the fact that I was rubbing against her thigh as she stroked my sweat-slick skin under my shirt.

She pulled back, breathing almost as hard as I was. Her dark brown eyes looked black under the dim streetlight. "I want to take you to my place. Is that cool?"

"Uh huh," I murmured against her neck. My hands were still buried in her jeans pockets and I made no effort to move them. "In a minute."

She put her hand on the back of my neck and gave my hair a little tug. "In a minute?"

"Yeah, in a minute," I said. "I'm not done kissing you."

I pulled her closer, feeling the hard edge of the door handle digging into my back. I didn't care as long as she was pressing against my front. We kissed for what felt like hours, until I was nearly panting with need. This time, I was the one who pulled back.

"Let's go," I said.

"Not yet." She nibbled my neck just below my ear. "I'm not finished with you yet."

I groaned in frustration. "Please?"

She laughed. "In a minute."

I opened my mouth to argue, but she did two things that prevented me from saying a word: she kissed me again and unbuttoned my pants. I gasped into her mouth as I felt her hand slide down the front of my pants and into my underwear. Her fingers found my wet, swollen clit and my entire body went rigid as she stroked me.

"Oh god," I moaned.

"Still want to leave?"

I shook my head, digging my hands into her ass. "Don't stop."

She didn't. Instead, she anchored me to her with one hand around my waist and the other down my pants. It was all I could do to remain upright as she played with me. If it weren't for her holding me up, I probably would have slid down the side of the truck and melted in a puddle in front of her.

She sucked on my neck, whispering to me in between nibbles. "You want me, baby? You want to get fucked right here in the parking lot?"

Part of me, the rational, reasonable part of me, was freaking out at the possibility of getting caught fooling around in public. The other part of me, the wet, horny part, didn't really give a damn if the entire city was sitting in beach chairs, munching on popcorn and watching Tina Marie get me off.

"Fuck me," I said, ignoring rational thought in favor of an earth-shattering orgasm.

"Good girl."

I tucked my head into her shoulder and closed my eyes as she slipped two fingers inside of me. She pulled them out and rubbed them, slick with my juices, over my clit. I whimpered and moaned against her, every muscle in my body screaming for release. Over and over, she repeated the motion, her fingers going deep inside of me before returning to my quivering, aching clit.

Finally, as if sensing I was at the breaking point, Tina Marie palmed my crotch and gave it a hard squeeze. I bucked against her, pressing my cunt up to her hand and gripping her shoulders as tightly as she was grabbing me. She pushed two fingers into me, never letting up on my clit. Standing there like that, with my pants now down around my ankles, Tina Marie's hand in my panties, and her fingers in my cunt, I came.

She didn't release her grip on me even when I pushed so hard against her we nearly fell over. She braced herself, holding me against the truck and riding out my orgasm with me. Every twitch of her fingers inside of me, every squeeze and release of her hand against my clit, sent ripples through my entire body. It was the longest orgasm I'd ever experienced, and when it was over, I couldn't do anything but lean against her and try to catch my breath.

Finally, I came to my senses and realized where we were and that it was very possible that someone had seen what we were up to. Tina Marie said something, but the blood was still roaring in my ears.

"What?" I asked, still trying to catch my breath.

She kissed me softly on the lips. "I said, are you ready to go back to my place now?"

I was but I wasn't sure I could move yet. So I just shook my head and smiled. "In a minute."

the flying hat

●

madlyn march

I studied journalism with two distinguished professors; worked as an editor on my school newspaper; won a college journalism award; wrote articles for publications in my spare time; and interned at one of the top publications in the country. I deserved—and desperately wanted—to be a glamorous editorial assistant at a big-time magazine in Manhattan. There was just one small problem: nobody wanted to hire me.

So I decided that if I couldn't be on the staff of a magazine, then I'd be a freelance writer. I began getting assignments, but, unfortunately, they weren't the kind that paid very well. I realized there was no way I'd be able to support myself on what I was making by writing. So after I saw an ad for a position at a nonprofit organization in Brooklyn—not even the hip part of Brooklyn, mind you—I sent in a resume. Shortly after, a woman from the office that placed the ad called me, asking if I could come in for an interview. But the position she wanted me for was practically full-time. I realized that if I took this job, I'd hardly have any time to write. So I told the woman I wasn't interested in the interview.

When I told my father I had refused the interview, he reminded me that I didn't live too far from the office and could write when I came home from work. Well, I thought, maybe he's right. (One day, when I come out to him—probably in the year 2066—I'm going to thank him for pushing me to take that job.)

So I called the woman back and recanted my no. Luckily, she wasn't mad and set up an appointment.

The interview was going well. I liked her. I sensed she liked me. And then a baseball cap flew past my head.

An obviously butch girl had just thrown her hat clear across the room. Ok, I thought. That was weird.

The woman interviewing me was, as you can imagine, none too pleased by this. But the girl, Bobbi (not her real name), offered no clear explanation for her action. I just sat there, hoping that I wouldn't ever have to deal with this lunatic.

Unfortunately, the interviewer told me that Bobbi was in fact the exact person I'd be working with. I tried getting out of it, asking if I could instead take a job in another department, but she wouldn't let me do that. What could I do? I needed the job, so I took it.

Once I started working there, I learned that, surprisingly, Bobbi was not the terror I thought she'd be. In fact, she was downright friendly and went out of her way to make me feel comfortable in my new position. (Later on, she explained she had been having a terrible fight with an ex-girlfriend the day she lost her temper, and that she felt bad for having scared me.) Bobbi was patient, explained things clearly, and convinced me I could do the cold-calling the job required. (I've always hated calling strangers—even though it's part of my job as a journalist.)

Still, despite Bobbi's warm personality, I was somewhat frightened of her in the beginning. It had nothing to do with her; I was just frightened of everyone back then. I'd had some bad experiences with people through the years—particularly with my ex–best friend, a girl I'd ended a fourteen-year relationship with a number of years ago.

So while I appreciated Bobbi's efforts to be my friend, I wasn't interested. I had decided a while ago that I was going to be alone.

Well, almost alone.

I had a boyfriend I'd been going out with for a while by the time I'd started the job. He was my first boyfriend. It was about high time I'd had one, too, considering all the years I'd spent looking. I was extremely picky when it came to guys. They had to look and act just so, or I wasn't interested.

Mark (not his real name) had somehow passed the test. He lived in my building and I'd had what I thought was a crush on him for years. Though I wanted to approach him, I never did when he lived in my building, simply because I was too shy. As luck would have it, he answered a personal ad I placed, and from then on we were an item.

I realize now though I thought he was cute, I wasn't ever physically attracted to him. I only wanted him because I was just so sadly desperate to be loved and to—finally—have my first sexual experience. I was twenty-six at the time.

Still, I thought I might be bisexual. I had actually even considered going to a lesbian bar a few years ago, to see if I really did like girls in that way, but ultimately chickened out. A part of me was convinced my wild sexual side was something shameful, and I was desperate to keep it hidden from conservative Mark. Mostly, my plan worked—except for one time, when he told me he had once dressed up as a girl on Halloween. I couldn't help myself—a look of pleasure and intrigue came across my face. He saw it, and teased me. As I recall, he said something along the lines of "I bet you would like it if I did that again, wouldn't you?" At the time, I felt extraordinarily embarrassed. Now, I just think it's funny as hell.

I eventually told Bobbi about my boyfriend, and she told me about her girlfriend. It didn't matter that we were involved with people, because we were just friends. And I liked our relationship the way it was, anyway.

The more I learned about Bobbi, the more I liked her. She was funny, intelligent, and extraordinarily humble. She made me feel like I mattered. But even more important, she was one of the nicest people I'd ever met. And her kindness extended to everyone.

And she wasn't the only cool person at the office. I found that a lot of the people who worked at this place were fun to be around. Sometimes it felt like all we did was talk and joke and laugh ourselves silly. I started to become more and more comfortable with everyone, and I began to let my guard down. The job soon started to seem less like a job and more like a sleepover that never ended. I started to think that maybe it wouldn't be so bad to have friends again, after all—as long as they were casual.

Though I enjoyed being with everyone, Bobbi was still my favorite. We called ourselves Big Chief and Little Chief—which referred to our unofficial positions in the company. She even made us paper hats that bore our "titles."

She would do special things for me for no reason, but "just because."

One day she bought me a stuffed animal from the nearby drugstore. We named him Kenny.

A few months into my job, when New York had a major blackout, Bobbi called to make sure I was all right. When I mentioned to her that I was having trouble with a computer disk I had saved a lot of stuff on, she offered to come with me to the library to see if she could fix it.

She couldn't fix the disk, unfortunately, but that day proved to be a very important one, because later, after we left the library, we stopped for some pizza and talked, and talked and talked about everything. It would be one of the many marathon conversations we'd have in the years to come, conversations in which we'd spill our lives and our souls out to each other.

It was an office tradition to dress up in costumes on Halloween, and I had decided to participate, since I'd loved dressing up as a kid, and it had been ages since I'd done it. But I didn't have a lot of time and had no leftover costume at home to wear. So I had to settle for a cheap clown costume from my local chain drugstore. I remember feeling very excited the night before.

Halloween came, and Bobbi was indeed shocked to see that I had dressed up. She told me she was going to see her girlfriend later on at the big Halloween parade in Manhattan. I tried to seem happy for her, but secretly I wasn't. At the time, I thought I was just envious of what seemed to me to be a happy relationship. (God knows I wasn't in one myself.) But it was deeper than that. Secretly, I wanted to be Bobbi's girlfriend.

I don't remember exactly when it started—though it probably was around Halloween—but somewhere along the line, I began to feel uncomfortable in Bobbi's presence. The best way I can describe it is to say I didn't want her getting too close to me. I remember once she put her hand on mine and I instinctively wanted to move my own hand away. I recall blushing after she whispered something naughty in my ear. Bobbi gave girls massages in the office—I know that sounds weird, but it was completely casual—and I flinched when she tried to give me one. Yet I was jealous when I saw her massage another girl.

Bobbi liked to flirt, which made me feel even more nervous. She told me gender wasn't that important when it came to love. She said she'd eat me into a screaming orgasm if only I'd let her. As soon as she said those words, I pictured her doing just that. The thought made me curious, frightened, and hot. Did Bobbi have a crush on me, and was this the only way she felt comfortable showing it? Though I played along, and even liked it at times, overall I really didn't care for her teasing. And I hated that she made me feel like I had to tease her back. I knew I was only leading her on. I had a boyfriend, and though Bobbi tempted me, I was trying to make the relationship with him work. Didn't she realize I couldn't go out with her?

At one point, Bobbi got sick. It wasn't anything really serious, but it was bad enough to keep her away from work for a while. She started to call me on the phone more often. At first, I thought she was calling just to catch up on what had happened at work. That was part of the reason, but she was also using it as an excuse to get closer. I found I really enjoyed our phone conversations. I felt I could talk to her forever and never run out of things to say. Bobbi had finally broken through my last wall.

Still, things got uncomfortable again when Bobbi finally got up her courage and asked me out. I wasn't sure if she was completely serious, but it didn't matter. I still had a boyfriend. I thought I had to be tough to show her I meant business, so I told her she wasn't my type. (To this day, I regret saying that. Bobbi, to her credit, never got mad at me, though she does tease me about it from time to time.)

One weekend, my boyfriend and I went away to Atlantic City. I always looked forward to spending time with him in private, because I thought it would help us get closer—though it never did.

This particular trip was the worst we'd ever had. I remember spending one entire part of our vacation just crying and not knowing why. Now, I recognize it was because I was feeling trapped in the relationship.

During the December holidays, Bobbi and I decided to exchange presents. I got her a science fiction book, since I knew she loved the genre. I didn't know what she had gotten me, though the way she was hinting around, I suspected it was a dildo or a vibrator.

It turned out not to be either of those things, though she did buy me one sex-themed present (a beautiful box filled with various fun items for sex). But the other present was what really took me by surprise. A while back, I had casually mentioned that when I was younger what I wanted most of all was a Snoopy Sno-Cone Machine. (I could still sing the jingle.) I thought they stopped making it in the 1980s, but apparently they hadn't, because Bobbi had managed to find one for me. The gesture floored me. I could barely remember mentioning the toy, and here she had not only remembered that I'd mentioned it, but thought enough to go out and search for it. And I had only known her for a little more than six months. I became emotional and hugged her. And though I didn't know for sure whether I was in love at this point, I did know I didn't want that hug to end.

We both broke up with our lovers around the same time. Though I'd felt badly about my breakup, I was also relieved. Bobbi's breakup, on the other hand, was really nasty. I felt terrible for her. But I also knew it was probably best for her to get out there and search for someone new. I tried to push her to go to a lesbian dating event, but she assured me that she was through with relationships. A part of me was relieved. Even though I'd been the one to suggest it, I didn't really like the idea of her seeing someone else.

But I had no problem looking for someone myself. I felt anxious (okay, desperate) to get back out there in the dating scene, so I went online and began looking for men. One day, I showed her a picture of a guy I was considering seeing. She didn't like the way he looked, and told me as much.

I was mad. How dare she do that! Why couldn't she be supportive and find something nice to say about him? Maybe she just wanted me for herself, I thought, and then, stupidly enough, expressed that thought out loud. Looking back, I know the real reason I was upset was because I was scared that my feelings for her were becoming intense. Bobbi got mad—rightfully so—and left the office in a huff. I started to worry we'd never be friends again, but eventually she came back. She walked over to me and took my face in her cold hands. (It was winter and she'd been walking outside for a while.) I was shocked by the odd gesture, but I knew that was her way of saying that she forgave me.

One day, I casually mentioned that I had never received flowers before. When a delivery of the most beautiful flowers I had ever seen came into our office, I wasn't completely surprised. I had a feeling they were from her. When I asked her, she confirmed it. And when I looked at the card, I saw there was a message: acts of kindness are never forgotten. (I had talked her out of a really bad mood a while back.) I went to her office right after receiving the flowers and felt a little odd. This wasn't meant to be a romantic gesture, and yet…Well, there was something in the air. That was for sure.

New Year's Eve was coming up soon and I was feeling lonely. A coworker was having a big party at her place and had invited me and Bobbi to come. I figured it would help me to go out. I didn't want to stay home and feel sorry for myself.

Bobbi had to stop at her own house first and asked if I wanted to go with her. I said yes. When she went upstairs to change, I found myself wondering what she looked like underneath her clothes. Okay. Now, the red flags were starting to go up.

She came down, wearing a beautiful gray sweater. While I had once seen her dressed in a skirt—for another special occasion—that was nothing like this. That look was far too dressy for her. But this…This kind of casual feminine dressing suited her perfectly. And sure, I was attracted to her as a butch, but seeing her with that sweater—and her hair down—well, let me just say it was enough to put me over the edge.

We went to the party and it was okay. I felt kind of out of place because I didn't really know everybody well. I was clinging to Bobbi. At one point, Bobbi went out on the terrace just to talk to another girl, and I felt that weird jealous feeling again. I was thrilled when she finally said she wanted to go back to her house to celebrate New Year's. She wanted me to stay at the party to socialize with the others, but I didn't want to. I only wanted to be with her.

Neither of us drove, so we had to take a car service back. As we waited for our car, she started engaging in horseplay with me. Though we'd had a pretty playful relationship up to this point, there was something different about this, namely in the way it made me feel. At one point, she pulled me to her by the sash of her coat. I was getting turned on again, but still, I said nothing.

Our car still hadn't come, and we were anxious to get back. A car from a car service stopped, but it was not the one we called. We hopped right in anyway. Big mistake. The driver drove as if he had a death wish, and at one point stopped at his home (in a really bad neighborhood) to go to the bathroom. I'm not exactly sure when she did it, but I remember Bobbi holding my hand at one point, to calm me down. An intense feeling of love for her flooded my heart.

Back at her place, we relaxed with her family and friends. I began wishing we had the place to ourselves so I could make out with her. Why was I thinking this? After midnight, she walked me to the block where my father would be coming soon to pick me up.

I was drunk as I was walking down the steps outside her house—so drunk I actually fell. I easily got up on my own, but a part of me wanted to be swept up in her arms.

While we were waiting for my father to come, she said she wanted to kiss me. I didn't know what to say. I sort of wanted to and I was sort of frightened. But ultimately, she didn't kiss me, and I was relieved when my father finally picked me up.

I struggled with my attraction to Bobbi until I finally realized that I was probably in love with her. But that didn't mean I should tell her. Sure, we were still both unattached at this point, but I knew having sex could kill our friendship. I couldn't lose that.

And there were other things to consider. What if I wasn't queer? How awful it would be to make her my experiment. And even if I was gay or bisexual, what if this wasn't love at all, but just an intense friendship? She'd had enough drama in her life and I didn't want to add to any of it. I realized after thinking about it for a while that I was 99 percent sure I wanted this. There was only one way to find out about the other percent.

One day, not long after that fateful New Year's Eve when we took a car service home together, I told her in a roundabout way that I liked her. When I got home, I asked her over the phone if she would go out with me. She said she'd have to think about it. I found myself worrying she'd say no, but thankfully, she didn't.

We both lived with our families, so the chances to have sex were few and far between. We had to take them when we could grab them, even if that meant—gasp!—using the office.

On Fridays, everyone cleared out early. Most of the place was closed up, but Bobbi had a separate office on the second floor that she had a key to. I had been upset when our boss had moved her there a while back, but now I wasn't. For this purpose, it was ideal.

I was somewhat nervous and yet, at the same time, determined to fully explore my feelings, and see whether they were real or not.

As soon as she hugged me, I knew. I felt like I wasn't hugging her so much as falling into her arms. This was what I'd been missing with my boyfriend.

Various memories from our office sex sessions stand out in my mind. I recall being knocked out by how incredibly soft her skin was, and looking longingly at her gorgeous black bra. I remember her putting her long black jacket out on the floor once, right before she went down on me, like a true gentlebutch. (I thought that she'd throw out the jacket after that, but she said it was even more special now that it had the lingering scent of me on it. Say it with me: Awww.) One time, I looked passionately into her eyes while she was going down on me, and I remember thinking that this was surely the most romantic moment I'd ever had in my life—and probably ever would.

The one time I had tried to have oral sex with my boyfriend, it was hard to get into, as I could tell he really wasn't into it himself. Also, the oral sex—like the intercourse itself—was lacking warmth (which was partly his fault, because he was a little cold, and partly my fault for going out with someone I really didn't like.) With Bobbi, though, it was completely different. I felt more strongly about her than I ever had about my boyfriend, and she turned out to be as warm a lover as she was a friend. Plus, I could tell she really loved going down on me.

When my boyfriend had gone down on me, I simply sat back and hoped that an orgasm would somehow magically happen. I didn't make any movements that might add to my pleasure, fearful that it would somehow crush his fragile male ego. But the first time Bobbi went down on me, I didn't feel that way at all. When I felt like I wanted to take an active role, I did, instinctively using my hands to maneuver my lips and clit up and down her tongue—all while she kept up her end, giving me a thoroughly good licking. The fact that I was controlling where the pressure went made the sex all the hotter. The build-up was intense. After what seemed like an unbearable stretch, I came. It was the first orgasm I'd ever had during sex. The first I'd ever had with someone I loved. The first one that really meant something.

There's another memory from those sessions. One day, when we were in the office and no one else was around, I lovingly stroked her sweet, soft pussy. I felt her wetness for the first time, and it was wonderful. Somehow, I was able to make this tough butch practically whimper beneath my touch. Unfortunately, she began to make so much noise I was scared she would be heard. So I decided we'd better stop for our own good. (I was a little paranoid. I'll admit it.) Still, I felt good knowing I'd at least given her some pleasure. (Bobbi was a typical butch in the sense that she got off on giving, but rarely on receiving.)

But we weren't just about sex. One day, I kissed her—during work—behind a door where nobody could see. I felt like I was having an out-of-body experience, the kiss was so intense. Even when I was doing something as simple as sitting on her lap, I thought I was in heaven.

A few months into our relationship, we went to a hotel room for a day. Being with her under the covers made me feel so cozy and so very, very hot, I wanted to stay there forever. Because she had her period, she spent the whole day making me come. She worked my clit so well, bringing me to such heights of pleasure, that on the subway ride home I felt like my face was glowing.

We'd also occasionally had sex in my house, when my parents went away. (Someone was usually at her house, so we couldn't do it there.) Those sessions were always nerve-wracking, since my parents could have walked in on us at any time, but still great. I remember screaming as she licked my clit, and groaning from the pleasure of feeling her naked breasts—which she pushed onto my back. And the box of sex items she'd gotten me back in December? Oh boy, we put those babies to good use! There was erotic massaging with warm oil, and tickling with a feather. Honey dust was everywhere. We had one hell of a good time!

As our relationship got more serious, we started going to gay clubs where she'd give me discreet hand jobs that left my knees wobbly and my head spinning. One time, when she slipped her fingers inside my pussy, I lost control like never before, inching my clit frantically toward her rapidly moving fingers. It was as if her hand were a wire and my pussy, an outlet—that was how electric it felt. There was such a mammoth orgasm welling up inside me, it was all I could do to hold myself up and pray no one was watching. Another time, she sucked on my breasts so intently and for so long I thought I would come from just that alone. And then there was that time she slipped her hand down my pants and teased my clit so that it felt like I had slipped into another world when I came. When I got my bearings, I was surprised to see all the other clubgoers dancing like nothing had happened.

Bobbi was shyer, outside than she was indoors but once she actually let me finger fuck her as she straddled a bench outside a bar. I delighted in pushing her just to the edge of orgasm, but not quite over (well, we were outside, after all).

In case you're wondering, Bobbi and I are still together today, and will be celebrating our two-year anniversary this January—by moving in together.

And to think, it all began with a hat.

do you floss?

●

therese szymanski

"Do you floss?" the beautiful Latina asked, leaning over the table to take my chin in her hand, acting as if she really wanted to carefully scrutinize my teeth.

As a big ol' geek, I've been known occasionally to attend…Well, it's not really occasional, since this was only my third, and I was totally dragged to the first, which was for a different show that I didn't even watch, so it didn't actually count or anything but…See, I'm not really an autograph hound, and getting a pic taken with someone just 'cause they're a bit famous kinda squicks me a bit and strikes me as being rather odd.

Plus, as anyone who really knows me knows, I'm rather shy and naive, and I hate that I'd probably sound like an even bigger dork than I am to any of these celebrity types. And I'd probably ask the stupidest and most commonplace questions imaginable, if I could even get my mouth to work.

Now my friend Amalia is totally different. She's an autograph/ picture/celebrity hound—and she has no problems walking up to them and chatting them up. She gets giddy coming up with good questions to ask them during Q & As. So at the cocktail party the first night of the convention, I wandered around with Amalia, taking her pic with all the celebrities in attendance, even though I was a bigger fan of the show, and had to keep cluing her in to who everyone was—"He played that really floppy-skinned demon who liked kitten poker"—"Oh, god, he played a bunch of different villains—we met him last year in Chicago!"—but then we got to *her*.

I told Amalia who she was, and I took a pic of the two of them. And there was something about her smile and the twinkle in her eye that made me hand the camera to Amalia as I shyly asked, "Can I get a pic with you as well?"

I hadn't really cared much for her character on the show. She was bossy and opinionated. She replaced a character I really liked, and kicked another out of her own house.

"Sure," she said, sliding an arm around my shoulders and pulling me close.

But the actress was not the character, and I was immediately swept up by her charm, and—oh my god—she was hot, and she was flirting with me!

"I don't think she got it," the actress said into my ear, so I could feel her warm breath on my skin.

She pulled me a bit tighter, so I wrapped my arm around her slender waist, feeling my knees go a bit weak. "Oh, would you mind if she took another?" I said.

"No problem," she said, pulling me in closer and pressing against me. "Why not one more, just to make sure?" she said, smiling at me after the second picture.

"Wow, she was really flirting with you," Amalia said as we walked back to our table.

"So it wasn't just me, then," I said, looking at Amalia and the hets we'd been hanging with that night. "She was flirting with me?" I normally didn't pick up on such things, but I'd thought maybe she had been…I started turning bright red, like someone poured warm…no…hot water over me.

"Oh yeah."

"She was flirting with you."

"Omigod, she so was!"

"Definitely."

She played a lesbian on that TV show.

And now she was holding my chin in her delicate, warm hand, smiling as she admired my teeth (which I know are none too admirable, given that I'd been a smoker for seventeen years and had only given it up seventeen months before).

And then I realized that, with me standing and her leaning over in

215

her low-cut top, I could see right down her blouse. And I, always big with the suave, finally choked out, "Uh, yeah. I do," as I tried to force my eyes back to her face. She had to know what she was doing. And I'm such a butch, folks can ID me from two hundred paces. She was playing me and having fun with me...

So I did it. With just one of those perfectly fabulous, right-on moves worthy of my slickest characters, I raised my hand to hers, bringing her hand to my lips so I could lightly kiss her palm. "I floss daily, as a matter of fact." I looked behind me at Amalia, and at all the other guests who were already assembling to leave the room, apparently for a break before nighttime activities, then back at the woman in front of me. "It looks like we're your last customers."

"Looks like," she said, taking the photo from Amalia's hand, signing it and returning it.

"I'm, um, just gonna get the rest of these people, before they leave," Amalia said, stepping around me to the guests we had not yet gotten autographs from.

"So you're gonna, what?" I said. "Take a break, get a bite to eat, then maybe go to the improv and dance later?"

"I was thinking about it, unless I get a better offer."

"Could I possibly take you out to dinner?"

"Possibly." Again with the teasing grin.

Amalia apparently overheard this, because she hurried back to whisper in my ear, "It's almost eight. If you hurry, you can use our reservations for tonight."

"What about you?" I asked.

"I'll be fine. You just have fun," she said with a wink as she rushed back to get the rest of her pictures and memorabilia signed.

"Have you been to the place down the road yet?" I asked, helping her gather her stuff.

"No. Is it better than this place?"

"Yes."

"Thank god!" Then, as we walked out to my car, "Are you two together?"

"Me and Amalia? No. No, we're not," I said, holding her door open for her.

"Good," she said as I got in. She reached over to take my free hand in hers. Her skin was warm and smooth.

No one at the other restaurant recognized her, so we were able to continue flirting over dinner…and I had the chance to look at her—really look at her. Her thick, black hair was short, but her eyelashes were long. Her lips were full, her smile wide, her teeth perfectly white, and her eyes a warm, inviting dark brown.

She was slender, and everything about her held an air of sophistication. And Hollywood. But she was here, with me.

And I sat across from her and realized I was a writer—I'd created worlds that had journalists calling to interview me about my plays and books. And folks had stopped me to get a pic with me, or an autograph from me.

Not to the extent she had, but…it was different, but still, I had some thought as to how she felt about it all. I could empathize with her.

I didn't cling to celebrities. She was just an amazingly beautiful, attractive, and nice woman.

And we drove back to our building. I looked over at her. "We could hit the improv, or I could just let you go to your room to freshen up, or whatever."

"Tell me, is that what you really want to do?"

"No." I reached over to bury my fingers in her hair and draw her head nearer mine, even as I leaned forward to catch her lips with mine.

"Then what do you want?" she asked between kisses. Her tongue was warm and wet. As I thought other places on her body might be.

I reached down to cup her breast with my hand. "I want to take you to bed." I caressed her side with my hand. "I want to explore you and give you pleasure."

"Oh, god…" she arched up, then grabbed my wandering hand. "Not here, not now."

"Not like this?" I whispered, sucking on her neck, her earlobe…

"Take me to your room," she said.

I didn't have to be told twice. And, in fact, although we didn't touch at all during the walk to my room, as soon as we were safely hidden by that portal, I had her against the wall, one leg wrapped around my hips as she pushed into me, opening herself to me.

"Oh, god," she said, burying her face in my neck. "It's been too long."

I cupped her ass, lifting her. She wrapped both legs around me and I carried her to the bed, kneeling on it before laying her down, and then laying on top of her, between her legs, our lips never parting.

Our tongues dueled. She tasted sweet, but her teasing teeth, nibbling on my lips and tongue, were a sharp alternate. Her skin was warm and she smelled a bit vanilla, and a bit spicy.

I wanted to explore every inch of her—touch her everywhere and make her scream my name. I got that this was a one-time thing, and we'd never be together again, but I'd make the most of these few moments.

I raised myself up on my arms and looked down at her. Her short, black hair was mussed, and her lips were full and moist. Her pupils were huge and she was panting for air.

"I'm so glad you don't just play a lesbian on TV," I said.

"Shut up and fuck me," she said.

I pushed her legs further open with my own, even as I held her hands over her head, against the bed, with one of mine. I trailed my hand down the side of her face, over her neck, to her breast. I caressed it lightly before cupping it.

I met her gaze as she squirmed under me, in a good way. She was enjoying herself.

"God, you're gorgeous," I said to her.

"I know."

She'd been told this all too often. She no longer understood exactly what it meant. I planned on showing her the truth of every syllable of it. "You're also way overdressed. Sit up." I helped her up, just so I could strip off her plain white top, bringing her bra with it. "That's better." I pulled off her light beige knit hat as well. Even while I looked at her, focusing on her eyes.

But, hell, no matter how noble or shit I was thinking of trying to be, she had really nice breasts—real ones. Not silicone. Not huge, but good handfuls…and hell, I'd been admiring her cleavage all weekend. I had to look at them.

And she leaned back, propping herself up with her arms, all cocky and shit. "Enjoying the view?"

Her nipples got harder every time I looked at them. I ground down on her, pressing myself into her cunt so she had to squirm against me.

"So are you just gonna wriggle like a dead fish, or are you gonna do somethin' about this?"

I had to grin. She had quite a way with words, and anyone who knew me knew I had a right hot thing for women with brains. A tart tongue made them even hotter.

I forced both her hands above her head and grasped them in one of mine, using my greater strength and weight to control her and keep her in my power.

I grabbed a nipple between a thumb and forefinger, then twisted and pulled it. Tightly and cruelly.

"Fuck!" she yelled, arching her chest up while I held the rest of her down.

"Yeah, I'll be doing that soon." I leaned down to lick her other breast… all around…till I focused on her nipple, as it hardened further…

Then I caught it between my teeth, biting it lightly as I tugged.

Then harder as I bit and pulled it. Brutally.

And as she cried and twisted under me, I slipped my hand from her left nipple down the front of her trousers, to cup her hot, wet, thong-covered cunt. I lightly fingered her through the satiny fabric.

"I'm gonna let your hands go," I said. "You're going to unzip your pants, pull them—and your thong—down, exposing yourself to me." She pushed against me, struggling against my hold, but I was firm. "Then you will put your hands back above your head—once you are naked from head to knees, so I can hold you down again. Got that?"

"Are you on crack?" she asked. "What the hell makes you think I'll listen to you?"

"The fact that I can make sure nobody pays any attention to your screaming," I pushed my thigh into her cunt and twisted her nipple—hard. "That and, well, I can overpower you."

She moaned and arched up as her eyelids fluttered shut. "No."

"We're in your room. You invited me in. Kinda like I'm a vampire. Now, when I release your hands, what are you going to do?"

"Besides…oh, god…claw your eyes out?"

"Yeah." I kept eye contact as I released her hands, adjusting my weight over her.

She looked up at me, her dark eyes looking right into mine. Into me. Challenging. She'd been giving herself to me up till now, but I'd raised the stakes, working at making fantasies come true.

If this was the only time I'd be with her, I wanted it to be memorable.

She used her now free hands to unzip her jeans and pull them, and her thong, down to her knees. Then she raised her hands over her head, so I could restrain her again, stretching her out to her full length, with one hand.

I looked into her eyes as I ran my hand over her body. As I caressed her perfect body. I cupped each breast, running my thumb over each nipple in turn.

I held her legs open with my body and my own legs. And I reached down to run my fingers up her. She wriggled under me, squirming.

I used two fingers, enjoying how easily my fingers moved in her wetness. Then I slipped the two middle fingers into her as I ran my thumb up and down her. It slid in her slick as I started slowly fucking her. I started playing her clit back and forth with my thumb even as I fucked her, slowly, gently, with my fingers.

She arched into me, panting, even as she raised and lowered her pelvis to bring me deeper and farther into her, then release me.

"Yes, please," she said, then closed her eyes.

I kissed her neck. I bit it lightly, ran my tongue up and down it. And I fucked her. Fingered her.

And then I released her hands. I brought my arm down to hold her—not restrain her, just…hold her.

I raised myself back up and looked into her eyes, which she closed.

"No, baby," I said. "Open them. Keep them open." I started collecting as much of her own lube as possible, coating all my fingers, and the rest of my hand, with it.

She finally gasped and opened her eyes to look at me.

"Do you want it?" I said.

"What…? Oh, god, that feels…so…good."

"Give it to me."

She looked back up at me, then spread her legs even more. She barely had to touch my wrist—reaching down between her legs to do so—before I understood.

I slid my fist up into her.

"Oh GOD!" she screamed, shoving her pelvis up against me.

And that's when I really began fucking her, but still I held her to me while we sweated and looked into each others' eyes.

Her eyes were wide, her arms holding me tight, as she used her legs to release herself from her jeans. "Please, yes, oh god. Oh, fuck me."

And so I rammed my fist into her, repeatedly. I fucked her hard. And I looked into her—meeting her gaze—and...I felt her convulse around me. I saw her come. I felt her come.

For me.

Again. And again.

And then she slowed up so she stopped coming and we both could just be...aware...of my fist inside of her.

I left it there.

And then we had this moment when we both knew I'd hold her all night. That I'd love cradling her body in my arms, spooning her from behind while I cupped her nonexistent tummy with my hand, till she raised my hand to hold it between her breasts ...

And it would all be terribly intimate. Even more so then me spreading her wide and fucking her.

I hadn't been with as many women as my rep indicated, and so I really did care to ensure each woman I was with remembered me as an incredible fuck.

And sometimes more.

"Okay, so who should I make this out to?" she said, after asking me if I flossed.

Is that the end?

"Reese."

"Oh, I like Reese's! But I bet you get told that all the time!" (She was obviously referring to the peanut butter cups.)

"Uh, yeah," I suavely said. "One of my friends says if I had kids they'd be Reese's Pieces."

She laughed. Then sobered up. "I'm sorry. That's funny. But I'm sure you're told that all the time!"

She was beautiful. So I shuffled myself along before I could be a bigger ass, and then, at the end of the last day of the conference, Amalia came up to me with the latest anthology I had edited. "Sign this."

"To whom?" I said, taking it.

"Here's the spelling," she said, handing me a program to ensure I got the spelling right.

My hand started shaking. "You're kidding me, right? What do I sign this to? How do I sign this? What better book for a vampire slayer?"

"Yeah, that's it."

three's a crowd

●

barbara johnson

It was 1975—Halloween night at All Souls' Unitarian Church in Washington, D.C. Thunderous applause boomed through the cavernous church as Meg Christian took her final bows. The women who filled the building to its rafters were standing, stamping their feet, and shouting. The very structure shook to its core. It was Meg's last encore, and she finally disappeared behind the stage. The lights came on as the clapping died down, and a collective sigh echoed through the chamber. The audience was sorry to see the evening end.

Kit glanced over at her friends, Casey and Mary. She could tell from Mary's angry gestures and frowning face that they were having a bad argument. Casey didn't appear to be doing much talking, and soon Mary stormed away. In response to Kit's upraised eyebrows, Casey sauntered over.

"Mary's mad 'cause she overheard me talking to you about Brenda," Casey said with a shrug of her shoulders. "She doesn't like it when I compliment other women. But what does she expect when she ignores me, as she's been doing all night?"

Kit looked over at the object of Mary's ire. She had to admit that Brenda looked particularly fetching tonight, dressed in jeans and an embroidered Indian cotton blouse. It was the blouse that had prompted Casey's comments. Brenda's ash blond hair, fashionably long and straight, swayed with every movement of her head, and her green eyes sparkled with animation. Kit was glad she'd been able to bring Brenda out that night for the concert. She and her lover attended different universities and lived at home with their respective parents while they worked to make enough money to move in together. It was hard to get

1111

111111111111111111

away together, especially because the parents were hostile to Brenda's and her relationship. Kit returned her attention to Casey, who was lucky enough to have parents who were completely supportive.

"So, what're you gonna do?" Kit asked. "You going after her?"

Casey shook her head. "Nah. I told her she could go home with her buddies."

Kit was a bit surprised at Casey's indifference. "You sure?"

From the vantage of their balcony seats, Casey looked down at the throng of women below. "She's probably already on the way home."

At that moment, Brenda joined them. "Where's Mary?"

Casey answered. "We had a fight. I told her to go home."

Brenda raised her right eyebrow but said nothing.

"Well," Kit said, "how about going out for a bite to eat? Blimpie's in Georgetown? Should be lots of interesting Halloween action going on."

Casey and Brenda nodded, and the trio maneuvered their way down the stairs and into the main hall of the church. The place was still crowded with women, and the high energy and excitement from the concert seemed to electrify the room. The three friends finally exited into the cool night air. The streets were busy. Lights from all the cars glowed like diamonds and rubies in the darkness. High overhead in a dark, cloudless sky, the full orange moon lent atmosphere to the spooky holiday. Casey quickly located her white VW bug. They paused on the sidewalk.

"You know, we'll have trouble finding parking in Georgetown," Casey stated. "Still want to try?"

Kit looked at Brenda's happy face. The little café whose specialty was made-to-order submarine sandwiches was Brenda's favorite. "Sure," she answered.

They folded themselves into the VW and drove off. Kit wished she'd been able to borrow her mother's car that night. It was nice of Casey to drive—like she usually did, being the only one of the three with her own car—but if Kit had the car she could take Brenda home tonight and maybe steal a few hours in Brenda's bed before dawn. They'd done it before, sneaking into the house and down to the basement where Brenda had her bedroom. Her parents' room was directly overhead, so there was many a time Kit had to cover Brenda's mouth with her hand to stifle her moans. An hour or so before dawn, Kit would creep out of Brenda's house and drive the hour back to her own. She liked to believe they had both sets of parents fooled, but she doubted it.

It wasn't long before they were cruising around the residential streets of Georgetown looking for a parking space. They got lucky; a Mercedes pulled out not three blocks from Blimpie's. The three women piled out of the car and quickly headed for the café, passing several groups of people in various costumes and stages of intoxication.

Once inside Blimpie's, they ordered their sandwiches at the counter, watched the cute redhead make them, and then carried their trays to the back of the café. Brenda found herself sitting between Kit and Casey, a not unpleasant situation. The closeness of the two dark-haired women stirred feelings in her that she had only dared fantasize about. She glanced at Kit seated on her right. She was broad shouldered and amply endowed, with dark brown hair that fell almost to her shoulders and laughing hazel eyes that crinkled when she smiled. Her strong arms and hands had driven Brenda to distraction on more than one occasion. She was much shorter than Brenda, a characteristic that Brenda found she didn't mind at all.

Kit and Casey were in animated conversation, discussing some upcoming sports event at the University of Maryland. Brenda bit delicately into her shrimp salad sub before letting her eyes wander over the woman sitting on her left. Casey was a bit shorter than Kit but just as broad shouldered. Her short hair, black as midnight, was thick and just made for running one's fingers through. The expression in Casey's dark eyes let a woman know exactly what she wanted.

Brenda squirmed a bit in her seat. She wondered what it would be like to make love with both women at once. It was an idea that had crossed her mind before. She felt the hot flush on her cheeks and guiltily closed her eyes. What could she be thinking? A ménage à trois? What would Kit think? What would Casey? She opened her eyes. The two women on either side seemed to be sitting nearer than ever.

"Well, well, well," Casey said in a low husky voice, "take a look at that."

Brenda and Kit followed her discreet finger. A stunning blonde in a black satin Playboy Bunny costume walked precariously on spike heels to the back of the café. A tall pirate accompanied her, but the three women paid him no mind. The blonde more than filled out her costume. As she slid around the table to sit down, the white puff of fur on her shapely ass seemed to tease and beckon.

"I wouldn't mind playing with that powder puff," Casey said with a twinkle in her eye. Her mouth turned up at one corner in a lecherous grin.

"You're not kidding," Kit replied with a glance at Brenda. She put her arm around her girlfriend's shoulders. "Why don't you wear one of those, honey?"

Brenda rolled her eyes in mock ire. "You two are terrible. You done? Let's head home."

The three found Casey's VW and headed out of the city into the Virginia suburbs. They were animated on the drive home, talking about the concert and upcoming midterms and the latest happenings at the women's center. Brenda envied Casey and Kit; they attended the University of Maryland, where such things as a women's center existed. She attended a conservative Virginia university that had barely heard of feminism.

All too soon they arrived at Brenda's house. Casey pulled into the driveway and cut the engine. Brenda was relieved to see that no lights were on inside the house. That meant her parents hadn't waited up. In the backseat, Brenda curled her hand inside Kit's and laid her head on Kit's shoulder.

"I don't want you to go," she said softly. "I don't want the night to end."

Kit tilted Brenda's chin to kiss her softly on the mouth. "I know, sweetheart, but Casey has to work early tomorrow."

Brenda felt daring. She touched Casey lightly on the shoulder. "You know, my parents have a sofa in the basement where my bedroom is. You can spend the night, too. I promise I'd wake you up in time to go to work."

Casey was tempted, but she had to be at work by eight. She looked at her watch. That was only five hours away, and the drive back to Maryland was an hour long. She looked at Brenda's pleading green eyes, and her resolve melted. Casey knew Kit and Brenda didn't have many opportunities to spend the night together. Who was she to stand in the way of true love?

"Oh, okay."

"You're a sweetheart," Brenda said as she leaned over the seat and kissed Casey on the cheek.

They got out of the car and walked quietly around to the back door of the house. Brenda unlocked the door as quietly as possible. She didn't want to wake her parents or siblings or dogs. No such luck. The dachshund and the fox terrier waited with wagging tails as she stepped into the kitchen. Brenda bent down to pet them.

"Shhhh. Go on to bed," she whispered as she pointed to the doorway leading out of the kitchen.

Obediently, the two dogs disappeared down the darkened hallway. Brenda motioned for Kit and Casey to follow her down the stairs to the basement. She breathed a sigh of relief as she turned on the light.

"I am so glad Mom and Dad weren't up," she said as she unfolded the sofa.

Kit bent to help her. "You and me both." She straightened and looked at Casey. "You're really lucky that your parents are so cool."

"That's what women tell me all the time," Casey replied with a grin. She flopped onto the bed. "Have fun, you two," she said with a knowing wink.

Brenda felt a blush warm her face. Kit pulled her quickly into the bedroom and closed the door, but not tightly. It was still the typical bedroom of a young girl—gold and white French provincial furniture, stuffed animals, posters on the pale green walls, clothes draped over the chair and on the floor. It was a familiar place to both Brenda and Kit, a place Kit secretly thought of as way too feminine.

They hurriedly pulled off their clothes in the dark and climbed into the double bed. The small window above the bed filtered in light from the streetlamp. The two women snuggled together briefly before Kit pulled Brenda to her and kissed her deeply.

In the other room, Casey listened to the murmuring sounds of love and squirmed in her lonely bed. For a moment she regretted her fight with Mary. Would she have been allowed to have Mary here in this bed? Most probably. Kit and Brenda took every opportunity to sleep together.

Casey knew she and Kit would probably leave before dawn to make sure Brenda's parents didn't know what had gone on in their basement. She looked up at the ceiling. Just where was their room anyway?

In the bedroom, Brenda momentarily stopped Kit's roving hands. Impulsively, she dared a suggestion. "Don't you think Casey is awfully lonely out there?"

Kit smiled and got out of bed without a word. She pulled on a T-shirt and went to the door to push it open. She could see Casey on the sofa. Was she already asleep?

Casey heard a sound and turned her head toward the bedroom door. It was open now as Kit stood there and motioned for her to come in. Casey sat up and pointed to the bedroom with a questioning glance. Kit smiled and nodded. Hmmm. This could prove interesting, Casey thought as she got out of bed and complied.

Kit quickly walked around the foot of the bed and got in on the right side. Casey, still wearing her underwear and a T-shirt, slid under the covers on the left. Brenda lay on her back between them. Casey could tell immediately that Brenda was naked. The very thought of Brenda's soft body made her lick her lips. She had always thought that Brenda was very pretty and sexy. She lay on her back and let her hand rest ever so lightly against Brenda's thigh.

Kit wondered what Casey was thinking. Did she realize that Brenda was naked? Did she want to make love to Brenda? Kit knew that Brenda had thought about making love with Casey. At first it had made her jealous, but now the idea of her and Casey driving Brenda crazy with lust was very appealing.

Brenda was dealing with a stirring of emotions that she had never felt before. She could feel her rapid heartbeat, the butterflies in her stomach. She concentrated on lying perfectly still and keeping her breath even. She could feel Casey's hand softly against her left thigh. Her fingers seemed to burn. Brenda felt the fire spread across her skin and between her legs.

As if on cue, Kit and Casey each rose up on one elbow and stared silently down at the woman lying between them. Brenda looked first at one, then the other. She shrank a little into the pillow, but not fearfully. Her dark-haired companions smiled and then leaned down to kiss her. Two pairs of lips on her neck; Brenda felt the rush of heat course through her body. Kit and Casey's hands slid across her body and met briefly on her stomach. She squirmed as their fingers edged lower, and lower still. She moaned deeply as Casey kissed her full on the mouth while Kit sucked a tender nipple into her mouth. Brenda arched her back and grabbed each woman.

Casey felt her own heart beat faster in response to Brenda's moan. She looked up briefly from her kiss to watch Kit descend on Brenda's nipple. She kissed Brenda's eager lips once more and then moved to her sensitive throat.

Kit changed tactics and slid from Brenda's breasts to her stomach and then lower still. Brenda's legs spread invitingly. Kit dipped her fingers deep; Brenda was wet and oh so ready. She took Kit's fingers easily. Kit heard Brenda's indrawn breath as she touched her tongue to Brenda's clit. She felt Casey's hand on her head, pushing her down. Or was it Brenda's hand?

It seemed only seconds before Brenda felt the waves of orgasm. Her legs tensed as her senses exploded with the intense stimulations all over her body. It was as if a hundred hands caressed her and just as many mouths kissed her and licked her and nipped her gently. And how many fingers penetrated her, pushed into her, reached far into tender places? Her moans were smothered by Casey's mouth. Or was it Kit's? She clutched the sheets, and then the strong shoulders of the woman between her legs. Her climax receded like a warm tide.

Brenda collapsed into the pillows. She took several deep breaths. The filtered light from the window only revealed shadowy forms above her. She couldn't tell who was who. But the two women who hovered over her weren't done with her.

Silently, Kit and Casey changed places. Casey's hand delved where Kit's had been only moments before; her mouth traced the same path that Kit's had taken. Kit kissed Brenda's swollen lips. As she watched Casey's head dip lower, she fought back a twinge of jealousy and instead smothered Brenda's cry with her mouth.

Unbelievable as it seemed, Brenda felt the beginnings of a second orgasm. She grabbed the hair of the woman between her legs and pushed into her mouth. She thrust her hips upward, taking Casey's fingers deeper still. The orgasm rippled across her body. The lips on her lips took her breath away, making her moan and yet stifling her moan at the same time. Exhausted, she felt her whole body go limp. Her exquisite torment was over.

Casey and Kit smiled into the darkness. They still said not one word. Casey moved up to rest beside Brenda. She lay on her left side, cradling her head in the crook of her elbow and placing her right hand gently on Brenda's belly. Kit nestled against Brenda and traced her fingers softly across Brenda's shoulders and down over her breasts until they too rested on Brenda's belly. Her hand touched Casey's. Their fingers intertwined. She smiled and closed her eyes as she felt her own body relax.

Across the bridge of Brenda's body, Casey smiled too.

meeting ftf

●

radclyffe

I pace restlessly on the corner opposite the small coffee bar in Old City. There are a few small, round, glass-topped tables out in front of the tiny establishment on the uneven red-brick sidewalk, and they barely leave enough room for passersby to get around them without stepping into the cobblestone street. "Street" is a generous term for what is little more than an alley, but the history-laden district with its three-hundred-year-old buildings has its charms. All of which are lost on me as I watch the café for some sign of her. No one is seated at the tables.

I'm fifteen minutes early. Still lots of time to think about the fact that she might not show up at all, and to worry that I haven't dressed appropriately for the occasion if she does. Plenty of time to spend trying not to think about the possibility that she won't want me—in the flesh. Nine months into our relationship, and now, fifteen minutes before liftoff, I get to worry about that.

Funny how it's all turned around. Usually it's the chemistry, that elusive indescribable irrational spark that gets things started. You see someone hot and give her a look. She looks back, and you're on your way. You spend a little time finding out if there's any more to it than heat, or you have a quick, sweaty tumble, but either way—you know. Then you go on from there, discovering, exploring, learning. Or you smile, say it was nice, and move on. Not this time. Now I'm in so deep I can't breathe, and I've never seen her face, heard her voice. Well, I know her "voice"—the cadence of her speech, the words she uses when she's angry or happy or horny. I can tell from the length of her sentences if she's stressed or tired or ready for loving.

And she knows me in ways I never thought possible and had given up hoping for.

She knows practically all there is that's worth knowing about me. My passions. My hopes. My dreams. What I fear. What I love. How I like to come. I know almost all those things about her, too—what makes her laugh, what makes her cry, what makes her come. I know she can turn me inside-out with a word. Or the absence of one. Silence has become my greatest fear. Even anger is better than that. Because when I don't hear from her, I am afraid that she is gone forever.

Although I can't remember who suggested it first, we both agreed that it was time. Time to make the final connection. Time to meet. Because there was too much between us to contain inside the perimeter of a four-hundred-square-inch high-resolution monitor any longer. We have five senses, and there is only so long that the critical ones can be denied. I had to see her, hear her voice, touch her skin, smell her scent, and taste her desire. Or die from the deprivation.

And now that I'm about to see her for the first time, at the same instant she sees me, I don't know if I'll pass the test. She has written that she likes androgynous women. Anxiously I wonder just how androgynous she really meant. I catch a glimpse of myself as I pass the wide plate-glass window in the storefront café, a pale blue denim (pressed and fitted) work shirt, low-cut button-fly jeans, black Doc Martens twelve-eye boots. No tie. Thought the tie might be a little too much, even for a liberated, out lesbian artist like her. My hair is as long as I let it get before it needs to be trimmed almost to the collar in back, long enough on the sides to brush the brown-mixed-with-gray at the temples back into casual layers. I run a hand through the unruly wave at the front that wants to fall over my forehead. It does. The gold signet ring on my little finger catches the light and glints back at me from the glass, and I survey the rest of the picture. Very thin-rimmed, tortoiseshell glasses—the professor look. Athletic build, not much heavier than when I was eighteen. On a good day I can still wear the same size jeans. Not bad, I guess, but I'm still nervous; she's younger—a lot younger. She might have fallen in love with my quick wit and irresistible charm, but I'm hoping to impress her in the flesh. Soon.

I check the street sign, double-check the address. Right name engraved on the discreet wooden sign hung above the door. This is the right coffee shop, all right. I take one of the sidewalk tables where I can keep watch in both directions without looking as if I'm at a tennis match. I try to amuse myself by observing the interplay of students, faculty, and staff passing by from the nearby campus. Snippets of conversation and laughter float to me on the warm afternoon breeze. I feel a little out of body. What the hell am I doing meeting a stranger who might just have been playing an elaborate game with me for the last three-quarters of a year? But she couldn't have been, could she? There are some things you just can't fake. Need is one of them.

Check my watch—five minutes to four. We'd agreed on four o'clock. We'd agreed no pictures. I know she'll be early. I know I'll recognize her. If I leave now, she'll understand. And I'll lose my mind wondering what could have been.

I watch the street. I see her now, crossing the intersection with an expectant expression—excited, it appears to me. She sure doesn't look as nervous as I feel. My height, but definitely not androgynous. Lustrous, wind-blown hair—thick and dark—almost to her shoulders. From here, I can't see the beginnings of gray I know are there. She told me about that right after I finally confessed my age. Maybe to make me feel better. White T-shirt—very white, no wrinkles, nice tits. Very nice. Jeans—not tight, but fitted enough to show off a tight butt and strong thighs. She's sexy and moves like she knows it; my pulse shoots up a notch. Our eyes meet—she grins. So do I. I stand up as she approaches. I watch her walk—confident, centered—all the time her looking me over, taking her time with it, too. Cocky—I knew that about her and love her for it. But then, love isn't the issue here.

I let her look, want her to look, hoping—Christ, praying—the packaging will do. Because this time I want to fuck her, skin on skin. She stops a few feet away, smiles with her eyes. Then her whole face lifts as she smiles with her mouth—a generous, very kissable mouth. I want her so much right then. Her eyes are very bright, shining, brilliant. I'm drowning.

"Hi," she says softly, even a little shyly. That surprises me.

"Hi," I answer, my throat tight.

"You look great."

"So do you." Jesus. So do you. I clear my throat. Try not to shake. Gesture to the table. "You hungry?"

There's no way I could possibly eat. All I want is to touch her. She shakes her head, her hand trailing lightly down my arm, brushing over my hand, taking my fingers in hers. Her skin is warm, her gaze so steady.

"Yes."

I try not to look disappointed.

She tugs my hand, pulls me around the table into the little street. "Come with me."

I follow. I would have gone anywhere as long as she held my hand. We walk, our shoulders touching, our strides well matched. We don't talk. We don't need to. There is no need to say what we both know in our souls. Love was never the issue here.

She climbs four stone steps, worn down in the middle from decades of use, and opens the door to a three-story, two-hundred-year-old townhouse sandwiched among a row of them, all now converted to apartments. I'm right behind her, almost brushing against her ass. She turns to me as I move to shut out the world, but before I have the door completely closed, my back is against the wall and she's pressing along the entire length of my body. I kick the door the rest of the way shut as her weight pins me. If she's worried about offending my butch sensibilities with a frontal assault, she sure doesn't show it. She's kissing me, and I'm kissing her back—hard, openmouthed, tongue-probing kisses that say you belong to me. We're both gasping, groaning softly at the physical sensations that are so damn familiar and so completely new. I pull her shirt out, slide my hands up. No bra—she did that for me. Another reason I adore her. She remembers what I need. Her nipples are already hard but they stiffen further as I clamp down on them, both at once, my hands cupping her breasts, squeezing. She moans and twitches and pushes into my palms.

"Apartment?" I ask desperately. This can't be smart, fucking in the hallway like this, but my brain is melting fast.

"Yeah," she gasps. Her hand fisted in my shirtfront, she dances and drags me ten steps farther along the dim corridor. Then, with my hand still tormenting her nipples, she produces a key from somewhere, turns a lock, and we tumble into a room. Two more steps and I bang up against the back of something—a couch, I think. She's got her hands on my ass, massaging my butt roughly, pulling me closer, fitting thigh between thighs, pelvis to pelvis, our mouths still fused.

Then she gasps, pulls her mouth from mine, and leans back in my arms to stare at me. She blushes. I have my hands on her nipples, she's feeling me up—and now she blushes. God, she's beautiful. I nudge the hard curve against her crotch a little, and her eyes widen as she realizes she really did feel what she thought she felt.

"Okay?" I whisper, holding my breath, praying again.

She slides a hand around my thigh—between my legs—finds the cock, and cups it in her hand.

"Okay," she murmurs, leaning to kiss me again.

She tugs it, my clit surges to twice its size, and my knees get so weak I almost fall down. She laughs. Quick learner. Still working the cock around in my pants, she gets her other hand on the front of my jeans and starts pulling the buttons open. I've got it easier. Her jeans zip.

I get her fly down in record time and push the denim down over her hips. No underwear either. She's more than a dream; she's a miracle. When her hand dips into my fly, I toss my head back and groan. There isn't much room in there with her fingers and the cock and my clit all smashed together, and I'm feeling every little movement of her fingers straight through to my spine. I look down, wide-eyed, as she fists me inside my jeans.

"Jesus!"

"Mmm, nice." She tilts her head, her eyes dreamy as she searches my face. "I want to jerk you off. Can I?"

I cover her hand from the outside, stopping the torment. "No...I mean, yes...you can, for sure but...I mean...not yet."

"Can I take it out?"

My head is about to come off. "Oh yeah, please."

She eases it free, kissing me again, pinning me to the sofa back this time. The length of it lies along my belly now, between us, as she surges against me again and again. The base pounds my clit as she pumps her hips into me. She's naked to midthigh, her T-shirt tented up over my hands, her bare belly rubbing over mine as she slides all over the dick.

Jesus! Who's fucking who here? Stupid question. She owns me. Has

235

from the first.

She's groaning as she bites my neck, kisses my jaw, my chest, my nipples through my shirt—I'm damn near coming from the sensations assaulting me everywhere at once. Someone is whimpering—I think it's me. My legs are turning to rubber and there's a dangerous quivering in my belly.

Fuck! She's gonna make me come.

"Baby, wait!" I cry.

She eases her hips away from me.

Oh God—I don't know what I want, but not that!

I start to protest; she laughs again. Then she shoves her hand between us and tugs my dick. "Are you going to fuck me with that thing or just tease me all night?"

My clit twitches like crazy when she says that. God, I'm crazy about her. She lets me turn her so it's her butt against the sofa now and I'm between her legs.

"Step out of your jeans," I growl as I drop to my knees, my cock brushing her leg as I move down. My hands part her thighs, my lips find her clit. She cries out in surprise. I groan, my stomach clenching at the first taste of her. She's so wet, so sweet, so goddamned perfect. Her clit is hard, waiting for my tongue, my lips. I suck it in, tug at the inner lips with my teeth, bite gently. She grabs my head, pumps against my face erratically. Her body is calling the shots, and I follow her rhythm. I'm licking the whole length of her, trying to swallow every drop of sweet come, stroking under the stiff shaft, up over the top, around the sides. The muscles of her sex contract.

"I need to come soon." Her voice is high and tight, her fingers twitching in my hair.

She needs to come alright, and I want her on the edge. I'm about to go over mine. Still licking her, I rub my clit under the cock. It's huge, heavy, throbbing. If I stroke it another few seconds I'm gonna be coming all over her. I'm close to forgetting why I should wait.

"Please, please, please," she sighs, her head rolling gently from side to side. "Fuck me, make me come…fuck me, make me come…fuck me fuck me…"

I'm so close to exploding I'm not sure I can even get it in her without coming. Standing on shaking legs, I grit my teeth, grab the cock, and guide the head between her thighs. Rub it against her clit—she whimpers, grabs my ass, tries to pull me into her. I spread my legs, tilt my pelvis forward, and angle the cock up with my hand. She feels it, helps me, her fingers on mine—leading me home. Between us we slide the cock in.

My head is pounding, and she's making little wild noises in the back of her throat. I can't stop my hips from pumping. I'm gasping and groaning and fucking her for all I'm worth. She's got her arms around my neck and she's fucking me right back, the both of us poised to come, neither wanting to give in. Her muscles finally squeeze down on the cock so hard that when I go to pull out for a long stroke, it doesn't come—so I just slam back into her, and my clit goes crazy.

"Ah fuck, I'm gonna come!"

My pelvis hits her clit, the cock bangs deep into her, working that spot that's sending her over. She bites my shoulder, trying not to scream. I'm coming now, can't stop it—great pounding waves shooting from my clit, rising through my belly into my chest. I shout meaningless words, jerking in her arms—inside her, and she screams. Screams and screams and comes all over my cock.

God, she's beautiful when she comes—her whole body resonates with the sound and fury of it. Her climax seems to go on forever, and with each contraction she moans, digging her fingers into my ass.

I'm afraid I'll crush her, I'm holding on so tight, still coming in slow, rolling spasms. With my mouth close to her ear, I murmur, "I love you."

"I know," she whispers brokenly, still coming. "I love you."

But we both already knew that. Love was never the issue here.

bios

TARA ALTON's erotica has appeared in *The Mammoth Book of Best New Erotica, Best Lesbian Erotica 2005, Best Women's Erotica, Hot Women's Erotica, Clean Sheets,* and *Scarlet Letters.* She lives in the Midwest and writes erotica because that is what is in her head, and it needs to come out. Check out her Web site at www.taraalton.com.

Having made attempts at several places and professions, **DEVON BLACK** remains in search of the city and career that fit her best. She thrives on sweets and exercise and loves to tour coffee shops, laptop in tow and head filled with sensual thoughts.

L. ELISE BLAND has published in *Faster Pussycats* (Alyson), *Shameless: An Intimate Erotica* (Seal), *Up All Night: Real-Life Lesbian Sex Adventures* (Alyson), *Back to Basics: A Butch/Femme Erotic Journey* (Bella Books), *Naughty Spanking Stories from A to Z* (Pretty Things Press), *Naughty Spanking Stories from A to Z 2* (Pretty Things Press), and *The Best American Erotica 2006* (Fireside/Touchstone). She has worked as a stripper, a dominatrix, a fetish model, a sex educator, and an actress in sexy lesbian movies. Her foray into the sex industry began with the lesbian adventure described in her first-time story, "Sugar Daddy."

GUN BROOKE resides in the countryside in Sweden with her very patient family. A retired neonatal intensive care nurse, she now publishes with Bold Strokes Books and writes full time, only rarely taking a break to create Web sites for herself or others and to do computer graphics. Gun's list of book publications are *Course of Action* and *Protector of the Realm.* She also has a short story, called "Aflame" in the upcoming Bold Strokes Books erotica anthology *Stolen Moments: Erotic Interludes 2.* Gun is currently working on her next romance novel.

JEN CROSS is held in thrall by the transformative power of smut writing and the fluid rigidity of gender performance. Her stories have appeared (under the name Jen Collins) in such anthologies as *Back to Basics, Best Fetish Erotica, Glamour Girls,* and *Naughty Spanking Stories from*

A to Z 2. She also performs as a member of the dyke erotica collective Dirty Ink.

GINA DE VRIES has been active in various struggles for queer and sexual liberation since 1995. She is the co-editor, with Diane Anderson-Minshall, of *[Becoming]: Young Ideas on Gender, Sexuality, and Identity* (Xlibris Press, 2004); a contributor to *That's Revolting! Queer Resistances to Assimilation* (Soft Skull Press, 2004); and a contributing writer to numerous queer zines and glossies. She is a graduate of Hampshire College, where she completed a creative thesis in memoir and sex writing entitled *"Passing: Short Stories about Queer Sexuality, Transgressive Gender, and Pervert Love.* De Vries is also a board member for the Youth Gender Project and an intern at San Francisco's Center for Sex and Culture. She has spent the past few years focusing her political energies on the fight for comprehensive, sex-positive sexuality education, the movement for sex-workers' rights, and the inclusion of bi and trans women in dyke spaces. She hopes she doesn't sound too humorless in this bio.

KATE DOMINIC is the author of *Any 2 People, Kissing* (Down There Press, 2003), which was a finalist for a 2004 Foreword Magazine Book of the Year Award. Her work is available in *The Best of Best Women's Erotica, Glamour Girls, The Many Joys of Sex Toys, Dyke the Halls, Ultimate Lesbian Erotica 2004,* and many other anthologies, magazines, and Web sites. Kate's column *The Business End* appears monthly at the Erotica Readers & Writers Association (www.erotica-readers.com).

KATE FREED is a writer and health educator who works with teens in New York City. She likes to skip town, ride her bike, and occasionally try her hand at Pilates.

SCARLETT FRENCH is a short-story writer and a poet. Her erotic fiction has appeared in *Best Lesbian Erotica 2005* and *Va Va Voom.* She is currently working on her first novel but is repeatedly distracted by the urge to write filth. "Sanctuary Girls" appears with thanks to Daniel F., who provided the space where this memory was created.

ISABELLE GRAY is the pseudonym of a writer whose work has appeared in many anthologies, including *Best American Erotica,* several volumes of *Best Lesbian Erotica,* and *Best Bisexual Women's Erotica.* She still remembers her first time fondly.

SACCHI GREEN writes in western Massachusetts and the mountains of New Hampshire, with occasional forays into the real world. Her work has appeared in five volumes of *Best Lesbian Erotica,* four volumes of *Best Women's Erotica, Penthouse, Best S/M Erotica 2, Best Transgender Erotica, Naughty Spanking Stories from A to Z,* and a thigh-high stack of other anthologies with inspirational covers. Her first co-editorial venture, *Rode Hard, Put Away Wet: Lesbian Cowboy Erotica,* was published by Suspect Thoughts Press in June 2005, and two more anthologies, *Dykes on Bikes* from Haworth Press and *Lipstick on Her Collar* from Pretty Things Press are due for release in fall 2006.

LYNNE JAMNECK is a South African writer and photographer currently living in New Zealand. A quiet butch and a science fiction geek, she likes Earl Grey and has a penchant for writing dirty stories. Her fiction has been published in numerous tasty anthologies, including *Best Lesbian Erotica 2003, Best Lesbian Erotica 2006, The Good Parts, Call of the Dark: Lesbian Tales of the Supernatural,* and *Hot Lesbian Erotica, The Merry XXXmas Book of Erotica and Erotica Vampirica.* The first book in her Samantha Skellar mysteries is published by Bella Books (www.bellabooks.com). She is the creator and editor of *Simulacrum: The Magazine of Speculative Transformation* at www.specficworld. com/simulacrum.html. She has a blog at http://www.blogger.com/ profile/10875090 and can be reached at samskellar@gmail.com.

BARBARA JOHNSON is the Lammy finalist author of the bestselling lesbian novels *Stonehurst, The Beach Affair, Bad Moon Rising,* and *Strangers in the Night.* Her short stories have appeared in almost a dozen anthologies. She has novellas in *Once Upon a Dyke: New Exploits of Fairy Tale Lesbians and Bell, Book and Dyke: New Exploits of Magical Lesbians,* and she has co-edited *The Perfect Valentine: Erotic Lesbian*

Valentine Stories. She still thinks about that Halloween night so long ago... She changed the names in the retelling to protect the not-so-innocent.

LAREN LEBRAN is the alter-alter ego of a well-known romance and erotica writer who believes that sex is language, and she never tires of hearing women speak.

MADLYN MARCH has had her work published on Afterellen.com and Blacktable.com. "The Flying Hat" is her first published erotic story.

ELAINE MILLER is a self-employed Vancouver leatherdyke who spends her time playing, learning, educating, performing, and writing. Elaine has been the BDSM columnist for *Xtra West* newspaper for over three years. Since her first publication in 1994, her short fiction has regularly appeared in numerous magazines and anthologies and quite a few tawdry porn sites. She's also a bit of a geek, and runs a Web design and hosting business so she has an excuse to spend yet more time staring at the computer screen. Her Web site is http://elainemiller.com.

AIMEE NICHOLS is a prizewinning erotica author who is slowly coming to realize that there is more to literary greatness than being a lush. Her work has appeared in *Ultimate Lesbian Erotica 2006, Best Lesbian Erotica 2001,* and numerous print and online magazines. She lives in Melbourne, Australia, and maintains a Web site at http://www.intergalactic-hussy.net.

JOY PARKS writes articles, interviews, and book reviews for the *San Francisco Chronicle, The Advocate* and many other GLBT and mainstream publications. Her book column, *Sacred Ground,* appears regularly on a number of Web sites and in print. She began writing fiction as a fortieth birthday present to herself, and her short stories appear in *Back to Basics, Hot and Bothered 4, The Call of the Dark,* and the Bella Books anthology, *The Perfect Valentine: Erotic Lesbian Valentine Stories.* She lives in Ottawa, Canada.

RADCLYFFE is the author of nineteen lesbian romances, the Honor (Above All, Honor et al) and the Justice series (Shield of Justice et al), the Erotic Interlude series (Change of Pace and Stolen Moments: Erotic Interludes, 2, ed. with Stacia Seaman) and selections in the anthologies *Call of the Dark* and *The Perfect Valentine: Erotic Lesbian Valentine Stories* (Bella Books), *Best Lesbian Erotica 2006* (Cleis), and *Naughty Spanking Stories from A to Z 2* (Pretty Things Press). She is the recipient of the 2003 and 2004 Alice B. Readers' Award, a 2005 Golden Crown Literary Society Award winner in both the romance category (*Fated Love*) and the mystery/intrigue/action category (*Justice in the Shadows*), and the president of Bold Strokes Books, a lesbian publishing company. She shares her life with her partner, Lee, and assorted canines in Pennsylvania.

AUDACIA RAY is a New Yorker, polyamorous pervert, nakedteer, sex worker, safer sex educator, and history of sexuality enthusiast. Knowing things gets her in trouble.

JEAN ROBERTA teaches first-year English classes at a Canadian prairie university and writes in several genres. The true story of her first lesbian experience is in *Up All Night: Adventures in Lesbian Sex*. Her rants and reviews can be found in her column, *In My Jeans* at www.bluefood.cc.

TINA SIMMONS divides her time between New York and her home town of Key West, Florida. She has a variety of writing credits, a couple of useless degrees, and a coffee habit she doesn't care to break. When she isn't writing, she can often be found outside, enjoying the sunshine—or a good rainstorm.

THERESE SZYMANSKI, an award-winning playwright, has written seven books in the Lammy-nominated Brett Higgins Motor City Thrillers, edited *Back to Basics: A Butch/Femme Anthology* and *Call of the Dark: Erotic Lesbian Stories of the Supernatural,* co-edited *A Perfect Valentine: Erotic Lesbian Valentine Stories,* has novellas in *Once Upon a Dyke: New Exploits of Fairy Tale Lesbians* and *Bell, Book and Dyke: New Exploits of Magical Lesbians* and has contributed tales to about two dozen anthologies.

Called "a trollop with a laptop," **ALISON TYLER** is naughty and knows it. Over the past decade, she has written more than fifteen explicit novels including *Learning to Love It, Strictly Confidential, Sweet Thing, Sticky Fingers, Something about Workmen,* and *Rumours*. Her stories have appeared in anthologies including *Sweet Life* I and II, *Taboo, Best Women's Erotica, and Best Fetish Erotica,* and in *Wicked Words* 4, 5, 6, 8, and 10. Ms. Tyler is the editor of *Heat Wave, Best Bondage Erotica, Three-Way, Naughty Stories from A to Z, Down and Dirty, Naked Erotica,* and *Juicy Erotica*. Please visit www.prettythingspress.com.

JANE VINCENT is a dyke-identified bisexual woman who loves the term "fluid" to describe her sexuality. She has a degree in sexuality, will soon be pursuing a master's in the topic, and no, you can't be her lab partner. She is a sexuality educator, certified sex coach, and (possibly former) sex worker. She has had more sex in more combinations and circumstances in the last five years than most people will have in their lives. She is a knitter, potter, and creative mess. And she just turned twenty-three.

KRISTINA WRIGHT'S fiction has appeared in over twenty anthologies, including *Ultimate Lesbian Erotica* (2005 and 2006); *Best Lesbian Erotica* (2002, 2004, 2005 and 2006); *The Mammoth Book of Best New Erotica* (Volume 5); and *Amazons: Sexy Stories of Strong Women*. She lives in Virginia and is pursuing a graduate degree in humanities. She can be reached through her Web site, www.kristinawright.com.

about the editor

RACHEL KRAMER BUSSEL (www.rachelkramerbussel.com) is senior editor at *Penthouse Variations* and a contributing editor at *Penthouse*, where she also writes the *Girl Talk* column. She writes the *Lusty Lady* column in *The Village Voice* and conducts interviews for Gothamist.com and Mediabistro.com. Rachel's books include *Up All Night: Adventures in Lesbian Sex*, *The Lesbian Sex Book* (second edition), *Naughty Spanking Stories from A to Z* 1 and 2, and *Glamour Girls: Femme/Femme Erotica*. Her writing has been published in over seventy anthologies, including *Best American Erotica* 2004 and 2006, *Best Women's Erotica* 2003, 2004 and 2006, *Best Lesbian Erotica* 2001, 2004, 2005, and *Best of the Best Lesbian Erotica, Juicy Erotica, Naked Erotica*, and others, as well as *AVN, Bust, Cleansheets, Curve, Diva, Girlfriends, Metro, New York Post, On Our Backs, Oxygen.com, Punk Planet, Rockrgrl, The San Francisco Chronicle, Time Out New York, Velvetpark* and others. She has appeared on *Berman and Berman* on the Discovery Health Channel, *Family Business* on Showtime, *Naked New York,* and *In the Life,* and has been quoted in *Celebrity Living* and *New York* magazine. She greatly enjoys spanking and being spanked in equal measure. In her spare time, she frequents comedy shows, co-writes a cupcake blog, and takes advantage of New York City every chance she gets.